ALRIK

rooted in place
woman. Abbiga

to send a woman like her to him. She was
seductively formed, small waisted with hips made
for a man to hold on to while he thrust inside of
her, and breasts that made his palms itch to hold.

She turned her back to him and waded into the
water like a brave enchantress. The sight of her
shapely backside and the sexy dip of her lower back
nearly sent him after her. Her legs were strong, with
just enough muscle that they rippled as she stepped
into the lapping water.

Was she testing him? Trying to taunt him with
something he couldn't have or wouldn't take?

Wait. He'd take it. Yes, he'd take it and so
much more if she offered her young lithe body to
him. After all the horrible deeds he'd committed in
the past, using her body would hardly fare against
them. He'd taken several steps towards her
retreating back before he stopped himself.

No, he couldn't touch her. They both needed
to stay focused. He'd had and lost his love.

Alrik made one of the hardest decisions of his
life then and turned around.

development and emotional depth demonstrate her tremendous growth as a writer. Grey has hit the mark with "The Fallen King"..." Amber L. Barr
-VAMPIRE AND IMMORTAL BOOKS

The Bellum Sisters Trilogy

"The Bellum sisters are a handful for sure and it's their feistiness that creates sparks for the males who have recently "acquired" them. Bravo!! Five stars to T. A. Grey for a series I am dying to continue."
-*THE BOOK LOVER'S REALM*

The Bellum Sisters

"The Bellum Sisters Trilogy" is a provocative look into the lives of three young women as they come of age in a paranormal world. Ms. Grey's world is not only magical, but erotic, enchanted, and deadly. In addition to the fiercely passionate female characters, Grey creates a fresh cast of male counterpoints who are seductive, gritty, rugged, and noble. "The Bellum Sisters Trilogy" is an encouraging start to a promising new series. I look forward to reading more from Ms. Grey in the future."
-*VAMPIRE AND IMMORTAL BOOKS*

Stock image by: Jimmy Thomas
www.romancenovelcenter.com
Cover design by: Char Adlesberger
wix.com/wicked_art/wickwix.com/wicked_art/wic
ked-cover-designed-cover-designs
Edited by: Brandi Fairchild
Copyright © 2013 T. A. Grey
All Rights Reserved
www.tagrey.com

ISBN-10: 1481922874
ISBN-13: 978-1481922876

ALSO BY T. A. GREY

THE KATEGAN ALPHAS
Breeding Cycle
Dark Awakening
Wicked Surrender
Eternal Temptation
Dark Seduction
Tempting Whispers

THE BELLUM SISTERS TRILOGY
Chains of Frost
Bonds of Fire
Ties That Bind
The Fallen King

STANDALONE WORKS
Capturing Jeron
Midnight Sex Shop
Ecstasy Overload
Evernight Romance Anthology –
'The Vampire's Mate'

The Fallen King

THE BELLUM SISTERS 4

T. A. GREY

Acknowledgements

I have the usual girls to thank plus a few special extras. I'd like to thank my editor Brandi for doing such a fabulous job, LuMary for being the greatest beta reader ever, and Char for creating such an awesome cover! I couldn't love it any more.

A special shout out goes to my ladies in The Alpha Squad! You gals are the best, and I mean that in the most sincere way possible. You have been so supportive in helping me to tell people about The Fallen King. You have also shown me more glorious pictures of sexy men than I've ever seen in my life. Thank you, ladies! I love you!

Happy reading, everyone!

T. A. Grey

Glossary

Dreenaru gina slinah – Demonic for "You are incredible."

futhorc – A small furry animal that lives in the rift.

Haute – Royal shahoulin demons

idummi – A bottom feeding demon from the deepest layer under the rift. They are aggressive, easily manipulated creatures with poisonous talons.

jaheera – Dark and dangerous demons that live at the lowest rung of the rift and are capable of incredible dark magic.

Kolan – A black, carnivorous bird that resides in the rift.

Krishnoe! – Demonic for "Silence!"

Protector – A male in charge of protecting and caring for a succubus.

rift – The division between earth and the nether-realm where demons of many kinds reside.

shahoulin - A breed of demon that lives at the top of the rift. They have magical powers and superior strength.

One

The dead girl lay on her back facing whoever had ended her life. Her left arm curved around her head in a plié and her right knee bent out towards the street.

"All right, Krenshaw, do your thing." Mike Waxell gave her a nod then went back to surveying the scene. Mike was the lead detective on the case tonight. She'd worked with him a few times before.

Abbigail sucked in a deep breath and blew it out through her nose. She already had her latex gloves donned and cloth booties covering her shoes. The booties weren't always necessary, but in this case there was so much blood the whole team had to wear them. Everything would have to be processed. With stabbing victims the murderer often cut himself too so the his or her blood may be on the ground too.

First, Abbigail took in the scene just as the detectives would do. It helped her to get an idea of how the attack took place. She was new at this, still had a lot to learn, but she was pretty good. She'd had an excellent mentor who'd trained her under his wing and helped her to get this job. God, she missed Stan.

They'd already determined the girl to be a shapeshifter from a local pack who'd gone missing two nights before. An elderly woman walking her poodle before she went to bed found the body at the back of an alley between two brownstone city apartment buildings. The residents of the Green Tree apartments peered down at her from their little windows up above. Others, mostly curious neighbors passing by, watched the team work from behind the yellow tape closing off the crime scene.

The alley was typical with A/C units and small windows facing each other from both apartment buildings. This path was only here for maintenance men who needed to work on the A/C units or for the utility companies to check their power lines. A six-foot tall fence stood at the back of the alley, and the girl's body was found right in front of it on a patch of concrete.

Abbigail looked back down the path where the faces watched with morbid, avid curiosity. She noted the alley to be only about twenty feet wide with the AC units taking up a good four of that from either side. A small pathway. She'd spotted the large community-sized dumpsters as she'd pulled into the lot. Why hadn't the killer just dumped her? Did he want the body to be found? Was he interrupted and had to be quick about it? If he just happened upon her here and killed her that'd make sense. Except that a shapeshifter being out this far away from her pack alone didn't make any sense. Shapeshifters stuck in groups, or at least the females did.

Abbigail squatted beside the girl. She had brown hair, the natural kind that had hints of blonde from being out in the sun. Her eyes were open, her face tilted towards the alley. The majority of the blood had spilled from a neck wound. Abby leaned down to inspect it. Could be a throat cutting or garroting, but more blood covered her abdomen wetting the girl's brown t-shirt to her skin. A cartoon cowboy riding a horse and lassoing a whip above his head sat on her shirt. Above it in pink scrawling text it said: Ride me cowboy! Abby cleared her throat and moved in with her inspection.

One shoe had come off which had been found at the beginning of the alley. The shoe probably came off during a struggle.

As associate medical examiner for the paranormal unit of the Fort Collins Police Department in Colorado, Abbigail got to touch the body first. She shouldn't even have the job she had. She was too young, but she'd graduated high school a year early then went through a special FBI program, a brand-new unit on studying supernatural cases. She'd been surprised to find her classes not filled to the brink. Who wouldn't find learning about the supernatural beings of the world utterly fascinating? Apparently many since her classes had sat half empty. That's when she met Stan Haubermann, a middle-aged detective turned behavioral profiler who'd started the program. He'd taken her under his wing and taught her everything he knew. Not that she was special; he'd done it to other members from her graduating class. She was just the only one to already have a job practicing his teachings.

Abbigail gently pushed the victim's head back, to the left, and then right. The cut was deep and clean. Not a serrated blade, and the wound wasn't thin enough to be from a garrote.

"Definitely a blade," she called out. "Rigor mortis has set in. She's been here at least four hours but probably no longer than twelve." Her skin had already begun to turn a purplish hue. Her muscles were beginning to tighten.

Abby arrived at the scene at a quarter passed eight. That meant the girl had been killed during the night.

The detectives quieted and came closer. Detective Mike leaned down next to her as his keen eyes professionally scoped out the body. Abby pressed her fingers around the neck to feel for splintered or broken bones but found none. She lifted the shirt and the detectives leaned over to peer.

"Stabbed her a good four times then took out her neck I bet," Mike said.

"That'd be my guess," Abby agreed, eyeing the deep red cuts in victim's abdomen. "Arm bent that way, I'd say he was holding her from behind and she'd reached back to try to get his hair or pull his arm away, something. That's when he slit her throat. She fell down just like that, still reaching for him."

"Check her hands," Mike said.

Abby lifted each of the victim's hands paying specific attention to her nails, fingers, and palms. "Defensive stab wounds." They happen during knife fights or on victims of knife homicides. The victims throw out their hands to try to dodge or block the swinging blade and their own hands get cut in the process. Blood was caked under the victim's fingernails making them look murky brown.

"How old do you think she is? The local shapeshifter alpha said the girl they're missing is about seventeen." He glanced down at his notepad. "She fits the description. Went missing last night."

"Yeah, I'd say that's right judging from the size of the body, the facial features, and her teeth. Definitely a teen. I'll know more once we get her back to the lab."

Mike stood, pulled out his notebook, and scribbled down some notes. "Anything else for us?"

Abbigail looked back down the path. "Definitely got stabbed at least the first few times at the beginning of the alley. Blood drops lead us back here to the body. He dragged her here and she lost her shoe in the struggle. She fought back, maybe even got away from him for a few seconds when he started slashing at her giving her the wounds on her hands. Eventually he got her turned around and slit her throat for the final killing blow."

"All right, we'll have the body sent down for processing. Let me know if you get anything else," said Mike.

"Will do." Abbigail walked down the path then removed her bloodied booties and gloves, handing them over to another crime scene investigator who held open a trash bag.

"Any luck?" he asked.

Abbigail shrugged. It was too soon to say.

She headed to her car and saw that it wasn't even ten in the morning yet. Time to head home and try to get a quick nap before they got the body down to the lab. She let out a jaw-cracking yawn then took off for home.

Two

Alrik lifted his knee high to his chest then slammed it down. His heavy boot caught the demon's chin smashing its bony skull into the ground with a fleshy crack. The idummi squealed a heinous, ear-piercing sound before Alrik let his boot connect with the demon's face again, ending the squeal.

Dragging in a heavy breath, Alrik turned to the temple and surveyed the grounds. The seer's home was a decrepit stone structure with two rock pillars in front acting as an archway to an empty, dark doorway set behind them. The home, if one could call it that, looked like a small rock hovel. The outside of the house was formed from hundreds of jagged rocks that varied in size and color. With the full light of day on it you could see chalky white areas and shiny black ones that glinted in the hazy sky's pink glow.

The one-story abode had no door but did have a dirty brown curtain that billowed in the breeze.

Alrik checked his surroundings once more then ducked inside the temple.

His lip curled. The one-story temple was anything but what he expected. Magic reeked in the place; it saturated the air like fog. The rocky structure was a hoax, a glamour created by the seer. Inside, the room traveled back for some distance, something not possible when judging from the outside of the temple. The floor and walls were made of flat, sanded-down stone, and torches burned brightly to chase back the shadows. The scent of burning wood and smoke hit his nostrils.

Alrik gripped his bloodied sword as he made his way down the long hall at the back of the room. The tunnel went on for some distance with no end in sight. No light lit the way and no light could be seen at the end of the tunnel. He hated these games but it looked like he'd have to play them. He did not come this far to not get the answers he sought.

Stepping lightly he made his way down the blackened tunnel. He kept his ears alert, all of his senses ready. He didn't make it far when a voice spoke and sounded as if came from all around him.

It sounded chipper as if it was laughing. "Found me at last have you, fallen king? Took you long enough."

Alrik's lips peeled back. To the darkened tunnel, he demanded, "Stop playing games with me seer. You'll speak to me—"

"Or else what, fallen king? You'll kill me too? As you did to that demon outside?"

"He was rummaging around your temple. I saved you from him."

The voice came back heavy with sarcasm. "Hardly necessary. No one gets in here unless I want them to."

Alrik's neck muscles flexed as he clenched his shoulders, but he didn't roll his head to ease it. "Then speak to me, old man."

The voice, that of an old man scratchy with age and hoarse, laughed again. The jolly sound only fueled Alrik's anger.

"The fallen king is desperate, his heart filled with anger. I'll tell you now that isn't the answer."

Alrik stopped walking down the endless tunnel with no light in sight and spun his head around trying to track the seer's voice. "I haven't even asked a question yet, seer."

"Ah, but I know what you want to ask."

"Then give me the answer!" Alrik shouted, his voice bouncing off the tunnel walls and echoing down the long corridor until he was surrounded by the shout. After many seconds, the echo faded leaving him in heavy silence.

He heard a long sigh which sounded laden with disappointment. "Very well," the voice said.

The walls around him shimmered and bubbled as if looking through the clear water of a waterfall as it fell to Earth. The dark walls became bright as if it was suddenly illuminated. Alrik turned and saw the black tunnel wall dissipate completely to reveal a large room complete with a large burning fireplace, a long wooden table covered in silver plates and golden goblets, and large iron rods around the room that held thick waxy candles that flickered orange light.

In front of the fireplace sat an old man sitting on a deep orange rug woven with magical symbols and Demonish words. Alrik stepped into the room. The old seer sat with his ankles crossed and knees pointing out. His long dark hair was pulled high atop his head in a curl and he wore a blue and red robe that shimmered in the firelight.

Alrik started for the seer.

The seer lifted his head from the floor and his eyes met Alrik. Alrik froze at the sight of those eyes, and he'd never seen anything like it. Black eyes with a brilliant blue center. He'd seen many demons in his life of varying colored skin, hair, and eyes, but never anything like this. However, the rest of the seer looked very human. Dark brown skin, dark hair, but those eyes were something different.

"So you've found me, fallen king Alrik."

"Not easily." Much blood had been shed, and even more time spent trying to find the seer. It had better be worth all the trouble. He was his last hope, and the only one capable of helping him on his quest.

"Nothing worth doing is ever easy."

"Spare me the proverbial talk, seer."

The seer looked up towards the ceiling, his expression dreamy with thought. "I must correct myself. Nothing important worth doing is ever easy. Seeing as how much you need me and my guidance and how important that will change things for you, I'd say it's going to be very important for you."

"Enough of the bullshit, seer. You know what I'm here to ask."

The seer looked at Alrik and smiled, his white teeth dazzling against his dark skin. "Shall you ask anyway? People like that. They don't enjoy knowing that I already know what they're going to say. I believe it makes them feel more comfortable."

"Where is my mother?"

The seer jumped up to a stand, surprising Alrik with his agility. The man sounded as if speaking was a chore yet he hopped up with the spring of a child.

The seer was guessed to be older than the kingdom of Harumina itself and yet he looked no older than Alrik did. Surely, he was a shahoulin demon like Alrik, because they aged much slower than some species of earth.

Still smiling, the seer walked to a cupboard hanging on the stone wall and grabbed something off the shelf. With a few more movements, the seer walked to the candle standing in the corner of the room, and with a smoke pressed between his lips he breathed deeply as the candle sparked. The smoke's end lit brightly as he inhaled.

"Smoke?" the seer asked without glancing at him.

"No," Alrik said, his patience waning fast. "Answer my question, seer."

The seer pulled the smoke from between his wrinkled lips and stared at the tip before turning it back around and casually sucking from the end. The scent of burning herbs reached Alrik's nostrils. The odor was not unpleasant but close to it.

"You're asking the wrong question, fallen king."

Alrik squeezed his sword then deposited it back in the scabbard across his back. "Stop calling me that."

The seer's dark eyebrows flew up in surprise, and Alrik wasn't fooled. The seer wasn't surprised by anything. "What? The fallen king? You are fallen, aren't you? Were you not banished from your home for all your...horrible deeds?"

Alrik's blood pumped hard with the need to lash out. The need to tear across the small space, wrap his hand around the old seer's throat, and squeeze—squeeze until his eyes rolled into the back of his head and his wheezing breaths stopped. He didn't do that though. Instead, he released a strangled breath and bared his teeth.

"Where is my mother?"

"Ah, yes, the fallen queen," the seer said, still smiling and puffing away at his smoke. "That's not the right question to ask. Try another, fallen king."

"How can I find my mother?"

The seer rocked his head side to side as if contemplating.

"You are very close to death right now," warned Alrik "I'd answer if I were you."

The seer tossed his head back and laughed a hoarse, wheezing sound. When he looked back at Alrik, his grin was broader and his dark eyes bright with amusement. "You can't kill me, fallen king."

"Want to bet on that, seer?"

The seer spread his arms out wide until his body formed a T. "You need me."

Alrik looked away. It was either that or risk tearing the seer apart limb by limb. God, just the thought of it sent a rush of pleasure through him. The howl of his screams would fuel him better than any food, the sight of his spurting blood like a balm to his heart.

"Answer the question," he said slowly, his eyes closing as he enjoyed the mental image of killing the seer with his bare hands.

Silence met him. Alrik pushed back the dark thoughts and opened his eyes to find the seer watching him, no longer smiling.

"How you can find her or where you can find her is not important, and you already know the answer."

"All that I know, seer, is that she's in the rift."

The seer shrugged a slender shoulder.

"I'm sure you know how big the rift is, seer."

"She's here. You'll find her eventually, but you already know that. You don't need me for that."

Alrik frowned. "Then why the fuck else am I here?"

Again, the seer smiled. "Because you don't know how to kill her."

Alrik's body stilled, each muscle tensing. "I'll slice her head off with my blade and if that doesn't work, I'll turn to magic as she has."

The seer laughed then sat back down on the rug at the fire, leaving a trail of smoke behind him. "But you can't kill her."

"What do you mean I can't kill her?" he asked slowly.

That's all he'd thought about, all he'd planned for years. He'd been searching for her for years, always either one step behind or completely off her trail through some form of her treachery. He was done. This would end soon. He'd make sure of it.

The seer looked him up and down. "Your curse won't let you. The queen isn't stupid. When she cursed you she made sure that if you ever learned of her deceit you couldn't kill her. Since surely you'd want to."

'Want' was such a lame word. He didn't want to kill his mother, he needed to. He needed to as much as needed air to live.

"How do I break the curse upon me then?"

"By killing her, of course."

Alrik's fists clenched until his blunt nails stabbed into his skin. He felt the skin give and blood bead. "But you said I can't kill her."

"No, you can't."

Alrik nearly saw red. "Then how do I kill her?"

"It's not a how so much as a who. See, you're not asking the right questions."

Alrik blinked, the only sign he gave to show the shock in his body. "Who can kill her?" The thought of anyone else ever delivering the killing blow to his mother had never, not even once, crossed his mind.

The seer laughed and rubbed his hands together. "The most unlikely person, naturally. A woman, a human woman."

Alrik took a hard step forward and pointed a hard finger at the seer. "Stop messing with me, seer. A human, let alone a woman, could never kill my mother and you know it."

"But this human is a witch." His eyes turned into a faraway look, unfocused and hazy. "Though there is a bit of a problem with that."

As if this wasn't a problem already. "And what's that?"

The seer didn't respond for several moments. His eyes were lost in thought. Finally, the haze left him and he tossed the end of his smoke into the burning fire. "She hasn't used her magic in a very long time. She shuns it."

Alrik shook his head. "This is ridiculous. You mean to tell me that the only way to kill my mother and lift the curse from me is through a human witch who doesn't even practice her skill?"

"Precisely!" the seer said with a smile.

Alrik looked away, lost in his own thoughts. "You're certain she is the one?"

"Oh yes."

A human witch. If she could kill his mother then she must be very powerful indeed. The human aspect would be a downside. That means he'd have to go to the surface to get her and she'd have a harder time adjusting to the environment in the rift. But, it could work. The fact that she doesn't practice her own magic would have to be remedied right away. He needed her power at its fullest for when they reached the queen.

"What is her name?"

The seer's lips lifted into another smile. "Abbigail Krenshaw."

Alrik frowned. "That's a strange name."

"Maybe to her your name is strange."

"Maybe so. How do I find her?"

The seer shrugged but a smart glimmer in his eyes said he did know. But he stayed silent.

God, the surface. He hadn't been there...in ages. The last time was before the Great War and even then he preferred his richer, brighter colors of the rift than the dull colors of the earthen-realm.

"Fine." Alrik turned without a goodbye and headed back towards the hall. He'd just stepped foot onto the dark path when the seer spoke.

"She'll die in the process."

Alrik looked over his shoulder at the seer. "Then so be it."

The seer's merry laughter echoed around him as he stalked away with his next quest on his mind.

Three

Abbigail stretched her tight muscles as she got out of the car. The sun was entirely too bright today...like it was trying to sear her eyeballs. Stupid sun. It wasn't the sun's fault she hadn't been sleeping well.

She'd never been a great sleeper because she woke at the slightest of noises. Her mother said it was paranoia. Whatever it was she had a hard time sleeping and it didn't help that she lived alone. At least with a roommate she felt some added comfort and could sleep mildly better.

Abby pinched her eyes into slits to hide the brutal sunlight and grabbed her mail from the mailbox. She pulled out a stack of mail and flipped through the envelopes as she strode back to the house.

"Bill, bill, wrong address, junk, junk, more junk..." she muttered.

She paused as her gaze landed on the last envelope. The envelope was tinted yellow, the paper thick and scratchy like parchment. It certainly didn't look like any kind of envelope she'd ever received before. Then again, companies that sent out junk mail did seem to be finding more creative ways to get people to open their trash mail.

The tall black cursive letters on the front read: To Abbigail Krenshaw then listed her address below in the same unique scrawl that looked like something from an older era. No return address, and Just a stamp. She flipped the envelope over and her brow drew down in confusion. A black seal made of wax covered the V-closing of the envelope.

Apparently, this was no envelope you licked closed. Certainly not something you'd see from a credit card company trying to get you to apply for a high-interest, low-limit card. She fingered the material and touched the seal feeling the waxy material under her fingertip. Some symbols marked the seal, but it was hard to make out. It just looked like something official. There were two poles curving left and right on the outside with a regal bird's head in the middle. Peering closer, she corrected herself. Swords, not poles. She could just make out the handles and the edge of the blades if she looked hard enough but not any details of the bird's head.

"What the..." she said under her breath.

Just to make sure she flipped the strange envelope back over and ensured that it was indeed her name on the letter. Yup, sure was. A strange feeling filled her, starting in her gut and working its way up to the back of her neck until the little hairs stood on end.

She had to sit down for this. Heading back to the house she plopped down on her sofa. Dropping the rest of the mail on her chipped coffee table, she propped her feet up on it and leaned back to inspect the letter.

She hadn't noticed something before. She had been taking in too many other things on the letter: the handwriting, the seal, but now she noticed it. The worn look to it. As if it'd been crumbled again and again or passed between many hands. Where the envelope should be smooth and firm, the paper was wrinkled and weak, and one corner was bent.

"I'm stalling," she muttered.

Taking a deep breath, she flipped the envelope over and peeled back the seal; it popped off with a soft snapping sound. A heavy ball formed in her gut. It was almost as if she knew what it was before she even pulled the letter out, which had to be impossible. Maybe a part of her did know, could feel it.

She pulled the yellowed letter out of the envelope, folded thrice. It too was wrinkled and crumpled. This paper was much thinner than the envelope and softer but not as wrinkled like the envelope. The front and back were covered in handwriting of the same elegant, heavily inked hand.

It took effort to keep her hands steady, but she managed it as she parted the folds and opened the letter.

She read it slowly, her feelings so confused she didn't try to control or understand it. As she read the last word on the page, her chest twisted so tightly that her heart felt like it was being wrung like a wet rag in someone's hands. She took deep breaths and read it again.

Dearest Abbigail,

I've started this letter so many times only to throw it away.

What does a man say to his child? His child whom he's never met, but watched from afar. I'm afraid, dear Abbigail, that there is no way for me to tell you any of this gently. I only hope that you read this and that you can understand.

I met the love of my life many, many years ago and I lost her. She was taken, stolen from me. She's been lost for a long time. I was nearly lost to despair, even with my own three girls to raise. I think that made it even harder. I couldn't break down like my heart wanted to. I couldn't hide or leave them to search for her. I had to be here because they'd lost someone special too. That woman was my wife, my Protector, Mary Bellum.

One day a new light entered my world. It was so unexpected. I don't know if I could even describe it. My children made me happy. They filled me with love, but there was and always will be a gaping hole in my heart. Nothing could fill it, or so I thought. The day I met your mother all of that changed. It was as if I could breathe a full breath of air for the first time in so long. I wanted to fall to my knees before her and cry in joy. Naturally, that wouldn't have been very brave of me, so instead I asked your mother out and she said yes.

She said yes. She changed my life.

Then, something else that I'd never thought possible happened. She had a child. Our child.

I can still remember the feeling. It was like so much happiness and joy had been shoved into my chest it might burst. I didn't know if I could contain it. However, things can never be perfect. I missed my mate dearly. Even though I loved your mother dearly, she could never fill the whole in my chest fully. No matter how much I wanted her to.

This is where I falter. What to say next? Nothing could ever replace my not being there for you, though from afar I was. I saw your pictures as you grew up, could hear your small voice in the background when I called your mother on the phone. I heard and watched you grow up into a lovely, smart, and charming young woman. A man and a father, dare I say, could never be prouder than I am of you, dear Abbigail. Please believe that.

The day your mother told me you punched a girl in the face after she started a fight with your shapeshifter friend, I grinned in pride. The day your science project won the highest reward in both high school and college brought me to tears. Your mind, darling girl, nothing, and I mean nothing, is more beautiful than that.

Now, for the hard news. I wish I didn't have to tell you like this. Just once in my life I wanted to pull you into my arms and feel you there, to sit across from you and hear your voice in person. It breaks my heart to think of it. Maybe I should have done more. God, it's something I've struggled with every single day since the day you were born.

However, I have one fatal flaw. I've loved one woman in my life and she is gone. Nothing and no one can replace that. I hope one day you understand that feeling.

You need to know that if you're reading this letter then I am no longer on this earth. I have met my Great Death and moved on to the next life. Perhaps it's my own cowardice waiting until now to send this letter, but I didn't know what else to do.

The point of this letter, the point of my writing you is to tell you that I love you. I love you so much that just writing the words on a piece of paper can't possibly show you just how much I feel or explain how I can love someone so utterly and dearly without ever meeting them. But I do. How I do, Abbigail. Please, if nothing else in this letter, believe that. Believe me. I love you.

I want you to know you have three sisters. Chloe, Willow, and the youngest Lily. You have sisters. If you're as courageous as I think you are then I know you'll seek them out, and I sincerely hope you do. It's my hope now that you can be a family together in a way I could never provide. I hope you can find it in yourself to forgive me.

With all my love,
May 15, 2011
Francis Jeremiah Bellum

Tears formed at her eyes. She blinked and two dropped onto the letter splattering wetly across the words. She rubbed gently at them as she sucked in a ragged breath. She made sure to be careful, not wanting the wetness to smudge the ink.

She sat the letter on the cushion next to her and stared off at the wall, her mind turning slowly trying to put the pieces together. After some time, her mind returned to normal speed. Her body slowly relaxed and the weight on her chest gradually released. The tight knot in her gut faded. Her body relaxed as best it could considering what just happened.

She knew what she had to do. She just wasn't sure she wanted to do it. But she had to.

She went to the kitchen, picked up the phone, and dialed the numbers she called many times a week. Her mother answered on the second ring.

"Hey, baby. How you doin'?"

She could hear the sounds of people chattering in the background. The soft Celtic music her mother always listened to playing gently. She was at work.

"I got a strange letter in the mail."

Silence. Abby's gut feeling came roaring back to life. She gripped the counter in her hand, squeezing tight to the surface until her knuckles locked and blanched. Her eyes fixed on some indescript point on the white stucco wall of her kitchen.

"Mom?"

"I think we need to talk," her mother said gently. She heard her mother's voice break. The sound crushed her heart as if a fist gripped it. She could never stand the sound of her mother crying without feeling the same emotional pull inside her.

Abby's fist clenched tighter around the lip of the counter. "About what?" she managed to ask over her own clogged throat.

"It's about your father."

It was then that Abbigail Krenshaw's life changed.

§

By the time Abbigail arrived at her mother's magic shop aptly named Magic Shoppe, her mother had cleared out all guests, sent the employees home, and closed shop. This left the parking lot completely empty except for her mother's green Volkswagen Bug parked off to the side. The shop didn't have many employees, and mom had two coworkers under her. Both were witches who practiced magic in the same circle as her.

Her mom even managed to pull in a decent amount of profit from her shop. Abbigail thought the idea was hilarious when her mom first told her some eleven years ago that she'd be opening a "new age" store. She stopped laughing when her mom sold her fifty-year old home with bad plumbing and shoddy insolation and upgraded to a brand new two-story house in the suburbs. It was far from a mansion but wasn't close to being a dump either.

She'd done well because of the "new age" fad that had come and gone but wasn't really gone. Her brand and business had stuck around well enough in Fort Collins even among the local humans.

Humans knew about magic, though some still didn't believe in it. Some even knew about demons, shapeshifters, and the vampires of the world. Most ignored it because if they didn't then they'd have to accept something most weren't ready to. So most humans stayed out of the paranormal business, except for the fundamentalists. Whenever they got involved, things always got bloody. A slain vampire here, a dead shapeshifter there. Abbigail knew all about it. 'Course it went both ways when humans wind up dead, but that wasn't the area Abbigail worked. It didn't help that she got to see it more often than other folks.

Abbigail stepped inside her mother's shop and stopped. She didn't want to do this, but she needed to. Her stomach twisted with nerves, and her hands fidgeted no matter how hard she tried to still them. Even her legs felt weak like she could fall down at any moment. The music was off leaving the shop quiet except for the soft whirr of the A/C unit. The A/C was a bit of a strange thing in the North of Colorado. Usually by now, the temperature had dropped and people were preparing for the cold wet weather to come with winter. Instead they'd had a surprising amount of heat that still lingered in the air.

"Abby, is that you?" her mother called from the back of the store.

This is it. She couldn't turn back now. All those years of never knowing who her father was, of asking her mother repeatedly for answers only to get shut down time and again, this was her chance. She'd never told her mother, but that was the reason she'd shunned her mother's craft. It was petty, she thought, looking back on it, but no matter. That's just how it turned out.

Her mother was a practicing grey witch which meant she could dabble in magic that could heal or hurt. Abby had the same power in her blood, but it seemed that each year that passed growing up, each new birthday she had, each holiday that came and swept away without knowledge of her father, she pushed her mother further and further away. Until now, she only saw her mother on those holidays and birthdays, and only talked to her on the phone a few days a week. Even the phone calls they shared didn't last long—Abby made sure of that. She just couldn't stand to be around her.

And now she knew who her father was. What she didn't know was how to feel about it or how to feel towards her mother. Her mother's soft footsteps came out of the office and Abby closed her eyes. Anger, she certainly felt some anger but that wasn't the overriding emotion surprisingly. No, she wasn't very angry with her mother.

"Abby, is everything all right?" her mother asked, her voice closer, wary.

Abby kept her eyes closed and focused on just herself and the emotions scattering and darting around inside her as if they too didn't want to be figured out yet. As if something terrible might happen if she did figure it out—something awful maybe. Abby felt as if she was swimming through her own heavy emotions, searching to figure out which one she was feeling. Her breath caught as she found it. It wasn't anger, surprise, or confusion she felt. It was pain. Pure and not very simple, pain.

The words came to the tip of her tongue, laden with every ounce of emotion riding her. Abby spoke before she lost them. "After all this time, I needed to know. I had to know and you couldn't tell me.

Not once. Not after all the begging and the tears and the pleading." Her voice cracked, tears slipped out of her tightly squeezed eyes, but still she went on. "And now that he's found me and I've found him, he's dead. I know who he is and I can still never know him. And I can never talk to him, never hug him, never know him."

Abbigail wanted to drop to her knees and curl up in her bed and let her numb body find itself again. She wouldn't do it, and her pride wouldn't let her. She only let one sob escape before she clamped her lips shut, slammed her eyes closed, and just rocked on her feet with arms wrapped around her waist. He'd wanted her to know about him. He hadn't wanted her mother, which hurt on a level of its own.

"I wish he wouldn't have even sent the stupid letter," Abby said, slowing her rocking. Her mother was oddly quiet, all things considered. "You know, mom, it feels like there's a knife in my heart that hadn't been there before. It's like I'm being taunted. 'Oh by the way, I love you and would have loved to be in your life. Too bad I'm dead now.' And the stuff he said about you. I don't know if I hate him or…"

Finally her mother spoke. "Let me see the letter, honey."

Long engrained to answer her mother's commands, Abby pulled the letter out of her back pocket and handed it over. She kept her eyes averted unable to meet her mother's sad eyes.

A few minutes passed while Abbigail listened to her mother's breath catch and tears clog her throat as she tried to control it.

"I'll tell you everything," her mother said.

Anger started to poke its head up. Now you'll tell me, Abbigail's inner conscious yelled. Now, after it's too late to do anything about it! Isn't that fucking convenient for you, mother. But she didn't say any of those things that she was thinking. Instead she got up, her back muscles feeling stiff like they hadn't been used in a while and went to her mother's office to take a seat in front of the desk. Her mother followed and sat behind her beat up wooden desk that was covered in a disarray of pamphlets advertising the store, eschewed paperwork, pens without the caps on, pencils with broken points, three cups of coffee that were probably days old, and God knows what else.

"H-how do you want me to start?"

"Just...at the beginning, mom." Abby temples pounded against her skull. She pressed two fingers to the spot and rubbed circles as her mother began to tell her the very thing she'd been begging for her whole life. Funny, but she wasn't relieved or excited to hear it now. Not like she'd thought she'd be.

"I met him twenty-six years ago. He was so handsome and charming. There was something old world about him, you know, as if he came from a different time. I felt something special about him and when he pursued me, I agreed. I realized he was an incubus then. I fell in love with him fast. So fast..."

Abbigail's chest felt like it was going to explode. That meant she was part succubus? Oh my God.

"Mom," she cut in, "can you skip to only the most needed details please?" She couldn't handle hearing the falling-in-love story of her mother and father. Not right now anyway when everything felt so raw, and especially after hearing how her mother had just been second best.

"Oh, okay, anything you want honey."

The knife in Abbigail's heart twisted even deeper at her mother's favorite endearment for her. It had to be unfair that she felt angry with her mother, right? Except for the fact that she'd asked for more than twenty years to know who he was and she never received an answer. She had to find out from a letter from a dead man.

"Well, um, I got pregnant. Pretty quickly actually, and, well, I know you know about it from the letter, but it's still hard to say. He had three daughters already. They were all so precious to him. I mean he worshipped them. Their mother was his Protector. You know how they are, they get that one person who is sort of like a mate to them and they stay together forever. He loved her. They don't have to love their Protector but he did—so much."

Abbigail turned her head to stare at a green metal shelf that held cardboard boxes, stacks of printer paper, more paperwork, and a bunch of her mother's witchcraft knickknacks. She tried to focus on the paper she saw and to read the words there, but it didn't distract her enough. She couldn't remove herself from this situation because she needed to hear this. She just didn't want to, not really.

"I was afraid. I knew that I could never compete with that. He never actually said it but we spent many years together, and he never asked for us to move in. He never asked to see you. He never wanted to marry me. After his wife went missing, he never stopped looking for her. I'm sorry Abby, but we were always the outsiders."

Abbigail finally turned to look at her mother. She had her head buried in two hands and her shoulders were sagging forward. She looked much older at that moment. Her mother looked at her with wet, sad eyes, and a frown.

"I was always second. I had no choice but to be that. I didn't...I couldn't..." she scrubbed her hands over her face and shook her head as if to get rid of a bad thought. "I'm sure I was wrong, but it's like...he was holding back something from me so I...so I..."

Oh my god. So that was it, Abby thought. "He held back part of himself from you, so you kept me from him. Talk about petty, mom."

Anger sliced in her mother's eyes. "It wasn't quite like that. He never pushed to see you at all. I'm not the only one who's petty, or who's made mistakes. At least I sent him pictures."

Her mother's words hit home just as she wanted to. She'd never become a practicing witch like her mother wanted her to. She'd never carry on her mother's legacy, and yes she actually had a bit of one. And yes she did it just to spite her mother.

"Yeah, I guess we're both petty, mom."

Abby stood up, but couldn't meet her mother's eyes. Her mother started to say something, but the phone in Abby's pocked buzzed.

She took it out and answered it.

"Yeah?" she said. "Got it." She closed the phone and pocketed it. "I gotta go. A case."

She left her mother in silence and rushed out to her car. That was good. For the best. She loved her mom no matter what and all of this would have been different if only her mom had told her who her father was. She didn't deserve to find out in a fancy letter written by a dead man.

Warm air had gathered in the car, and it suffocated her in its heat. She started the engine then rolled down the windows to let in some cooler air. The breeze made her sigh as the tight muscles in her back relax. But no matter how hard she tried, she couldn't keep from crying.

Four

Night set by the time Abby got home from the lab. The dead shapeshifter case was going to be a hard one for detectives since they had no witnesses. Either that or anyone who witnessed the crime wasn't coming forward. Some people get scared in situations like this and don't want to come forward. It could be to their benefit or demise in cases where they recognized the killer. The knife used to commit the murder still hadn't been found and until all the blood and evidence was processed, nothing could be done. It was a waiting game until they got another hit.

"What a day," Abby said as she unlocked her front door and stepped into her house. It wasn't really her house; just a rental but she loved it all the same. It had three bedrooms, two baths, and a single-car garage to boot. Going from college dorms to the small apartment she shared with her friend Jenna after college to this was like hitting the lottery.

Her stomach growled. She hadn't eaten since breakfast that morning but her body was so tired she just wanted to pass out and not wake up for a week. She couldn't do that though, nope. She had to face her problems. She needed to contact her step-sisters.

She wondered: what would they think of her? Would they like her, accept her? She doubted it. She couldn't say she'd be so agreeable to accept a step-sibling that she didn't know about until now. Still, she had to try. As soon as she got some sleep she'd do some research and find some addresses. A spark of hope filled her that maybe, just maybe, they'd be wonderful. She'd only ever had her mom and no one else. She'd had friends but that wasn't the same as family. Jenna was always there if she needed her, but they weren't as close as they'd been while in college.

Abby set her lab bag on the kitchen table, snagged a yogurt out of the fridge and spoon from the kitchen drawer, and then headed to the bedroom. She needed to get a pet, a cat or maybe a dog. Something so the house wouldn't feel so empty every time she got home.

She scrubbed her face and changed into her pajamas as she finished her yogurt and tossed it into the trash bin. She'd just pulled down the comforter, ready to let her exhausted bones rest, when a bang came at a door.

Not a knock, a bang.

She jumped, her heart starting a fierce pounding beat in her chest. Her hand went to her chest, and her eyes flew wide open. She checked the clock: ten o'clock. Who the hell would be banging on her door like that? That sounded like the knocking SWAT officers used before breaking down the door when they had a search warrant.

Getting control of herself, Abby opened her nightstand drawer and pulled out her gun. She had a permit for it and she knew how to shoot. The banging persisted.

BAM! BAM! BAM! BAM! It never relented, never paused.

Abby crept down the hall on the balls of her feet as her heart thundered in time to the knocking. She kept her thumb over the safety on her gun, ready at a moment's notice to flick it off and use it.

Just as she reached the door, the banging stopped. She froze, straining to hear something. No whisper of breath, no sound of movement; she only heard the cacophonous thud of her own heartbeat. She breathed as quietly as she could as she tried to slow her racing heart. She was glad the lights were off in the house. Maybe whoever was there would assume she wasn't home and leave.

Then the banging came again, this time even harder. She flinched, her hand tightening around her gun warming the cool metal as the door shook in its sturdy frame. God, whoever it was must be strong. She wished like hell she had a peephole or even a window at the door but she had neither. The nearest front window only showed as much as the driveway. The front of the house blocked the doorway from view.

Only a door stood between her and the person knocking.

BAM! BAM! BAM! BAM! BAM!

Finally finding her voice, she called out in a hard voice, "Who's there?" Well, she'd tried for a stern voice but it still came out sounding scared, alert.

The knocking stopped as if it never happened. Only a resounding echo and her racing heart showed she wasn't crazy.

She heard a muffled voice, deep, unintelligible.

"What?" she said, yelling louder through the door. She wasn't stupid enough to open it. Hell no. Her thumb traced over the small safety lever on the gun, itching to release it.

"Abbigail Krenshaw," the deep voice said.

Her stomach fell to her knees. Fuck, what did she do now? Somehow this man, it was definitely a masculine voice, knew her name and that scared the shit out of her. She looked around, feeling as if dozens of eyes were watching her but she didn't find any. Only her empty dark house stared back at her. The green clock from the kitchen stove still lit the kitchen up in a dim glow and nightlights in the hallway and living room were dim but showed enough light to see that no one waited to jump her.

"What do you want?"

The voice didn't answer. All went silent. Abbigail swept her gaze around her house again as if, at any moment, a window would burst and some crazed maniac would jump through her window ready to gut her like the victim she saw this morning.

"Open this door." It was a command, an order.

Abbigail had no intention of answering it. Instead, she slowly raised her gun, keeping her thumb near the safety, and pointed it at the door. Quietly, she backed up towards the kitchen and to her phone.

BAM! BAM! BAM! BAM! The knocking started again, unrelenting.

Her breath caught at the sound of cracking wood. Her eyes darted around the door trying to see a crack, but she couldn't see any broken wood. She could have sworn she heard it crack. He knocked again, louder, the banging sound ringing in her ears amidst more splintering sounds. God, he's breaking down the doorframe, tearing it down!

She turned and ran to the phone. She faced the door, gun ready as she dialed. Her fingers slipped in their haste, and she had to end the call and try again twice before she got the three digits dialed—911.

"911, what's your emergency?"

"A man's trying to break into my house," Abbigail whispered, but her voice sounded just as panicked as she felt. The knocking continued, never stopping. "Oh my god, do you hear that?"

"What's your address ma'am?" Abby related it quickly. "Ma'am, get to a back room with a lock on it and lock yourself in there. Stay on the line. Patrol officers are on the way."

Abby started towards the bedroom then stopped as she felt the cord to her phone pull taut.

"I can't take the phone with me. It's not wireless." God, she felt really stupid now. She thought the corded, old-fashioned phone was cute and trendy when she bought it. It was one of those vintage, dark yellow ones that hung on the wall. She liked it because it came from the fifties and had a certain flair to it.

"Then set the phone down but do not hang up if you can. Patrols will be there shortly."

No sooner than the operator declared that the door shook violently.

"He's kicking it," she said, part in fear and part in disbelief.

Abby waited no longer. She turned and ran for the bedroom just as she heard the door burst open in an explosion of splintered wood. The front door bounced off the wall with a resounding crack just as she entered her bedroom, slamming the door closed and flipped the measly turn lock.

Her thumb swept the safety off her gun and she sprinted into her bathroom as another bang came at her bedroom door. No way would that weak wooded door last nearly as long as the front door.

She slammed the bathroom door shut, locked it and moved as far back as she could in the tight space by wedging herself between the toilet and shower. Shaking and scared out of her mind, she raised her gun, index finger poised over the trigger and waited.

BAM! BAM! CRACK!

The bedroom door slammed open. She heard it beat against her nightstand with another blow. She started praying for the police to come, and she didn't want to be another body like the ones she found for a living. Her arms shook. As she looked down the peephole of the black gun, the hole wavered, wobbling around in waves that she tried to steady but couldn't.

She kept waiting for him to come, kept waiting to hear the banging on the bathroom door. But it never came. A minute passed. Then another. And another.

A part of her told her to check the door, open it just an inch and peer outside. Maybe he was gone and she did have a gun after all. She could shoot if he charged at her, but the smarter part of her mind told her to wait there. Wait for the police. They shouldn't be that long. After all, she lived close to her job and her job which was with the police department.

Sure enough, another minute passed and she could hear the faint howling of sires in the distance. As they got louder, her heart rate slowed and her muscles relaxed, but she never dropped aim no matter how hard her arms shook.

She heard men entering her house.

"Abbigail Krenshaw!" a voice shouted.

She'd never been more relieved to hear another person's voice in her life. She collapsed against the toilet. "Mike, I'm in the bathroom!" Footsteps bounded in her bedroom but something made her stay in the bathroom. As if she had to be certain it was safe and this wasn't all some gimmick.

A soft triple knock came at the door. "Abbigail, are you all right?"

Mike's voice was tense, not that she was surprised. He was a sweet guy. A good cop and she'd probably just scared the shit out of him with her call. She stood on legs that didn't feel like her own and unlocked the door. She opened it slowly, peering out as she'd wanted to before. She met his dark blue eyes and light head of hair then let the door open all the way.

He had a hard look in his eyes, the kind he used when surveying a crime scene. "You okay?" His eyes traced her quickly from head to toe ensuring all parts were accounted for.

She nodded and before she knew it, he wrapped her in his arms. It was beyond unprofessional but she hugged him back. After the insanity she just went through, the least she deserved was a hug, right?

She pulled back first and gave him a tight-lipped smile.

"Now tell me why your doors are busted in and what the hell happened."

Abby shrugged then told him what happened. His frown got deeper and deeper as she continued. No matter how hard she tried to describe how terrifying it all was, she couldn't. No words could describe that.

"Stay in a hotel tonight. Use cash."

It was Abby's turn to frown. "What? No, why?"

He lifted a dark blonde eyebrow at her. "Because you don't have a front door."

Her face flushed and she nodded. "Right."

She packed a bag, being sure to put her gun in there, and changed out of her pajamas. As she left her house, she saw the detective unit making a crime scene out of her home.

Mike watched her walk to her car from the front door. She didn't like his scrutiny or that she'd needed help like this. These were good cops and had much better cases to be working on then spending time in her house. However, Mike insisted.

This whole thing was all so bizarre. Too many questions rang in her head: who had beaten in her door, and why did he want her?

She opened her car door and tossed her hastily stuffed duffel bag into the passenger seat. Strange, she didn't feel tired now. She felt as if she could run a mile at a full on sprint and not even be out of breath.

"Damn, hey, Abby." Mike took a step towards her, but then stopped.

Abbigail blinked. What the... he didn't stop, he froze. No, not just him, everything had frozen. The air that had been stirring the hair around her face stopped. The strands dropped flat against her. The trees swaying from the breeze stopped up and down the street leaning in mid-sway as if reaching for something. The voices in the house ceased. All went quiet, dark.

She felt him before she saw him. A roar filled her ears. She turned around and leaned back against the car for support. Time seemed to slow or maybe it was just her adrenaline pumping that made it seem like time slowed. What was that sound, the roar? Shoot, it was her heart racing.

"Mike!" Her one last chance for help, she called out. She darted a glance at Mike and saw him still frozen with one foot forward, his body in mid-step, and eyes locked on her, unblinking.

It dawned on her then...magic. The man coming for her was using magic. She should have realized it sooner, but she was so out of touch with it.

She felt him coming.

Spinning around, she stared at her neighbor's dark house. Her neighbors were older and paranoid and they always kept their outdoor lights on and several inside the house at night. Now the house sat completely dark and empty looking. Somewhere in the back of her mind, she realized the streetlights were off too leaving everything dark with only the moon light to guide her eyes.

The man appeared before her very eyes. A cloaking spell to disguise his presence,, that took strong magic. He didn't move towards her, just faced her from her neighbor's yard.

Her breath caught, heart stuttered. The first thing she noticed was his eyes. The darkest eyes she'd ever seen, too dark to be human. Pitch black. Her eyes moved away from his face. Curiosity had her digging to learn more about him. Just who was this and what did he want with her?

"Abbigail Krenshaw." Her stomach trembled at his deep voice. He had a deep voice. It could be sexy if it wasn't so terrifying. The way he said her name was unusual too, Abb-ee-gyle Kreenshaw.

She sensed the question in his voice though she hadn't heard the upward inflection normally there in a question. Maybe it was fear or the strangeness of everything, but she answered. "Yes."

He started towards her. Coming closer, out of the shadows, she could see him more clearly. His long, dark hair was as black as the empty pit of his eyes. His hair came down to his shoulders but was cut unevenly at the ends, not straight. She saw ebony skin that was so dark it was to the point of being black not brown. He wore a strange looking shirt that reminded her of a tunic. It was black, knitted, long-sleeved but with an open collar, black pants, and tall black boots. None of this kept her attention for very long because as he came closer, she saw the glint of metal on his back. Two weapons, swords actually, were strapped in an X pattern across his pattern.

"What are you?" she whispered. He was handsome, tall, and looked strong enough to pick her up and snap her in two she'd bet. He also didn't look entirely human.

He stopped so close she could feel the heat from his body. For some reason, she found she wasn't scared anymore. Maybe it was finally seeing her pursuer, but she didn't get the vibe that this man would slit her throat and leave her for dead. It might be dangerous, but she trusted her instincts on this. She craned her head up to see his face. No, he wasn't handsome. He was stunning.

His hair formed from a peak at his broad forehead. He had a brusque, distinguishing nose and high cheekbones that gave a hollowed definition to his cheek line. Dark stubble covered his jaw line and chin, but underneath that she could see he had a hard, jutting chin. He had full, masculine lips with the top just thinner than the bottom. They weren't perfect but that's what made them even more intriguing. All of his features on closer inspection were too perfect, and they shouldn't have formed a good-looking face. He should look too fierce, too sharp but somehow his features came together in a way that drew the eye.

"Demon," he answered.

His voice drew her out of her inspection. She'd forgotten she'd asked him a question. He's a demon? She knew about them. Most humans just pretended they didn't exist or only did in a religious or mythical way, but she knew about the supernaturals. Heck, her best friend Jenna could shapeshift into a panther, and Abby had once autopsied a vampire. However, she'd never met a demon. To say they were uncommon would be an understatement.

Her mother had spoon-fed her lore of the great wars fought by the vampires against demons long ago. Weapons manufacturer and wealthy tycoon, Telal Demuzi had come out publicly when heat grew on him about his strange appearance some years ago. He'd admitted to being a demon, he'd embraced it, said he was over a thousand years old, and it'd shocked many humans. You wouldn't think

they could be shocked. Vampires were all the rage—
real ones anyway. They were slowly coming out but
most still lived in secluded communities across the
globe. Many more had called him a liar and still
believed he used makeup and hair dye to achieve his
unique look. They said it was a marketing gimmick.

But, Abbigail knew better. Her best friend
Jenna was a shapeshifter, something else many
humans pretended didn't exist, however many knew.
Humans just didn't seem as interested in the beings
who could shapeshift. Abby had seen Jenna shift
before—it was one of the most frightening and
beautiful things she'd ever seen in her life.

Yet the creature before her was neither vampire
nor shapeshifter nor witch for that matter. He was
the stuff of nightmares.

"What do you want?"

His answer came fast. "You."

Her stomach knotted then dropped right out of
her.

A flutter moved inside her. Pleasure.

Oh, don't be silly, Abby. He's probably going
to kill you. She should seriously not be flattered that
a good-looking demon said he wanted her. It had to
be hormones because she could feel the beginnings
of a blush stir.

Before she could say anything, he wrapped a
strong arm around her shoulders pulling her close
and then she felt the earth sway at her feet.
Darkness enveloped her eyes, and she went blind.
Then she felt nothing under her feet. She was falling
in space, seeing nothing but empty blackness and

hearing nothing but her own fast breaths. The strong arm holding her drew her in tighter as her heart thumped louder in her ears.

Five

The human was different than he'd expected. The presence of magic surrounded her like a bright cloud. How could she not be using it if it was wrapped around her so? She must still be practicing. The seer must be wrong and this meant only good news for him. This meant she'd be ready to kill his mother much quicker than he'd originally thought. Perhaps with a little additional training from him she'd be ready in no time. They could leave to track the queen in as a little as a week if luck stayed with him.

Alrik shifted the slight weight of the human girl in his arms—she was a light thing—and scanned the area around him before swimming down into the lake and resurfacing in the hidden cove that lie under the slope of the beach. He rose with the human, water dripping from their hair and clothes. Thanks to the effect of porting, she still slept. Many couldn't handle it especially for their first time.

His boots splashed in the ankle-deep water as he made his way into the blackened cave that'd become his impromptu home. He'd had many 'homes' since being banished by his brother Telal. Sometimes on his travels, he would find a desolate shack or old farmhouse that he'd steal a few nights away in, but the further he'd gone from the kingdom the less he saw of other people.

Not much lived outside the kingdom, and the kingdom offered the only protection against idummi attacks. They had a highly trained militia of shahoulin demon warriors—the best in the rift. The lethal venom idummi carried in their fangs would kill anything it bit unless treated promptly by someone who knew what they were doing.

Alrik hadn't slept well in years it seemed. Since he was forced from his crown, his journey seemed to stretch on endlessly. He had no one. He'd never known how much he craved companionship, even just idle conversation, until he no longer had it.

He couldn't even relax let alone get a full night's rest. Not when the idummi targeted him like he'd be their next juicy snack. He'd interrogated enough idummi before ending their lives to learn his mother stood behind the attacks. He couldn't say that surprised him. She knew he was after her and that he was shunned from his kingdom. Which only meant that she knew he wanted to kill her. Alrik had prepared the best he could for her because few were smarter and more cunning than his mother. She'd set a target on his back the moment she learned of his banishment. Now it was just a matter of time to see who died first.

Just how many idummi she'd managed to rally to her cause, he didn't know. If his mother was one thing aside from insane, it was smart. She might have an army bigger than he could imagine. He'd just have to prepare for the worst. He did have one benefit on his side—determination. He wouldn't stop. Nothing would get in his way until her royal wet blood slipped between his fingers.

The cove he'd chosen to use was off a small, freshwater lake in the rift. The cave was well hidden around sharp rocks and a dangerous, steep slope that led down to the water. From atop the slope it looked like it went down into the water and nothing else, but when one actually walked down the slope and swam down, the slope actually gave way underneath to a large, cavernous space.

The human mumbled to herself, her head lolling left and right. Something tightened in his gut as he looked at her. He didn't like it. Gazing upon her stirred something deep inside of him.

Alrik cursed.

Who was she to try to compete with his Arianna? She was no Arianna. Arianna was a goddess. Beautiful, shining, dark black hair fell down to her slender waist and a graceful figure and demeanor that could only be obtained with the best of haute, aristocratic blood in her veins. This human looked nothing like his Arianna. She had hair the color of wet dirt. It looked thin and not heavy like Arianna's hair. She had wide hips and more curves than Arianna, but Arianna didn't need blatant curves. Her graceful figure brought about attention alone.

Simply put, she wasn't his Arianna.

Then why did his gut clench just looking at her?

Too long without a woman, maybe. His gaze trailed over her form once more taking in the slight span of her waist and the flare of her hips. The sight stirred something hot buried deep inside him. He wondered how she'd feel pressed tight against him…bare skin to bare skin.

His cock hardened like steel.

Enough!

Alrik charged into the dark cave. He didn't need his sight in his place; he knew it like the edge of his sword. He went far back into the cave, sidestepping the fire pit he'd made before he'd left to find the human. Then he dropped the human on the sandy floor. He wasn't gentle about it and she gave him the response he'd been looking for. Her eyes shot open, mouth forming a big circle as pain pinched her features. She let out a low, husky groan that did nothing to alleviate the pressure in his groin.

"What the hell," she groaned, turning on her side to rub her back.

"We will talk now."

She hadn't been aware of him, he realized. Now she was. Slowly her head fell back, her eyes turned up to meet his. Recognition dawned slowly. Her eyes darted wildly around the cave filling with panic and fear. She stood in a rush then wobbled on her feet. Panic had her in its grip. She swung her arms out, found the wet cave wall with a hand and then leaned towards it to steady herself, pressing both hands against it.

"What the hell's going on? Oh my god, where am I?"

"Be quiet. I will talk and you will listen. Do you understand?" He hadn't met a human in years. In his previous experience, some were smart and others not so much. He hoped his salvation didn't lie in a daft girl who looked entirely too young to have the amount of power the seer spoke of.

She turned and glared at him. The spark of anger was good, and the cleverness he spotted in her eyes even better. Good, she wouldn't be daft.

"Excuse me? How about you tell me who you are, demon, where I am, why I'm here, and what you want with me?" She crossed her arms and set her light green eyes on him.

Alrik had the distinct urge to stalk over to her and tower over her just to see her quiver in fear. She will learn her place soon enough. Her attitude would go even quicker. He was a king, and some lowly human would not treat him like a servant.

Alrik straightened and let the darkness in his heart bleed out to the air around him, stifling it, biting out the oxygen she so desperately need. The human sensed his magic. Her eyes traced the air around her as if she could see it. Maybe she could.

Then she gasped, choking. Her hands flew to her throat as she gagged, her lungs working hard to suck in air. Her knees buckled and only then did he release his magic. Stepping close to her, he looked down at her puny form with a sneer. "You do not order me around, human. Stay down or what you just felt will only be a taste of what I'll do to you."

When she looked up at him it wasn't with fear as he'd expected but...anger. Alrik took a step back, then another. He had to stay away from her. Maybe she was more dangerous then he'd originally given her credit for. She had fight in her. She wasn't stupid and she wasn't easily scared. Hmm... Maybe this could turn out to be in his favor. Having a strong witch under him, a smart one even, would be much better than a weak one. She wouldn't cower in fear when she saw her first idummi demon, which she surely would see many of during their journey.

"Good, your lack of fear gives me some confidence that you'll do after all."

"For what?" she spat, her eyes glaring fiery hatred at him.

He loved the look. His body absorbed the hatred and when he sucked in a deep breath, he almost felt fuller, more whole, and some feeling close to happiness. He loved the hatred as much as it loved him. He smiled bearing his teeth. "You'll aid me in killing my mother."

She choked in surprise, her eyes flying wide and jaw dropping. He could see the edge of her pink tongue and jerked his gaze away as a blaze of something wrong flew through him. Kneeling by the fire pit, he set to work stacking logs and began lighting them with a quick spell. He needed something to do other than stare at her. Something unsettled him when he looked at her.

"Excuse me, camp master, but I'm not helping you kill anyone. Where am I?"

He waited until all the logs caught and the orange glow lit up the cavern. His gaze caught on her face. She wasn't beautiful like Arianna, but something about her was pleasant to look at he just couldn't put his finger on it yet. Overall, she almost looked plain, simple even, but something about him stirred him.

"You're good to look at too that will make things easier," he said.

Her face scrunched, then relaxed, and then scrunched again. "What?"

He shrugged and then pulled his swords off his back laying them next to him, but away from her in case she got any ideas. "A pleasant face is easier to look at than an ugly one."

Her mouth dropped open again. She did that a lot, he noticed. Her entire face was active, flashing from one emotion to the next at any moment. It'd make her easy to read. He smiled into the fire. The seer might just earn a reward after his mother's ashes were burned to crisp. He'd chosen a worthy witch it seemed.

"Answer my questions, demon," the little witch said. A hint of threat lingered in her words. He'd tolerate her insolence for a little longer. She'd realize her place soon enough.

"Stay silent and hear me well, human—"

"I have a name," she cut in.

His fists clenched. "Do. Not. Interrupt. Me." He waited until she slumped against the wall before he continued. "I was told by the seer that you will be the one to kill my mother. I thought I could do it, but that's not the case. With the curse on me—"

"You're cursed?" She didn't look angry so much as curious. Her eyes skimmed over him leaving him unsettled. He fought the urge to cover up his darkened skin, to turn away from her.

"Don't look at me." He hadn't meant to say it. It had been a knee-jerk reaction. He could do nothing to take back his words though.

She scoffed. "Really, I can't do that either? Get real, demon."

Inwardly, he breathed a sigh of relief that she didn't notice his revealing words. "I am very real, I assure you, human. My name is King Alrik and you will call me thus. As to where you are, leave it said that you're in the rift—the demonic nether-realm."

Her head fell to the side. "A king? Really?" Her eyes rolled in a way that sparked irritation. "Come on just take me home and I won't press charges."

Now Alrik frowned in confusion. "How do you press a charge? You're speaking nonsense, human."

Her face flashed with annoyance, her small shapely mouth pinching together. "That means I'll go to the police, you know the authorities."

God, maybe he had been wrong. She might just be daft after all. "Abbigail Krenshaw if you think your human police as you call them could ever contain me, you'd be very wrong."

She started to say something, then slammed her mouth closed and leaned back against the wall with a defiant cross of her arms.

"Fine, continue your little story then."

He stiffened as anger flowed through him. She thought to speak to him as if she had control of this situation? He took a deep breath as anger filled his blood thick and hot like syrup, warming his cold body. The rush of it went to his head like a bolt of lightning, quickening his senses. "You will kill my mother."

"Why?" she shot back.

"To remove the curse that binds me." He'd already considered the other part of the seer's words and figured it better not to reveal the probable ending to the human's life. Knowing she'd die in the process would not help her decision to join his cause.

"What kind of curse is it?"

Alrik jerked his sword into his lap and pulled out a smooth rock from his pocket. Bending over the blade in the firelight, he began pressing the stone to the edge of the blade and slowly dragging it down in long strokes. The soothing motion of sharpening his blade helped him to think. He hadn't planned to reveal his curse to her. It brought about too many problems, problems he didn't want to think about. His blade hissed over the metal.

"One that I must remove. That is all." He left it at that.

She shook her head in disbelief. "Fine, but I'm not doing it."

His gaze shot across the fire to her. She flinched. Good, he thought. "You might want to rethink your words, human. I know of someone very precious to you. Someone whose life I could take as easily as I stole you from your home."

She shot to her feet. "My mother?" she yelled, her cry echoing off the walls.

Alrik let out a stuttering breath as her anger caressed him like a soft hand. His eyes fluttered closed, hand flexed over the hand of his blade. "Yes, I know who she is and where she is. If you are wise you will abide me on my journey. After, you can return to her unharmed both of you will live." He let his lie hide beneath his dark eyes. He couldn't stop from noticing the way her heavy breaths moved her quite full breasts up and down in the most erotic way. He jerked his gaze away and stared into the fire, focusing on banishing the unwanted, lustful thoughts.

"Let me get this straight, if I help you kill some woman I don't know then you'll return me to my mother?"

"Yes."

"I'd sooner believe I could throw you through this wall than a bunch of horseshit like that."

Alrik tensed. He needed her to believe him or this would never work. Standing tall, he stepped into her, backing her into the wall. Her chest flattened against his and he stifled a groan. Quite full breasts indeed.

Her gaze darted anywhere but at his face, but he stared down at her until finally, without a choice, she lifted her chin and met his stare.

"I do not lie." Lie. "You do this with me and I'll protect you every step of the way." Truth. He needed her alive. "After the deed is done, I'll return you to the earthen-realm and you'll never hear from me again." Partial-truth. She'd never make it back to the earthen-realm.

He tried to read her eyes—did she buy it?—but they revealed nothing other than a stony stare.

"Get away from me," she said. Did his ears betray him or was that a tremble in her voice? His chest expanded and his gaze fell to her mouth. Her lips looked soft, welcoming. A soft sound caressed his ears...a hitch in her breath. A hot knot formed in his chest and shot down to his cock at the sound. Those shapely and pouty lips beckoned a man like a sin.

Before he did something to hurt his cause, he stepped back and took his seat by his weapons.

Picking up his whet stone, he scraped it hard across his blade. For the millionth time he wished things were different, that he was different, but he couldn't change what was. Couldn't change who he'd become. But he could kill his mother and hopefully right some past wrongs.

With an edge to his voice he said, "You will help me or I'll slit your mother's throat before your eyes. I'll force you to help me anyway and kill you after the deed is done. You have your choices, now decide."

The human pressed a hand over her heart. The pained expression on her face hit him strangely in the chest. For some reason the look didn't fill him with a rush; instead, strangely, guilt ate at him. He didn't have time to study the emotion he hadn't felt in so long because he ruthlessly shoved it away.

The human straightened her spine, lifted her chin, and stared down at him with a loathing he welcomed over guilt. "I'll do it."

"Good choice."

In a flash, the look on her face changed. Her arms flattened to her sides, fingers spreading open to the earth. He had only a moment to feel the magic swirl around him before he felt invisible binds wrapping around his body, locking him into place in less than a matter of seconds. Under different circumstances, he might have been overjoyed to see her magic skills used so well. She didn't even need to speak a spell to cast magic, but he wasn't overjoyed now.

His eyes flashed to hers and found her light green eyes shining bright like a light in the cave. The binds twisted tighter around him, binding his legs together, his arms to his side, snaking around his chest and squeezing just enough to make it difficult to breathe.

"Stop this, witch," he warned, his own eyes beginning to glow.

Her body relaxed and she stumbled backwards hitting the wall. She winced, then ran up to him. He sucked in shallow breaths through the invisible binds as he brought forth his own magic. He started chanting the words to break the binds as she picked up one of his swords. She started to lift it but she'd underestimated how heavy demon steel was and dropped it back in the sand before taking off on a sprint.

The last of his spell left him and the binds loosened the magic around him. "Abbigail!" he roared.

He surged to his feet with blazing fury roaring through his veins as he charged after her.

Six

Water engulfed her. Her mouth filled with it and she swallowed the fresh, cold liquid. The frigid temperature slowed her movements but still she slugged through it and thrust her arms through the water, kicking her legs until her muscles burned. Finally, she saw light above her and shot towards it. She burst to the surface and sucked in a breath of air. Her heart raced and she quickened her movements, paddling swiftly to the surface.

Her feet sank into sand as she stood and, without time to take in her surroundings, she rushed into the forest. It looked strange. The leaves too green, the flowers too pink and red on the buds. Not a tree she'd ever seen before. Aside from the gray and pinkish swirl of the hazy sky above her, the forest looked familiar and she stuck to it, her lungs burning with every breath she took.

She raced through the forest. He had magic skills she'd never witnessed before. Hell, the fact that she'd been able to bind him when she hadn't used magic in years surprised the hell out of her. She'd just been so mad, so desperate to get away from the demon that some deep-seated magic had come forth.

It didn't take long for her gait to slow and her muscles to burn. She didn't run much. In fact, never. Her lungs felt like they were on fire but she couldn't risk stopping to catch her breath. She could almost feel him right behind her.

The demon was insane. Straight up fell-way-off-the-tree crazy. How did he find her? Why her? Why did his mother curse him? These questions roared in her head with the need for answers.

The forest broke and she stopped, her gaze swinging behind her searching for a dark, deadly man. Maybe his magic wasn't as good as she thought because he was nowhere in sight. Good, really good. She took in the scene in front of her. The strangeness of it was enough to make her want to stick to the forest but it didn't seem very big or like the best choice right now. In front of her was rocky, dirt-laden land. Two crumbled stone buildings looking ages old reminded her of an ancient battlefield. What she didn't find was anything that looked like a city or town and no people.

A sound made her freeze and flatten her back against the tree. She strained, pressing her lips together and breathed as quietly as she could through her nose as she listened. There it was again. The whoosh of leaves being brushed. He was closing in on her!

Without a second thought, she took off on a sprint for the stone building where a small rocky hill led up to it. The incline was too steep to run up so she went on hands and feet and crawled up, kicking up chalky rocks and sending them tumbling down behind her. She winced at the noise she made but continued.

Breathing hard she made it to the top. Her energy waned fast and she found it took her longer to stand up and run for the temple than she wanted. She made it and breathed a sigh of relief as she darted inside. With her back to the cold stone, she tried to collect her wild thoughts. The ceiling of the temple had caved in on one corner, and the inside was empty save for the stone floor.

"Abbigail!" the wild demon roared.

She squeaked then slapped her hand over her mouth to stifle the noise hoping like hell that she wasn't too late. God he sounded close.

He yelled her name again, this time sounding farther away and off to the left. Her eyes shot wide at her one chance. He'd check in here for sure. Hell, she knew she would if their roles were reversed. She spotted her next goal out of the crooked opening of the temple and saw a fierce mountain in the distance. It looked unused and old. Trees and foliage grew thickly up to the white peak. She didn't need to go up it; maybe if she could get to the base she could trek around it until she lost him. The forest looked thick enough that she might be able to lose him.

"Abbigail!" His voice came back, closer to the temple.

This was her chance.

She tore out of the opening, her feet slapping against the dirt and rocks. She didn't turn back to see if he saw her, just kept her eyes on the mountain and mentally calculated the distance. A couple hundred yards at least. The land wasn't flat but lifted and dipped in waves. Eyes wide, more scared than she'd ever been, even when the demon had come to her house, she let her instincts burst inside her, and flat-out ran.

The mountain came closer and closer, getting bigger as she neared. The heavy, thick tree line surrounding it beckoned her with welcome arms. Something flashed in the trees. She kept running. An animal. A stroke of fear went down her spine but still she ran straight towards it.

A distinct sound came from behind her. Her heartbeat pounded like drums in her ears as she pushed her body harder. He'd spotted her and his heavy steps were coming right after her.

Another flash of movement darted in the forest. She had no clue what kind of wild animals lived in the nether-realm where a variety of demons resided, but none could be as bad as the demon after her. None of them had threatened to kill her mother.

She smiled with joy. Less than fifty yards— nearly there. She'd make it. She heard him calling her name, his heavy steps beating the rocks. After she got a safe way in the forest she'd turn and look back, but not now.

Movement flashed again in the forest. Something shorter than her. That's all she got to see before it disappeared behind a mass of wide tree trunks. She neared the forest but never got to enter it.

A creature stepped out and she dug her feet into the ground to stop. A scream curled up in her throat but never escaped. Something nasty and very scared uncurled inside her. This thing would kill her without blinking, she just knew it.

It looked like something out of a nightmare. Evil yellow eyes with red spider web veins glared at her. Its bony body looked undernourished with knobby knees, elbows, and knuckles with extra-long fingers sporting a set of black hooded claws worthy of a bear. Surrounding its bony body was a layer of hard looking muscle. Its greenish skin looked leathery and rough to touch. Black claws stuck out sharp looking from its fingertips. The creature peeled its blackish lips back and hissed, bearing rows of sharp pointy yellow teeth.

She'd heard about other demonic creatures in the rift. Evil, horrible ones that feasted off living flesh, whose poison could kill within minutes. Was she staring at one of these creatures?

Abby started walking backwards. Her hammering heart pounded recklessly as the creature took a step towards her and didn't stop. She wanted to turn and flee but couldn't give this strange, hairless creature her back. It had green skin and was short probably not even five-feet tall yet its small size didn't ease any of her fear.

Its jaw snapped open wide like a snake's mouth detaching its jaw to eat a large prey, then a horrible ear-piercing cry split the air. Abby couldn't fight her instincts anymore. She turned and ran—straight into the arms of the crazy demon.

"Stay back!" he demanded.

Finally, an order she could comply with. He thrust her away and she toppled backwards landing hard on her butt. Half scooting backwards on her butt, she watched as the demon lifted his arms over his head and unsheathed the two swords from his back.

The creature's eyes swung to the tall, dark demon, then sprang jumping the clear twenty feet that separated them as if he had bounced off a trampoline. The demon didn't move. Abbigail watched wide-eyed as time slowed. The demon's teeth bared, its claws spread open ready to slash as it fell towards the king with a nasty cry. And yet he never moved.

Abby crushed handfuls of dirt in her hands. Her muscles tensed as the creature neared the demon. "Watch out!" she screamed. She didn't know why she'd decide to help the demon now but she couldn't take back her scream.

She didn't need to say anything apparently because as the creature nearly landed on the demon, he slashed his swords in a cross pattern. The creature howled in agony and goopy green blood spurted from its body. It dropped almost neatly at the demon's feat, twitching as it died.

Abby couldn't catch her breath. She knew she was shaking but couldn't do anything about that either. The demon stepped over the creature, and then turned so he faced her. With a cold, hard look in his eyes, he lifted his sword then swung it down in an arc.

Abby screamed as the creature's head flew from its body, severed.

She couldn't catch her breath. Her heart wouldn't slow down. She was breathing too fast and she knew it. All she could do was watch as the demon strode towards her, sheathing his blades with practiced ease. He stopped in front of her with an expression she could only describe as enraged. His hands hung at his sides, curled into tight fists.

"This land is dangerous and you're not going anywhere. You need me," he said.

She agreed, but she couldn't form any words. He studied her, a slow frown forming at his rather nice looking mouth.

"Breathe slowly, Abbigail."

She shook her head hard. No, she couldn't. Her breaths came too fast and shallow. She knew a panic attack gripped her. She'd had them before. The most embarrassing of which happened during her first real crime scene.

The demon knelt beside her and wrapped an arm around her shoulders. She tried to push away from him but couldn't do anything more than raise her hands to his chest and curl them in his wet shirt.

"You must breathe slow and deep. Do it now!"

She wanted to slap him for trying to order her not to have a panic attack, but she couldn't manage to do that either. So there she was. Her escape plan had failed and she now sat in the arms of the man who had threatened to kill her mother and wanted her to murder someone she didn't even know. Not that knowing the person might make this any easier, but still it was the principle of the matter.

He cursed harshly. Or she guessed that's what he did because whatever he just said was in Demonish not a language she understood. Pulling her around like a ragdoll, he settled her back against his chest then flattened a hand across her collarbone. Sucking in ragged breaths, she tried to pull away but his hand held her tight.

Then he spoke. *"Iridona tradeen k'loshka."* He repeated the strange words and with each passing, her breathing came easier. Her lungs relaxed, air filled her, and her mind calmed.

Exhausted, she relaxed into his arms. Her body felt so weak she didn't even care that she was using his body as a prop to lean up against. Okay, she cared a bit. After a minute of full normal breathing, she started to lean up. Just what did she say to him? Thanks for saving my life? She didn't know what social protocol dictated in this kind of situation.

His hand stopped her from getting up. The demon was entirely too strong for his own good.

"What are you doing?" she whispered, her voice ragged from what she hoped was her panic attack.

He didn't answer. He just held her in this strange position with his arm around her. He was close enough he could choke the life out of her, but he didn't make any threatening moves, just kept her back to his chest and his hand flat to her collarbone. His thumb swiped once across the bare skin of her neck and something warm pulsed inside her.

"Let me go." She swallowed over the lump in her throat.

His hand fell away from her, then his body was gone. She teetered backwards before she caught the motion.

"How am I supposed to help you?" she asked.

He gazed out at the land. "Kill my mother, the queen."

"How am I supposed to do that?"

"The seer says you have great magical power inside of you. You are the key to killing her."

Abby's brow flew up at that. "I haven't used magic since...well since in the cave, but before that...I mean it's been years. A really long time. And what seer?" A seer knew about her. Had she met the seer before and just didn't remember it?

"The Great Seer, one of the last living seers in the nether-realm. He has great wisdom. He told me to find you. He says only you can kill my mother, for the curse upon me won't let me."

Finally, he looked back at her. She hadn't realized she wanted him to until he did. His dark eyes were interesting to look at, especially when they weren't looking at her like he wanted to rip her head off. "I will help you to train your skills. You will be prepared for the fight."

A thought hit her like a gunshot. He wanted to train her to use her magic? She didn't know about this seer or about her being all-powerful or any such nonsense, but she did have some powers. If he helped to train her and make her strong then maybe she'd be strong enough to bind him for much longer or to even knock him out, then she could port home. She'd heard of witches porting, it could be done from such a great distance. It would just take a lot of strength.

"All right, I'll do it."

His eyes flared. She'd surprised him.

"Good choice," he said.

Yeah, except that she was lying.

Seven

"Try harder!"

Abbigail wiped the sweat from her brow and glowered. "If I tried any harder I might collapse. I am trying."

Alrik shook his head in frustration and paced in a tight circle. "Obviously not, witch. This isn't good enough. Close your mind off to everything but your power and feel it inside you. Then push it with your mind out towards me."

Abby made a gargled noise of frustration. "I've been trying to do that this whole time."

He stalked to her, anger slashing his handsome features into a mask. "Obviously not. Obviously not well enough since you haven't budged me an inch. Try again."

"I'm tired and hungry. I need a break."

His eyes looked up to the sky and he laughed. The sound wasn't pleasant. "We are not stopping now. I told you, you can eat after you move me with the spell I taught you. Now, try it again."

Abby wanted to strangle him. They'd been going at this for hours. Magic always took a physical toll on her and right now her body screamed at her to lie down and sleep for a few days. She didn't know why the spell wasn't working. Maybe because she'd never tried a spell that would push a person back or maybe because of the spell she used yesterday to bind him had just sapped her abilities for a short time. Hell, she didn't know but she wished she did. All she knew was that her stomach wouldn't stop growling, her eyelids kept drifting shut, and her limbs felt heavy as if she'd been holding weights all morning.

Alrik, or, she corrected, King Alrik as he wanted to be called, grabbed a small branch and stood it up against a tree. Crossing back to her, he stepped up behind her and her teeth ground at his proximity. He unsettled her, and boy did she want that feeling to go fast. Apparently, though her mind didn't trust him one inkling, her body was more than happy to feel him press up against her back. The demon was big in many ways—tall, heavily muscled. He had that whole tall, dark, and handsome thing going for him in a big way. What that little phrase should include is tall, dark, handsome, and insane. The demon was not right in the head. However, she did wonder if it was the curse on him that made him so angry all the time.

Alrik bent low so his voice fell in her ear. His hands grabbed hers and thrust them forward. "Focus on the branch, witch. See the branch falling over, flying back, anything. Just make it move."

His impatience only fueled her anger. Abby envisioned herself snapping her head backwards and busting his straight nose open, but she couldn't do that. If she ever wanted to get out of this wretched place and back to her life, she'd need to grow strong. And for that, she needed his help.

She took all that anger, hunger, and exhaustion inside her and focused it on the thin, gnarled tree branch. She pictured her magic thrusting it, sending it flying away from the tree. Her breathing deepened as she narrowed her eyes on it. Nothing happened. She strained, sweat beading her brow and falling down her face in rivulets. The muscles in her arms strained, she squeezed his big hands in hers and willed the stupid branch to move. It didn't budge. Not even a slight shudder.

"Gah! I can't do it." She pulled her hands out of his and stalked away.

"You can't keep giving up." He sounded disappointed. A small part of her actually felt guilty about this as if she didn't want to disappoint him.

She threw her hands up and spun around to face him. He wasn't the one hungry. He wasn't the one tired. He wasn't even breaking a sweat. "I'd say working for hours on this and not seeing a result should win me a break at the very least, dammit."

His eyes closed and a shuddering breath escaped him. "I'd watch your tone, witch."

She snorted. "And what's wrong with my tone?" If she didn't do one thing wrong, she did another in his mind.

His eyes opened, pierced her. "Your anger fuels me. It's the nature of the curse."

Oh, well she didn't know what to say to that. Her anger fed his anger? Why? To what purpose? To make him a bigger jackass? She wanted to ask, but his eyes flittered away from her and she swore she saw a flash of—uncertainty, vulnerability, or maybe even shame.

That strange look in his eyes made her gentle her voice. "Listen, just let me eat and rest then I'll try for as long as you want."

He ground his jaw but made his way to the animal he'd killed earlier. It was a strange looking thing about the size of a rabbit but feathered like a chicken. He called it a fruthorc. From his tall boot, he pulled out a knife and fileted the animal into bite-sized pieces. Once upon a time, the sight of a bloodied animal might have made her disgusted, but she'd seen mutilated bodies. Nothing compared to that. It took something pretty gruesome to roll her stomach anymore.

He stuck the chunks of meat on a slender stick and handed one out to her with a watchful look on his face. "You surprise me again, witch. This dead animal doesn't faze you?"

She shrugged and took the stick that looked like a shish kabob. She held it over the little fire he'd built earlier. "After you've seen some of what I have, it doesn't really bother me that much."

He stared into the fire, rolling his stick slowly so the flames licked each side of the meat. "What do you do if you're not a practicing witch?"

Her gaze jerked to his. He wanted to know something about her? "I'm a medical examiner trainee for the supernatural department of the police department. The whole division just started a few years ago. I'm still new, in training, but with a little more work I'll have my certification to work without supervision." He looked over at her, his brow furrowed and she realized he really was curious. So she went on. "That means when someone is found dead, I'm sent in to inspect the body and try to decide how they died whether it was natural, an accident, or a murder." She left the part out about how she examines bodies in the lab, cutting them open in some cases. To do that work alone, she still had another certification program to go through. In the meantime, she still worked under the steadfast eye of her supervisor Stan.

"I couldn't imagine you working with the dead in such a way. You look so fresh and young."

Ignoring the flutter in her belly at his words, she pulled the now cooked meat out of the fire and started blowing on it to cool it faster. It smelled delicious even without any seasoning. She nibbled a piece and moaned. The meaty flavor tasted like steak. She wolfed down the rest of the meat, careful of any splinters that might have gotten stuck in it.

Belly full, she sighed and laid down on the grassy ground. No sooner than her tired eyes closed, Alrik stepped up beside her. "Time to work."

She groaned. "Let me sleep for a little while."

"Work now. This isn't up for argument."

Grumbling, she opened her eyes to glare at him. Fine. She slowly stood. "Fine, then tell me what you're the king of."

He stiffened, apprehension filling his features. "Why do you care to know?" he asked, suspicion clouding his voice.

"Because I'm bored and you want me to kill someone I don't even know. The least I deserve to know is a little about my kidnapper, right?" And maybe a bit more about this curse and the queen.

He shook his head and walked back to their designated spell casting area some twenty feet from the stupid branch that refused to fall over.

"You don't need to know anything about me. Just do what I say, human."

"My name is Abbigail. If that's too hard then call me Abby."

Again, his eyes met hers and she felt his look in a warm flutter down to her belly. The demon had a penetrating stare that never ceased to unnerve her with its intensity.

"I was the king of the shahoulin," he said at length.

She focused on the branch and put the conversation on the back burner of her mind. She tried to conjure her magic and focus on knocking the branch back as he'd shown her he could do so easily.

"That means you're a shahoulin demon then, right?"

"Yes." Again, he seemed hesitant to reveal anything about himself. For some reason, that only made her want to learn more about him.

She was adjusting to the crazy demon because when he stepped up behind her she didn't stiffen. Her body warmed as it did when she used magic, and she thrust her magic out at the tree branch willing it to move. Nothing happened. She took a deep breath and tried again. She couldn't let frustration get the better of her. She never worked well that way.

"Why aren't you king anymore?"

He stood just off to the side behind her so she saw his jaw flex in anger. "Stop asking so many questions, witch."

She wanted to growl. "Stop calling me witch," she said slowly. The whole 'witch' thing got old— fast.

He crossed his arms across his big chest. "You do not order me, witch."

Anger flared inside her and she focused it on that branch. The branch shuddered then toppled over to the ground. She let out a squeal and commenced her jumping up and down victory dance. She turned to him, a big smile on her face, and held up her hand for a high-five.

He looked to her hand with a puzzled express then slapped it away. "Don't try to cast magic on me again, witch, or you'll regret it severely."

Her hands curled into hard fists at her side. "You are such an ass. I wanted a high-five. I wasn't trying to cast any damn magic on you." He didn't look swayed in the least. She held out a hand to the toppled branch. "Uh, hello, I just used my magic and made that branch fall over. I call that a good job"

He didn't say anything, but went back to the tree branch. "Then do it again," he said propping the branch back up against the tree.

The demon had to be the most insufferable man she'd ever met. What she wouldn't give to slap him good and hard across the face just once. She started to focus on the branch again, then paused.

"No, you answer one of my questions and then I'll do it. I'm not going to get nothing outta this deal." She didn't state that fact that she wanted to grow her magical powers so she could port home. Some things a girl had to keep to herself.

He growled—an actual growl that sounded too bestial to come from a person's mouth. "You are the most frustrating woman I've ever met. If we were in my kingdom I'd have you sent to the dungeons."

"Oooh," she taunted in a high-pitched voice.

His dark eyes narrowed on her. "Be cautious, witch. My patience is at an end."

"Yeah, well, so is mine. What will it hurt to give me some information? It's not like—" she stopped herself short. Shit, she'd nearly said "it's not like you're not planning to kill me anyway."

"It's not like what?" he asked.

She shook her head and focused on the branch again. Anything to distract him. It took longer this time, sweat fell from her brow, but she knocked the branch over. It landed softly on the grass

"Good," he said righting the branch, "but not good enough. You should be able to make it fly through the air at great speed and power."

"That's what I'm trying to do," she said between clenched teeth.

"Then focus harder. You aren't doing it right."

That's it; she either strangled him or exploded. She chose the latter. "Whatever! I'm done with this. You knock the fucking branch over."

She turned on her heel and marched for the beach. She needed a damn bath and the thought of that only pissed her off more. She had no soap, no shampoo, not even a dang toothbrush. Oh and no change of clothes either. Yeah, this was going to be a great little vacation.

"Abbigail," he called in a warning voice.

She laughed and didn't stop or turn around. "Oh, now he uses my name. No, I don't think so, demon. I'm done for the day. You hear me, d-o-n-e, done."

God, she'd never been quick to anger. She'd always been a slow boiler but boy did her temper roar at a boil right now. She swore if he so much as laid a hand on her to try to drag her back up to that stupid tree branch she'd scratch his eyes out. Heavy footsteps followed her but she ground her jaw and pretended to ignore it. She broke through the trees and came upon the dark blue lake near their little cove in the water. The water lapped softly at the sandy edge.

"You are not done working, Abbigail." He sounded pained to say her name as if he couldn't say it without yelling it. "Get back up there or I swear I'll--"

Oooh!

She spun around and let all the frustration and anger that had been building throughout the long day fly from her mouth. "Or you'll what? Magically force me to cast a damn spell? Sorry, but I don't think even you can do something so ridiculous. I think I did good today. I started not even able to make the stupid little branch move a hair. Now I've made it fall over twice, and you know what? I'm wiped. Totally freaking wiped. I'm hot and sweaty, my skin feels sticky, and all I want to do is wipe the dirt and grime off me. And nothing you can do, I mean nothing, will stop me from doing just that, you got me?"

To prove her point she grabbed the hem of her shirt and whipped it over her head. It had to be the emotions riding her that made her wad the shirt into a ball and throw it at him. It didn't come near hitting him but he didn't seem to care. His eyes were locked on her chest. She had a moment of panic before anger overtook that too.

She propped her hands on her hips. Maybe she wouldn't have been so cocky if she didn't have a bra on, but right now she felt like she could command an army. "Are you gonna stand there and watch me bathe too?"

Something changed in the air. Energy crackled. His eyes turned hungry. That's the only way she could describe it. His gaze darkened, eyes smoldered and devoured her body as if seeing her as anything other than "the witch" for the first time. He had the look of a man that wanted to eat her up. She could almost feel his gaze caressing her breasts. Her breasts pulled tight at the predatory look—the look of assessing a female.

Her breath caught. "Alrik?" she said hesitantly. Something about his stiff stance, the way his eyes glowed brighter, made him look as if he was fighting some inner war with himself.

His eyes flicked up to hers. His voice sounded thick, heavy, and slow. "Yes."

Breathing became difficult, as if all the oxygen around them had disappeared. "Yes what?"

He blinked. "Yes, I'll watch."

She swallowed over the knot in her throat. Oh.

Abbigail had never purposely taunted a man for any reason. Even with her previous boyfriends and other short-lived flings during college, she'd never teased a man on purpose. She'd never had any reason to. Yet, she wanted to with him. Partly because he pissed her off, she wanted to unsettle him and watch him suffer. Another part, a much bigger part that she didn't quite understand, wanted to see if she affected him, and to see if her body could sway the tall dark demon whom she couldn't help but find physically appealing. A feminine charge spiked through her blood making her flushed, her movements slow.

She reached behind her back and unsnapped her bra. The white material floated to the ground.

Their eyes locked together in a fiery battle and then she tugged down her jeans.

She heard his deep growl as she shoved her underwear down her legs.

§

Alrik couldn't move. He was rooted in place not by a spell but by a human woman. Abbigail. Surely, life couldn't be so cruel as to send a woman like her to him. She was seductively formed, small waisted with hips made for a man to hold on to while he thrust inside of her, and breasts that made his palms itch to hold.

She turned her back to him and waded into the water like a brave enchantress. The sight of her shapely backside and the sexy dip of her lower back nearly sent him after her. Her legs were strong, with just enough muscle that they rippled as she stepped into the lapping water.

Was she testing him? Trying to taunt him with something he couldn't have or wouldn't take?

Wait. He'd take it. Yes, he'd take it and so much more if she offered her young lithe body to him. After all the horrible deeds he'd committed in the past, using her body would hardly fare against them. He'd taken several steps towards her retreating back before he stopped himself.

No, he couldn't touch her. They both needed to stay focused. He'd had and lost his love.

He could not turn so easily to another woman with Arianna's death still lingering on his hands.

But it's been a year since she died, a voice in his head taunted.

Abbigail ducked into the water and came up with a splash that glistened from her hair and bare shoulders. His mouth watered at the sight of naked skin, and his cock throbbed and hardened to a painful point.

Breathing hard, he stepped away from her, away from the temptation. She wouldn't welcome him. He could make her but the thought of that didn't sit well in his gut. If he touched her, something terrible might happen—he might begin to care. No, he couldn't risk it. He couldn't risk gaining any feelings towards her lest he be unable to go through with his plans. He needed her to die to save him. He finally had a chance to become the man he'd once been and he wouldn't lose that chance no matter what.

He'd already lost one woman he cared about, he wouldn't put himself in the same situation twice. No matter how the light glinted off her body. She cupped handfuls of water and scrubbed her face. She turned just enough so that he caught a glimpse of the side of her breast. He groaned low in his throat. He ached to know how she'd feel in his hand—heavy and full or light and firm? His cock became a heavy, throbbing mass.

He couldn't do this. Not for him and not for Arianna.

Alrik made one of the hardest decisions of his life then and turned around. Back at the camp, he sat next to the fire. Air filled his head making him feel light and dizzy.

The human Abbigail was proving to be trouble. How could he ever look at her again and not see her naked in his eyes? He must harden his mind to her and hurry her spell casting lessons. The sooner she became strong enough to defeat his mother, the quicker he could be rid of her and live some semblance of his old life. He craved that relationship with his brother that they'd once had. Now that his mother's cursed potions weren't in his body and overriding his thoughts, he felt for the first time in a long time some of his own emotions. Not everything had come back with the curse still overriding him, but now he could feel something. These feelings seemed foreign to him, like someone else's emotions, but they were his. And what he wanted more than anything was to be back at his brother's side. He'd do anything to have that, even if that meant using and sacrificing Abbigail in the process.

A far off cry caught his ears. Alrik turned his head to the sky and his body tensed. Far off in the distance, coming from the south at a quick pace flew a flock of birds. Not just any birds but kolans, a large black bird known for eating anything found dead along the way. That wasn't what sent Alrik to his feet and running down the path to Abbigail.

A dark foggy cloud surrounded the black-winged creatures and in that fog flew evil. The birds moved at incredible speed and as they neared a roar became louder and louder. The sounds reminded him of battle, where men yelled and screamed only the sounds of the birds was much higher.

"Abbigail!" Alrik roared.

She came up from the water and hearing the bird's cries, turned to see the dark mass charging at them from high in the sky. She turned quickly and started for him. Smart witch. He thanked the seer once again that his savior was a smart witch.

She met him at the beach just as he reached it. Without hesitating, he grabbed her clothes in one arm then latched onto her hand with the other. He dragged her to the rocky slope that led down to their hidden cove.

The roar became deafening. He didn't know what magic was at play, but he had an idea and it wasn't good. The bright sky darkened to a murky grey. He had a moment's hesitation that he hadn't put out the fire at the camp, but as he looked up at the sky with the dark birds nearly upon them he knew he was out of time.

Swirling black masses formed around the birds. The trees shook and whipped with fierce winds. The bird's beady eyes narrowed on them, their yellow, beaked mouths open. More cries screeched through the air.

Alrik pulled Abbigail to the bottom of the slope just as the birds ducked low and flew over them. Adrenaline rushed through his blood making him faster and stronger.

Turning quickly, he snatched Abbigail into his arms and pushed her into the rocks to shield her. Sharp bites pecked at his body. Blood beaded on his neck and back where their bites tore through his clothes and skin. A crack of thunder sounded overhead. A bright bolt of lightning flashed in the forest.

"What's going on?" Abbigail asked. She sounded scared and unsure but he had no time to explain right now.

"In the cave," he shouted over the deafening roar. She nodded and then they both ducked down into the cold water and swam under the slope. They reemerged in the hollowed out cave and ducked into the dark cave. He didn't stop moving until he had her safe behind him at the very end of the tunnel.

"What are those birds? Where did they come from?"

Alrik ignored her. He focused his attention on the sounds coming from above them. The birds shrilled endlessly as thunder boomed again. A loud crack of lightning tore through the sky and then rain rushed down in a fierce torrential downpour. The water seeped through the earth and sprinkled over them.

"Alrik?"

The sounds of the bird's angry wings flapping and their cries slowly faded as they soared past.

"They're moving away." Still, the thunder boomed and roared up above. Trickles of rainwater spilled down the cavern walls in rivulets moving faster. His eyes narrowed on it and then the entrance of the cave. He started for it to investigate when a hand on his arm stopped him.

He turned to her and there she stood, arms wrapped around her naked waist, wet hair plastered to her wet face, and shivering in the cold. She nodded to the clothes in his hand and he jerked his arm out to her. With a bright blush, she took her sodden clothes and started pulling on the wet material. His body warmed at the sight her nakedness. Bare breasts, jiggling as she bent over to pull on her wet pants could be in his hand if only he stuck out his arm. The wet material of her clothes only clung to her body in ways that the haute demons would deem inappropriate and lascivious. Though, he'd have to admit he rather liked the sight on Abbigail.

"Stay here," he ordered, his voice husky

"What's going on?"

He ignored the question. He wasn't convinced yet what had happened. Creeping to the end of the cavern, he watched the ankle-deep water lap at the cave entrance. He stood there with rainwater spilling down over him and watched the water as it grew steadily deeper and deeper around his legs. It reached his knees in a matter of seconds.

"We must get out of here."

Abbigail ran up to him and gasped at the sight. "What kind storm is this?"

"Not normal." His mind worked to search for an answer and only one kept coming to mind. "The queen has very strong magic," he said softly.

"She's doing this?"

He nodded slowly. "She sent the birds to find us and when they did they called back to her and she let loose a storm."

Abbigail shivered and rubbed her hands up and down her arms to warm herself. "Does that mean she's close?"

"No, it just means she's looking for me."

A whip of lightning sounded above striking the ground. The earth shook and rumbled from the attack. The rain came down faster, pelting the ground like wet darts above their heads.

"We must leave this place now." Alrik grabbed Abbigail's small hand in his brute, dark one then they dove into the water and swam out of the cove. Water pelted the lake's surface up above like a rain of bullets. Abbigail tried to swim to the surface but he halted her and pulled her close. She wrapped an arm around his back and looked up at the surface just as wary of the darkness above as he was.

He caught her gaze. Even in the dark water, he saw her brilliant gaze. She looked scared. She was completely dependent on him. She didn't have the skill yet to bypass his mother's magic. Nodding towards the surface, she jerked her chin in acknowledgement then they kicked their feet and swam for it. They broke through and sucked in ragged breaths.

Sharp drops of rain pelted them. The rain fell so hard and fast the forest looked like a murky environment in the distance. Wind whipped at them hard. Alrik acted quickly and jerked Abbigail into his arms, wrapping both of them around her waist as the harsh gales pushed them sharply to the side. His side hit the rocky coast near the cove and he had only a moment to register the pain in his side before they were once against jerked the other way.

The wind whipped them down under the water. It sucked them in like a giant creature's mouth taking a bite out of them. He kicked them back to the surface and worked his legs hard in the heavy water for what he hoped was the beach's surface. He couldn't see a thing, only the dark grey of falling rain. What he thought looked like the green of the forest looked too far away. It should be closer. Had the wind drifted them out to sea?

An even stronger gust swept across them as if trying to tear them apart. Abbigail screamed, the sound barely audible over the roar of the storm, and latched her arms around his neck. His grip on her waist slipped, her arms slipped and with a shout she went flying from his arms.

He swam hard through the water, following the white streak of her shirt. She appeared then disappeared again and again as water sucked her up and down. His arms burned but he dove towards her. Fear caught him. He couldn't lose her now, not when he'd come so far.

"Abbigail!" he shouted over the storm.

He barely heard his own words over the whooshing windstorm. He heard her shout, the sound so faint in the noise around him. He went with his instincts and swam hard towards where he guessed she'd gone. White flashes struck the sky. Dark clouds thundered up above with menace.

He swam some thirty feet before he felt a lump at his knees. Ducking under the water, he opened his eyes and found her drifting, eyes closed beneath the water. He screamed, swallowing a gulp of water and rushed to the surface to take in a much needed breath of air before diving down to snag her limp body about the waist.

Together, he took them to the surface. His body worked harder than he ever had before by swimming against the violent current of the storm and towards what he hoped was the shore. When the water grew shallower around them, he could have cheered. With a final burst of energy, he sprinted until he finally stood at the shore. He lifted her small body into his arms and raced from the storm, his booted feet slipping in the wet slop.

Still, the rain gushed over them, drowning his vision, and making it hard to see. He found a canopy under some trees and laid her under it. The trees barely managed to keep the vicious rain at bay. He breathed into her mouth again and again.

"Abbigail! Wake up!" He pressed a hand to her chest and felt the subtle rise and fall. She wasn't dead. Relief swamped him and he sagged over her, burying his face in her sweet-smelling hair.

KEER POW!

Lightning struck too close to be comfortable. The ground shuddered beneath him and heat seared him to the bone. He didn't hesitate another moment. With gentleness he didn't know he had, he cradled Abbigail in his arms and ran out of the storm, hoping it wouldn't follow.

THE FALLEN KING

Eight

Abbigail pushed herself up with a groan. Her whole body felt stiff as if she'd had a vicious workout. The muscles in her arms, back, and legs throbbed with a fiery burn. It took some effort but she forced herself to stand. Her knees wobbled and she gasped as blood rushed to her feet creating a burning pinprick sensation that poked her from the inside out. Her hand shot out to steady herself but didn't grasp onto anything. She teetered to the right, and then straightened up by locking her knees to stop from falling.

She then realized she wasn't in their little cave hideout beneath the beach. Not even close. She was in a building of some kind. It looked similar to the temple she'd hidden in from Alrik, or at least she was assuming it was temple of some kind since she wasn't exactly adverse in demonic architecture. Colored stones in dark greys and shiny black covered the room's walls and floor creating a medieval, yet beautiful look. A doorway paved out of the same stone, stood at opposite stone wall. Bright light poured in. She could see trees waving in the wind some distance away. She blinked against the brightness as her eyes adjusted to the light.

Where was Alrik? What happened? She thought back and fought to remember. She remembered the birds. Birds have never scared her before, but those did. And then, the storm. That storm...

It was as if it was after them, trying to kill him. She'd never felt anything so ominous before. The storm seemed to have one goal in mind: to swipe them down into that lake and make sure they didn't return for air.

She didn't want to think about how powerful his mother must be if she could send a storm that powerful after them, and he'd said she wasn't even close to them. She could perform that kind of magic from great distances?

Abbigail shivered as dread filled her. No way could she kill a person, even if she wanted to. No way she could go up against someone that powerful and win. Hell, she was a medical examiner not a combat-trained witch. Alrik showed greater magical powers than she did. Right, but according to some seer, he couldn't kill his own mother because of the curse. Again, she wanted to know more about this curse. What kind of woman would curse her own son and to what purpose? Just why.

Abbigail walked out into the light. The day was surprisingly cold. Wind blew making her shiver. Abby hugged herself against the biting chill. Her clothes were dry now but she still wore the jeans and t-shirt she'd changed into after the police came to her house. She didn't want to think about how long she'd been wearing these clothes. Nope, she wasn't going there.

She took in the scenery outside. If the rift was one thing—beautiful was it. The landscape rolled up and down in hills some ways in the distance. The ground was covered in vibrant green grass, golden flowers, or maybe they were weeds to the demons, that were short or sometimes as tall as her waist. Trees were taller here; trunks thicker and older looking as if they'd never been cut down, never had to grow a new one. Everything looked so similar to a forest she might have visited in a park before, but it was the small details that made the difference.

Something made her pause her surveying, some niggling feeling at the back of her head. Slowly, Abby turned then stilled. Even her breath stopped.

Alrik sat on his knees, ankles behind him with his back facing her. His shirt lay on the ground beside him. His dark, black skin showed almost shining in the reflection of the light. His back was a piece of art. If someone had asked her what the perfect man's body would look like, she would have fumbled for an answer before. Well, now she had an answer. It'd look like Alrik.

Smooth sinew rose over strong shoulders and down a tapered, thick waist. A strong enough waist she could wrap her legs around, squeeze, and it wouldn't break him. Her chest grew hot and breasts pulled tight and heavy as she pictured doing just that.

His arms, which hung loosely in his lap, were nothing to sniff at. Even relaxed, his shoulders rounded out hard then cut in over solid triceps and bulking forearm muscles. He looked smooth and completely hairless. His dark ebony skin was like looking into a sky without any stars.

She'd taken a spinning class at her local gym a few years back with her friend Jenna, not that Jenna needed the workout, she practically had a six-pack from just walking which wasn't fair. But even at the gym she'd hadn't seen a man like this. She'd seen strong men, men who worked to get cut and hard, but nothing about Alrik's body shouted "muscles obtained by gym-membership." He wasn't bulky; he was thick, strong, and cut. She flushed all over. Need gripped her and chose that moment to remind her how long it'd been since she touched a man. She hadn't been physically intimate with anyone since college. Yeah, that would be two years ago now. Yikes.

"Are you done staring at me?"

Alrik's deep voice jolted her. Abby's face burned red and she started to run back into the little stone house but that'd be cowardly. Instead, she stood her ground, blush and all. However, she still hoped he wouldn't turn around and see that blush. What did it mean that she found him so deliciously attractive? It couldn't be good, not at all. Every instinct she had told her as much.

"I just woke up." Crap, that didn't answer his question. She searched for something else to say, but no words came. She was at a loss all because of some bare skin. Bare, strong skin.

Alrik planted his hands on the ground in front of him and then stood with a fluid motion. He turned to her, his dark gaze instantly locking on hers. Her stomach did a little fluttery flop. She swore if she'd met him under nearly any other circumstance she'd be happy, maybe even flirty. She didn't normally chase after men but in this case he'd be worth it. If only circumstances were different.

He moved towards her and didn't stop. Abby's mouth dried up at the sight of all that skin. A slow, heavy thump started in heart. Each step he took her heart banged. An awareness came over her.

His chest was just as delicious as the backside, maybe more so. Smooth and hard. Would he be as soft to touch as he looked? His chest had two defined pectorals that trailed down to rows of ribbed, packed muscles that disappeared beneath his pants. For the second time, something wild, strange, and raw crackled between them. A dark colored tattoo covered his right side, but the paint was so dark against his skin she couldn't tell what it was.

Her gaze flew back to his and her breath caught in her throat. She couldn't have moved if she tried. A dark heat glinted in his eyes. She had to see what he was going to do, and even though she hoped he wouldn't, a part of her wished like hell that he'd touch her. She had to know what he'd do because what she felt she saw mirrored in his dark eyes.

He stopped before her, his heat warming her from the chill. They were so close to touching and yet so far. He seemed completely unfazed by the chill in the air. His hands came up and cupped her cheeks. A stuttering breath escaped her. Warmth permeated off his body. He had such strong hands, the kind meant to cup and cradle a woman. Something about the mixture of heat and hands brought a shiver between her legs. The look in his eyes spoke of only one thing—hunger. Her body answered the hunger with a growing need of her own centered deep within her body. Her skin tightened, entire body poised waiting for him to kiss her.

Only, he turned her head left then right, his eyes not low-lidded as she expected hers were, but hard and searching now. Something had changed in a flash. After that, he picked up each of her arms and checked them too. When he reached for her shirt, she was so surprised by the action she didn't get to protest before he jerked it up.

She jerked to pull away and that only made her sides flare sharply. Instant blazing pain seared up her side and along her back as her muscles pulled. She winced and caught his hands to halt them.

A finger traced along her side softly. Still, it wasn't soft enough and she hissed before latching onto his wrist. His eyes flicked up to hers. She swore she spotted a hint of lingering heat there, or maybe it what she wished she saw.

"You've sustained some serious bruising."

Abby looked down and gasped. Serious bruising was no joke. Her entire left side was black and a dark ugly blue. She twisted around and saw the bruising covered a decent portion of her back too.

"How did I get this?"

"From the storm. The waves swept you up into the rocks near the cove. It wasn't gentle."

"I don't really remember that to be honest."

Alrik nodded, the action sending locks of dark hair over his shoulder. "Not surprising, you hit it so hard you went out like a light. I brought us here."

Abby swung her head around. This didn't look like the little beach coast with forest directly behind it like she'd grown accustomed to. "Where are we?"

He looked out behind him, a hard look on his face. "South."

The hairs on the back of her neck stood up. The way he said it put her on edge. "Is that all? I get the feeling there's more to it than that." Which probably didn't bode well for her. Nothing seemed to lately.

"I haven't traveled this way in many years. Used to be that a band of rogues formed a settlement south of here."

"Rogue demons. Is that what you are?"

His body stiffened, muscles hardening as he turned back to level a lethal glare on her. She might have been nervous at the deadly look but it lost some of its power considering he'd never hurt her. He needed her too badly.

"I was banished, but I'm still a king. Not a rogue."

"What makes the rogues so different?" She didn't mention it but his hand still lingered on her bruised skin, the touch light. She liked him standing this close. He blocked out the cold wind, and, honestly, he made her warm all over.

"They didn't enjoy life at court so they left. Let's just leave it at that."

"Okay." Something about the warmth of his body, his soft touch on her skin had her eyes drifting back down to his mouth.

"You shouldn't look at me like that, Abbigail." An ache traced in his voice.

"Like what?" she asked, her voice breathy. Her whole body started a slow burn deep and low inside her working its way out. How did he make her feel so much with the barest of touches? His head dipped in low. Her eyes darted to his firm, shapely lips and wondered what they'd feel like against hers, what he would kiss like. Wild, hard, and a bit crazy like him?

"Like you want something I can't give you."

"Why not?" She blushed at her knee-jerk response but held firm to it. She wanted to know, needed to know. This was more than curiosity. Something else had taken hold of her and guided her words and actions now from some need that he'd brought forth.

He leaned in closer. His hand flattened against her cool skin in a possessive caress that sent her gaze low and hooded. His lips closed in, then stopped a scant inch away. Heat bloomed in her chest and between her legs. She panted against his lips. It took every bit of strength inside her not to reach up and curl her fingers around his shoulders

When he spoke she felt his warm breath on her lips. "Because the last woman I kissed ended up dead."

Abby jerked away from his touch. Her shirt fell back into place. "What?" Just like that the heat was doused into nothing.

He stepped away and shrugged, a strange glint shining in his eyes. "Don't worry about it. It's none of your business."

Her heart beat wildly. "Oh, I think this is all my business. I'm here with you all alone in this god-forsaken place and you're so closed mouth about everything I just want to rip my hair out. You can't leave me hanging with that. How did she die? What happened?"

Who was she? She didn't voice that question. It seemed too personal and a spark of anger flashed inside her at the thought of this woman. Jealousy? No, no way.

She saw him transform between her very eyes. He stood tall once again, unbreakable and strong. His gaze sheltered his thoughts; his face had shifted into a blank, unreadable mask. "I left some food in your shelter. Eat it then we'll get to work."

Abby paced an agitated circle. "You seriously can't think to keep me out of the loop on this. What's with you and talking about death and murder like it's second nature to you?"

"Because it is."

Abby stopped dead. Something in his voice, in the harsh look of his eyes made her feel something she never would have thought she would for Alrik.

She pitied him. He looked tortured, if only for a second before the look faded away to resolute anger. A strange realization came over her. He didn't like who he was. He didn't like this person the curse had created. This was a person who'd relish a bloody fight or seek out anger instead of compromise. He hated himself.

"Alrik..."

"Eat, witch." He strode away and slipped his shirt back on. He didn't stop walking.

"So we're back to that now are we," Abby muttered.

One step forward, three steps back. Whatever, she could use some time to collect her thoughts. One second she's devouring him with her eyes, the next she's practically begging him to kiss her, and then he's giving her ominous warnings.

Abby found some cooked meat sitting on a big plant leaf in the stone house. She ate it with relish and by the time she came back out Alrik had returned looking tightly in control of himself. She sighed and scrubbed her hands down her jeans.

"What's on the agenda for today?"

"We'll work the same spell again and this time practice on just me. After you get me to move, we're heading south."

Her eyebrow rose. "South where the dangerous rogues are? Why are we going there?"

"I need supplies. I might be able to get some there." He walked some twenty paces away from her then stopped and faced her. "My mother will also be south."

Abby wracked her mind for times and dates. Her mother must have heard about what had happened to her by now and would be worried sick. She'd been gone, what, three days now? God, she wasn't even sure.

"Just how long will it take to reach your mother?"

"I don't know."

Abby rolled her eyes, her patience waning. "Well, try to guess, please."

He was silent for several moments, his gaze calculating. "It may take three weeks, maybe longer."

She choked. "Three weeks or more. I can't be gone that long!"

His dark eyes narrowed. "If your magic was at the level it needs to be at then we could head there now. As it stands, you are not nearly strong enough to fight my mother. She'll kill you in an instant."

"Isn't that nice..."

"Do not take this lightly, Abbigail. The queen has strong magical blood in her veins. She's spent years using it, harnessing it behind closed doors. I can only guess at how powerful she's really become."

"I wasn't being...oh, whatever. Let's just do this."

Alrik nodded and crossed his strong arms across his chest. What a shame he'd put his shirt back on, but it was for the best. She couldn't do with getting distracted by a pretty body.

Abby called upon her magic. It filled her body making her skin warm and her eyes burn with glowing light. She focused with her mind on Alrik. She envisioned throwing him far back. But she didn't let her magic couple with the vision. She worked up to that. This was practice to get her focused.

"Do it already!" he bit out.

Abby clenched her jaw then raised her hands to him letting the magic fly from her fingertips. Burning energy soared from her like not needed lightning escaping from her fingertips, blasting against Alrik knocking him clear off his feet and sending him flying back through the air.

An ecstatic squeal escaped her as he landed hard on the ground. He was slow to stand, so she took that time jumping up and down and doing a fist pump.

"I did it! Ha! Take that, Alrik. I wiped you clean off your butt."

He wiped dirt off his pants then came back to the spot he'd marked before. "Do it again."

Her jaw dropped. "No way. There's no way I'll be able to do that again." She could already feel her body tiring just from that one exertion.

"Do. It. Again."

She started to yell or say something biting but clamped her mouth shut. Bitterness filled her. "Can't I even get a 'congratulations' or a 'good job'?"

He crossed his arms across his chest in response.

Of course not. God she hated him.

Abby went through the whole process again. This time she was determined to send the jerk even farther.

Yet, she couldn't do it.

She kept trying as hours passed. Sweat formed and fell down her cheeks, the warm beads reminding her how cold her skin was. Light faded from the sky turning it dark and hazy. Alrik still stood there without saying more than "do it again."

After God-knows-how-long, she dropped her arms and sank to the ground. Her entire body hurt including her head which sported a massive, pulsating headache at her temples.

"That's it I can't take it anymore." Hours of work led to nothing. She'd moved him right off the bat and that was it. No more progress, and if that was progress she couldn't tell.

She saw the disappointment and anger on his face that she was quitting but it didn't faze her one bit. She was done for the night, totally. If she continued with how she felt now she might accidently curse him.

"Fine, I hope you're ready for a cold night of sleep."

She groaned at the thought. Her breaths didn't form clouds but it was close. She shivered and walked gingerly with her aches back into the stone house. The floor was too cold to sleep on so she huddled back against the wall—not much better. Before she realized it, exhaustion took her and she fell into a fitful sleep.

She never saw or felt Alrik come into the room and pull her close, wrapping her in his heat. And she never saw him put her back where she'd been come morning.

Nine

Alrik woke at first break of light.

Something soft, warm, and feminine was curled in his arms. He stiffened; he'd almost forgotten. He'd been so angry with her for giving up on him last night after making so much progress that he'd wanted her to suffer the cold.

Yeah, well, he hadn't managed to keep that goal. When he came in to sleep she'd been tossing and turning, her brow pinched, and arms wrapped tightly around her. Something had softened in him. He told himself he was just protecting her for his own purposes, that if she stayed cold remove she may not stay in peak health like he needed her to be, but even he wasn't sure if he believed that.

She was steadily breaking down something inside of him. First, by flashing her bare skin at him at the lake. Then taunting him yesterday with her heated eyes and pouty lips. It had nearly undone him not to kiss her, and she'd wanted him to do it. To have a woman look at him with desire…no one had done so since Arianna. He'd brought forth passion in Arianna with his touches but Abbigail had looked at him with passion without his touch. She did it of her own free will and that had thrown him. He'd wanted to give in to her so he could show her what she was asking for, and mostly so he could taste her and feel that passion for himself.

He didn't know how much more he could take before he caved. Already he felt his resistance waning. Every moment around her, he had to remind himself that he needed her for a purpose that could lead to her death. It wouldn't do giving in to the carnal heat she awakened inside him. This task was proving harder to deny than he could ever have imagined.

She rested in his arms so perfectly. Her backside pressed into the curve of his body with his arm tucked around her slender waist. She'd snuggled against him in the night. Her delicately scented hair taunted him and he couldn't escape it. He'd had no choice but to bury his head there and breathe in her unique scent all night long. She smelled feminine and gentle, as a woman should. The scent stirred his cock.

After he took her in his arms, she'd stilled for a moment before falling into a deep sleep while he'd slept on and off all night. She fit him well. Small and delicate, curvy and soft where he wasn't. It didn't help that the image of her naked body haunted him. Hardly a moment passed that he didn't remember her heart-shaped bottom, firm thighs, and rounded hips.

Morning light spilled over her now casting her hair into something much prettier than he'd originally thought. Shafts of gold and copper colored her hair. He shouldn't have slept with her. What if she had woken during the night to see that he'd taken her into his arms?

Her bottom moved against him again making his body stir and his blood heat. His cock filled with blood, turning hard and demanding against her. He stifled a groan at the erotic sensation. He'd lingered too long already.

Moving slowly, he placed her back against the wall where she'd fallen asleep. He cast one last look at her, then shook his head and left her to find more food.

He hunted for nearly an hour and slew two futhorcs. Good, they'd need the meat to give them enough energy for the traveling they'd be doing today. He couldn't be sure how far south they needed to go, but he recognized the rolling hills in the distance. They were on the right path.

By the time he came back, she was up and moving about. Her eyes were bright and the circles under her eyes gone. She hadn't slept well since he'd taken her. After just one night of good sleep, she looked refreshed and, his chest tightened painfully, more beautiful. She looked over at him as he approached and a small smile teased her lips.

"About time you woke up," he scowled.

The light in her eyes dimmed instantly. He wished he could take back his words, but this was for the best. He didn't need to make his job of sacrificing her any harder. Distance would be good.

"If it's a problem then you could always wake me up early."

He ignored her valid point, lit the fire, and started skinning the small animals. From the corner of his eye, he watched her mouth flatten and anger flash in her eyes. She didn't argue, for which he thanked the lucky stars. Her anger only fueled him in a way he craved entirely too much.

She took a seat across from him. "Well is there anything I can do?"

He eyed her pensively. Warily he grabbed a small knife from his ankle holster and tossed it into the dirt next to her. Her legs jumped to the side and she gave him a wide-eyed look.

"Make some skewers." She picked up the knife and handled it in a tight, awkward grip and not like a warrior would. Still he had to make his point clear. "Make any move at me with that and you'll regret it."

Her jaw clenched, but then she gave a mock bow. "Yes, my Lord."

His mouth quirked with a smile and he saw surprise light her features. Quickly, he killed it. He had to remember his purpose. He couldn't let her get under his skin. He needed her for one purpose only.

After she finished making skewers from thin sticks, they ate and he packed up the rest of their belongings. They didn't have much and he needed some blankets for them and maybe some soap for her. He stilled in mid-motion of putting his swords back on the holster on his back. Was he making plans for her to be more comfortable? He jerked his mind off the thought. He wasn't going there because that's not what this was about. They'd both enjoy the added comforts.

They headed south by mid-morning and it didn't take long for her to grow restless. He saw it first in the way she sighed, then when she started to open her mouth to speak but stopped herself. He didn't encourage her even though a part of him was curious. Just what had her fumbling so?

They stopped around mid-day to eat more and rest. He found himself wishing she would speak. It was while he surveyed the hill that sloped down gently before them that she finally let it out.

"Oh my god, I can't stand this. You have to talk to me. I feel like I'm losing my mind here."

Alrik barely contained his stunned expression. She wanted him to talk to her. What about?

"Come on, we're heading back out. I want to reach the Drego river before nightfall. We'll sleep there."

She sighed and came up beside him. She was much shorter than Arianna. She didn't even reach his shoulders. Damn. Why was he even thinking these crazy ideas?

"What? I don't even see any water."

He pointed south. "It's there."

Her gaze narrowed on the distant landscape and then she shrugged. "I don't see it." She sighed even louder. "We have to walk all that way. That has to be, like, ten miles."

"At least."

She groaned and his lips twitched. He quickly schooled the emotion before she saw it. This was new for him—finding humor in something. He hadn't felt that in...a long time. He couldn't even remember the last time because not even Arianna had made him laugh.

"Fine, let's go before I lose my motivation."

She started down the hill without him. He followed behind; his gaze locked on a part of her he really shouldn't be looking at, but couldn't help himself. The way her pants fit her was almost indecent. Shahoulin women wore long, beautiful dresses that complimented their beauty. Abbigail, a mere human, managed to stir desire wearing nothing but tight pants that cupped her in ways that made his palms itch to feel for himself.

So wrapped up in his baser thoughts was he that he didn't react for a long second when her foot slipped on a rock. Alrik snapped out of it as her scream ripped through the air and she started tumbling down the hill.

"Abbigail!"

He charged down the hill, his heart pounding in his throat. Something intense and terrifying filled him. He reached her just as she rolled to a stop at the bottom of the hill. She lay on her stomach facing away from him, her arms bent under her, and her legs squeezed together.

He turned her over and her eyes squinted up at him in pain.

"Ow, that one hurt." Her lips pinched together as her brow furrowed.

He knelt beside her, his hands touching her everywhere. "Where are you hurt?" She stiffened, but he didn't realize it. That intense feeling still held him in its tight grip.

Her voice came out breathless. "Didn't hurt anything new except maybe my ego. A few rocks just jabbed into my bruises."

He lifted her shirt up ignoring her squeal of protest to inspect her bruise. A part of him expected to find blood there, but her skin was intact just colored in an ugly way. Relief filled him and he collapsed over her, burying his head in her hair. A wild staccato beat pounded in his chest. He'd only ever felt that feeling once before he realized, when Arianna stepped in front of him to take the blow that would have ended his life.

"Alrik?" she asked hesitantly.

He pulled back and found her face a mask of confusion. Something changed inside of him then. Now with the panic passing, he realized he had her practically in his arms. His gaze dropped to her mouth; soft pink lips that were pouty and full. His gut clenched and what happened next he was lost to.

He slanted his lips across hers and gave in to the need inside him. The first touch was like being zapped with an electrical charge. Every ounce of his body burned, roaring at him to take more, take all that she'd give, and then take even more. She was soft and warm, her lips delicate in a way that brought out the animal inside him.

He held back the beast and savored the press of her lips but his body strained to keep it caged.

Soft, pliable lips pressed gently against his as his mouth fluttered across hers. His cock was a mighty weight between his legs, roaring at him to have her hand curl around the shaft.

Then she pressed back against him and he snapped. A shiver tore down his spine.

A feral growl sounded, surprising him. The sound came from him, from the need he'd buried deep inside of himself. As her soft lips kissed him back he did something wild and utterly stupid. He did something he'd wanted to do since he met her and thrust his tongue deep.

The sweet taste of her flooded his senses, firing his already yearning body. Then she surprised him. Her hands swept into his hair, clenching his head to her as if she didn't want him to move.

Oh god. The way she touched him. She made sexy little noises in the back of her throat and the way her tongue met his in a wet sweep brought the need in him shooting down his spine to his cock.

He never thought...

He never knew...

She touched him as if she never wanted him to stop.

His cock throbbed, feeling ready to explode. One of his fists curled into the grass beside her head before he did something he'd really regret--like touching her. Touching her in ways they both craved.

Her tongue stroked his, wet, soft, and eager. She made a soft, needy noise in the back of her throat and her body pressed up into his like an undulating wave. Her breasts crushed against his chest, the pebbles of her nipples scraping him through their shirts. His hips jerked with a needy thrust.

He broke away, stumbled back away from her as his chest pumped hard. Her eyes were fogged with passion as she looked at him. Her cheeks were flushed, lips wet and swollen. Her chest rose and fell in fast waves, straining her breasts against her shirt.

His emotions teetered all over the place. He had to find some semblance of control before he went right back over to her and finished what had started. Just the thought sent his gaze between her thighs. Her hips jerked in response as if she felt his touch there and he nearly groaned. So badly did he want to feel her soft femininity. He clenched his hands as if to keep his fingers from wanting to dip into her jeans and feel her soft sex. How wet was she? How hot? Would she burn against him? Another shudder wracked through him.

He couldn't touch her though, he wouldn't.

So he said the one thing he knew would work. "Don't ever touch me again."

Hurt flashed across her face and he hated himself for putting it there. Then, just as quickly, anger surged and she jerked to a stand. "You kissed me."

His jaw popped he held it so tightly. "Come on." He strode past her. He had no other choice. He had to ignore her or else he might do something irrevocably stupid. He hid the tremble in his hands by curling them into fists.

He had about two seconds of peace before she stormed beside him marching like she was taking her anger out on the grass. "You are un-fucking-believable. I mean really. You are such an ass."

"Watch your tongue, Abbigail," he warned. He'd only take so much of her insults.

"Watch your tongue, Abbigail," she mimicked in a high voice. She darted a lethal gaze at him. "You watch it, demon. With how I feel right now you don't want to piss me off."

He almost laughed, actually. "And just what do you think you could possibly do to me."

No sooner had she sucked in a deep breath did he feel the warmth of her magic surrounding him. He realized he'd made a mistake just as he went flying through the air. Air rushed past him, blowing hair in his face. His stomach felt like it was kissing his spine. Surprise kept him from responding, or at least that's what he told himself. He landed on the grass some fifteen feet away feeling as though he'd just been run over by a horse.

He jumped to a stand ready to exact retribution, but she squared her shoulders and spread her feet looking ready to fight. Her eyes glowed dimly from the magic running through her veins. She looked so small yet stood as a warrior ready to battle at the front lines. She looked more beautiful than ever.

His anger fled as swiftly as it came. His lips twitched again and he stifled a laugh. The emotion felt so odd he didn't know how to hide it.

"Glad to see you're improving on your skills."

With that, he turned and continued south.

Her soft growl brought a full smile to his mouth.

Ten

Abby didn't know how she managed not to freeze her butt off during the night, but she slept surprisingly well. She'd asked Alrik to build a fire and he'd refused, said it'd leave them vulnerable. She didn't get that and when she pressed him, he shook his head in a condescending way then explained that: "If we leave a fire lit it only brings dangerous eyes to our position while we rest unaware."

Well he may have a point but she didn't like the idea of another freezing cold night without a blanket. However, now that she thought about it, she woke up warm and comfortable each morning. Strange.

Not to mention she needed new clothes badly. She'd give almost anything to have a pair of fresh jeans, a shirt, and a warm jacket. Scrubbing her clothes in streams and lakes worked only so much.

Alrik was already up and moving around when she got up but she figured he hadn't been up long.

The strange light in the sky, not a sun but a bright enough light that looked as if it always had a hazy fog covering it, just broke into the sky.

Abby stretched the sore muscles in her body. She was getting more of a workout with all the hiking than she'd had in a long time. She could already feel her stomach slimming some. Normally she might be happy that she'd slimmed down, but in this case it made her jeans bag on her and without any replacement clothes it just served to remind her how much she needed to be home.

Alrik set a packet of cooked, dried meat on the ground then announced, "I'll be back."

A flicker of panic instantly swept through her. He was leaving her? He'd never said any such thing before. When he started walking into the woods, underneath a high-rise cliff on their left, she hollered out to him.

"Where are you going?"

He kept walking for a few steps then seemed to debate with himself before he stopped and turned back. Her breath squeezed tight in her throat, her entire body caught fire just having him look at her. All because of that kiss. She swore his masculine, sexy taste still filled her mouth. It surprised her, but if he came to her right now and took her mouth she'd gladly give in.

Not once in her whole life had she ever been kissed like that. It was as if kissing her had been the most pleasurable act in his life, as if he couldn't get enough, and as if it took every ounce of willpower in his entire body not take her body. And she'd felt the same. She hadn't wanted it to ended, not even for a second.

A shiver quivered down her spine. Her breasts pulled tight and her nipples hardened. She gulped but hoped, and didn't hope, that he would notice.

His dark eyes caught hers and she swore—he knew. He knew every sensual thought she just had because he'd had it too.

"I'm going to the lake to bathe." He voice sounded even deeper than normal.

Her eyebrows flew up.

As if sensing where her thoughts were leading her he jabbed a finger in her direction. "You will not follow me, Abbigail. You will stay here and eat until I return. If anything seems amiss, cry out and I'll be here."

Abby looked around in dismay. A stream of cool water trickled down over the rocky cliff above and flowed down southwards, bubbling over rocks and crags. He told her it all poured out into the Drego lake, but a thick expanse of forest kept it from view.

This forest looked different from the ones she'd seen before. There were many bushes and shrubs colored dark yellow like mustard, bright yellow like a cheery tulip, and a beautiful dark cherry red. Some were as tall as her waist and others even taller than she was. They fit amidst the thick trunked trees creating a beautiful, earthy juxtaposition. Their leaves were heart shaped but elongated and thinner with the ends coming to a point. They brought a smile to Abby's face with their earthly beauty.

Alrik followed her gaze and he scowled. "And do not touch anything. Some of these plants are dangerous to the touch."

Abby's smile died. The forest just went from a pretty little garden she might explore to something dangerous. She took in the beautiful shrubbery one last time. Looks like she wouldn't be going in there without her little guide after all. Sighing, she took a seat on a rock that had a smooth flat surface.

"Fine, I'll wait here." She popped her chin up on her fist and gave him her bored expression. She was trying to play it bored, but truth be told she didn't like the idea of being here alone. The crazy demon was all she had in this strange world, and she needed him as much as he did her.

Alrik turned and followed along the cliff before disappearing around the bend.

Abby fidgeted then moved to sit Indian style. When that didn't bring any comfort, she kicked her legs out in front of her and crossed her ankles. Time seemed to slow after he left. She was never one to idle, always preferred to keep moving.

The peaceful quiet of the woods didn't help that any. The wind blew by rustling the leaves of the trees creating its own form of music. She sighed with disgust. This was no good. Sitting alone left to her thoughts to fill the silence.

She probably lost her job. If she made it out of this ordeal then she might be able to explain to Stan and get her job back. He was a good teacher but harsh. He'd probably make her redo her entire internship and that'd leave her back at square one working towards her supernatural medical examiner's certificate. God, she wanted it so badly she could almost taste it.

She wanted that laminated badge with her picture and name on it. The one stamped ME on it by the state. Not her intern's badge. She wanted to finish her autopsy training and be in there with the victims, finding cause of death, and helping detectives like Mike to find murderers. She wanted to be someone who helped to make things a little better in the world. She didn't want to stand by as bad things happened. She could do something to help and she wanted it so bad she could taste it.

With a grunt, Abby fell back against the slab of rock and stared up at the strange sky. Out of all the doubts she'd ever entertained about her job, she never once figured she might get her dream job because a sexy demon would kidnap her. Yup, can't say that ever crossed the mind, she thought.

Maybe not being smart enough for the job or not being able to stomach what she saw—those were legitimate fears she'd had. The thought of a cursed psycho storming into her house and kidnapping her into a dimension filled with different kinds of demons never entered her mind. Not even once.

What that meant for her was almost too scary to think about. Could she really be that powerful? If the queen was as powerful as he said, and if she sent those birds with the deadliest storm ever after them, then she must be. That meant she might be more powerful than the queen and the thought terrified her. What if when she finished harnessing her power to get out of the rift it went to her head? What if it corrupted her or changed her? She didn't want to change. She was perfectly happy how she was.

Okay, maybe that's not entirely true. She'd been stuck in a rut, bored when not working, and living without really living life. Her daily routine had consisted of getting in her internship hours and staying at home. Ever since she'd been out of college her relationship with her best friend Jenna had even started to deteriorate. If anything, they should be spending even more time together what with all the free time Abby had.

Well, she was certainly living life now just not in the way she'd ever thought possible. Now she was in a strange world with a strange man. No, a demon, she corrected. Alrik was no man. He was too powerful, too mysterious, too sensual, too dangerous...too everything to be a man.

And, he kissed her like she had always wanted to be kissed. Heck, like any woman would want to be kissed at least once in their lifetime. Like she'd been his air. Once his lips touched hers, something zapped between them, something too powerful to be contained. Her stomach fluttered and she ran her hand over it to settle it. Her lips felt suddenly dry and she darted her tongue out to wet them. She wanted that again. She wanted it so badly it was a physical need telling her to go after him and make him kiss her like that again. She wanted to see what else he was capable of, and discover what other passions existed between them.

A twig snapped nearby. Abby jumped up, her gaze searching in the direction of the cliff where Alrik had disappeared behind. She held her breath as her heart thumped in her chest. She despised the jumpy feeling she got every time Alrik left her. Her instincts were on full alert, preparing her body for fight or flight mode. She recognized it which only made her eyes widen further to see what had made that noise.

The sound of leaves rustling came and then Alrik stepped around the bend of the cliff. Her breath wheezed out of her in a long rush, and she collapsed on the rock as her muscles relaxed.

"What's wrong?" he asked his voice curt.

Abby sighed and pushed herself back up. When she looked at him her breath caught in her throat. He was shirtless, again, and very wet. His hair was slicked back over a set of broad, hard shoulders. Water dripped down his chest and dampened the top of his pants. He must have just done a quick wash and pulled his pants on. Saliva pooled on her tongue.

"Abbigail?"

Her gaze met his eyes which were dark again. Well, they were always dark, but they had fire to them now as they did after he'd kissed her. Breathing suddenly became a difficult task as her chest squeezed tight.

"You startled me, that's all."

"Pull your gaze away, Abbigail." It was a command. God, his voice sounded so deep and husky.

Easier said than done though she didn't say so. She couldn't help but be fascinated with the hard play of muscles on his chest. They looked soft to the touch yet hard at the same time. She found herself wanting to run her fingers over his stomach and find out which it was.

"What are you doing?"

The edge in his voice brought her gaze up to his again. His eyes were wide, his body language tense. It was then she realized she'd gotten up and started walking to him. She stood only a few feet away and had no recollection of moving.

She swallowed and looked back at the rock she'd just been sitting on then down to the ground where she stood. His question left her fumbling. How did she explain that she'd wanted to touch him so badly that she'd just marched right on over to him without even realizing she was doing it? That couldn't be explained without horrible implications on her part. So, she said something else.

"I like your chest."

Oh my god! her mind screamed. What the hell did I just say? A hot blush crept over her cheeks. "I mean..." her eyes followed a droplet of water sitting in the hollow shell at his collarbone. He moved a little and the drop went running down his chest and over one hard, defined pectoral muscle. Between her legs, she grew tight and hot.

Alrik eyed her warily then pulled his wet shirt on over his head. The shirt clung to him in ways that fascinated her. It fit along his arms like a second skin, showing to perfection his cut biceps. What a shame, though, to cover such beauty.

"Perhaps you are tired. Did you eat?"

"No, no I didn't." She'd been too lost in her thoughts.

He shook his head at her and grabbed the food off the ground, shoving it in her hand. "You'll eat as we walk. We have to get moving while it's still light out."

"Why is your shirt wet?" She couldn't help but ask. The wet shirt clinging to him bugged her. He'd come back without it on, yet it was wet. As his dark eyes narrowed on her, she knew she must be steadily making a fool out of herself.

He grabbed his supplies and sheathed his swords over his back. "I washed it."

"Oh." Of course he did. The idea of him soaping his own clothes in a cold lake made her smile. He cut a look to her catching it.

"What?" He sounded defensive.

Her lips twitched. "I didn't know you could do laundry. Bet you miss your slaves for that."

His gaze dimmed and she knew she'd said something he didn't like. "Slaves didn't do my laundry but servants did. Let's move."

Abby couldn't hide her frown. She'd meant it as a joke but obviously she'd messed up and insulted him. Great, just what she needed. She didn't know whether to apologize or let it be so she chose the latter.

On their hike through the dense forest, Abby took in her surroundings and nibbled at her cold dried meat. The meat reminded her of beef jerky, one of her favorite snack foods. The futhorc meat wasn't quite that tasty though. It had a chewy texture and it was cold which made it hard to bite into and even harder to swallow. She swore if she ever got back to her normal life she'd appreciate life so much more, even little things like beef jerky.

"What's up with the bushes?" she asked.

He grunted. "What of them?"

She nodded at a yellow bush. "You said not to go near them. Why?"

He shrugged, jostling the swords on his back. She liked walking a few paces behind him because he walked so much faster than she did which gave her the opportunity to take time to admire his body without him knowing it. It was sneaky but worth it. The man had a backside just begging to be nibbled.

He sounded frustrated at having to answer her. "Gringum the plant with the bright yellow leaves is contagious. One touch will leave you with a rash that brings fever and rupturing boils. Gargum the dark yellow bush causes hallucinations if inhaled, and gumrosh, the red bush, is most lethal of all. If eaten, you'll die from its poison."

Abby's eyes widened as she eyed the plants and mentally thanked Alrik for walking them far around them. "So how far until we reach this rogue camp you were talking about?" They had to be closer. They'd reached the lake last night, and he said it they only had some miles left to go from there.

"I'm not sure. I don't know if they're still there. They could have moved on long ago."

"And what is it you hope to get from them if you do find them?" She felt it more then saw it—the tension radiating from him.

"Supplies," he said shortly.

His odd response didn't go unnoticed but she didn't know what to make of it. The man could get tense from the smallest things. Who knew what went on in that mind of his.

"The things I would do for a bar of soap and a change of clothes," she sighed.

Angry dark eyes cut to hers immediately stamping out her little daydream of getting a sweet smelling bar of soap. "You need only what I get you and nothing else."

O-kay. Well, it's gonna be a long day, Abby decided. Mr. Tight-Lipped wasn't being any fun at all. She had the urge to grab his face and plant a big fat kiss on him just to see what he'd do.

The day trudged on and still they walked. The forest grew denser so that some trees stood only a foot apart from one another and they had to squeeze in between the trunks. After some time, they walked out of the dense forest and into an area where trees grew further and further apart.

The light had just started fading from the sky. Unlike on the earthen-side when the sun went down some light still lingered from the moon, here in the rift, it stayed quite dark. Not completely dark, some hazy pinkish glow still shone from somewhere far in the distance, but it was hardly enough to see where you were walking. Abby hated walking at night.

They walked on until they stepped out of the forest and came into an open vista. They stopped so he could examine the area, and she took the opportunity to catch her breath.

The land looked to go on forever. Yet, unlike on the earthen-realm where light poles and electrical lines staked across the country alongside houses, developments and cities filling in the every inch of land, this was on open unused piece of earth that flowed up and down in rolling hills and rocky crevices. Towards the right a steep hill rose, almost as tall as a mountain but not quite.

"We've made it," he said.

Abby frowned. "This is it? Where are the rogue demons then?" She stepped up beside him so she could read his expression. She'd expected a camp or houses or anything. He didn't look happy. A frown marred his lips, and his eyes were tense with thought.

"They must have moved."

For some reason she wanted to comfort him. She shouldn't. Her future with him wasn't exactly certain. However, certain things couldn't be denied. She couldn't deny that he had the ability to make her heart race or for her breath to catch. She also couldn't deny that she wanted to know everything about him and how he came to be cursed.

Something was happening between them. Maybe it started with that kiss or maybe it started before that, she couldn't be sure. They spent so much time together that it was all beginning to blur. Still, once she got powerful enough, she was porting her butt out of here and leaving him in the wind. If he came back after her, she'd be powerful enough to keep him away. Of that, she felt certain. He already said his mother was more powerful than he was and only Abby would be able to kill her, which technically made her more powerful than him too. Just, not yet. She was getting there though. Her powers were growing, becoming easier to reach and use.

"What are we—?"

"Krishnoe!"

He held his hand up at her, stopping her mid-sentence.

A new wave of tension poured over him and she stilled too. She didn't know what he just said but she got the gist of it. Even without thinking about it, her body tensed, breathing turning quiet as her eyes scanned the distance. Something was very wrong.

Alrik silently lifted his hands and grabbed the handles of his swords. With only a soft hiss of metal on the leather casing, he lifted the swords over his head and freed them.

They had no warning when it came. It all happened at once.

The sound of dozens of feet pounding the earth sent Alrik and her spinning around. From the forest, she spotted a small army of idummi demons sprinting for them. Abby backed up behind Alrik without realizing she'd done so.

"These aren't the demons you were talking about, right?" She tried to insert some humor into the situation because right now, she had to fight the urge not to run in the other direction. He couldn't possibly win against so many demons. Before there had only been one and he'd taken care of it quickly. But now there had to be at least twenty headed right towards them.

"No they are not. Stay back!"

That was all he said before he let out a roar that threatened to deafen her and charged into the forest. Abby pressed a fist to her mouth, teeth biting down. The man was a warrior.

He caught up to the first demon heading the pack and slew him to a bloody mess in seconds, but there were too many. The demons narrowed in on him, their line formation closing in, circling him. They jumped at him at once, their heinous cries and squeals piercing her ears.

But, something else caught her attention. That eerie feeling of being watched. Abby froze and slowly looked left. There, three demons had broken off from their friends and slowly came towards her, their knees bent, arms dangling low with sharp curved knives at their belts.

Abby didn't think—she acted. In a blast of magic, she shot the demons back. They flew into the trees, barreling into them with a hard whack. She didn't stay to see what happened with them—she ran.

She never ran as hard in her life as she did in that moment. She didn't know how she knew that the idummi would get up and come right after her, but she did. They were going to kill her. An ear-splitting war cry followed right behind her. She flinched knowing that sound was directed at her and what she'd done.

Pounding feet sounded behind her. Abby strained to make her body move faster. She just had to go faster, that's all.

Her lungs worked hard to suck in air through the panic. Any strain on her limbs didn't register as she was in panic mode. She raced flat-out across the plain, swiftly stomping down patches of grass and flowers in her wake. She headed for one of the hills towards the left. Some thought that she could hide there came to mind and she charged forward with her only goal to escape.

The pounding feet closed in on her. The creatures made clicking, gnashing sounds with their teeth. She pushed her last reserves of energy hoping it'd be enough, but a hard body slammed into her. Abby cried out as she went flying hard to the ground, the momentum of her speed banging her head into the ground and making her ribs kiss her spine.

She groaned, unable to move. The thing that tackled her growled and grumbled in a hissing deep voice. It spoke garbled, strange sounding words at her. She was flipped, not gently, onto her back and another painful groan escaped. She had to move. She had to fight back and get away, but her body had given up.

The fall had knocked the wind out of her and sharp pains made each breath she took a chore. Her right knee throbbed with a fiery, burning sensation from the landing. Her bruised sides pulsated in anger at the treatment.

Her eyes flashed open as an idummi climbed over her, one leg on each side of her waist. Its teeth gnashed together in a chomping motion making yellow spittle drop from its mouth. The spittle hung from its thin green lip for a long second. Then it fell from his mouth. The spittle landed on her shirt and started to sizzle, a tendril of grey smoke swirled up. It burned straight through the shirt leaving a black hole. Then it touched her skin. Abby cried out as burning pain engulfed her. She scrambled and wiped with her shirt at the spittle until the pain ebbed.

Breathing hard, she stared up at the demon. It had a nasty sort of smile on its face that only served to bear sharp, pointed teeth.

Only straight meat eaters had such teeth. That thought popped into her head at that exact moment, and it scared the shit out of her. She wasn't going to become a meal for this thing.

Sucking in a deep breath, she thrust her leg up in a brutal kick catching the demon between its legs. The demon's hands flew between his legs as its knees buckled. Before it collapsed over her, she scrambled backwards. Now that she wasn't running, her body started sending warning signals to her brain to let her know her body hurt in a bad way from that fall.

The demon screeched and its yellow, strange red-inflamed eyes narrowed on her. She had a moment to gulp before it launched itself at her landing on top of her. All the air whooshed out of her at its weight. The thing was shorter than she was and bony, yet had a layer of hard muscle over it. It seriously weighed a hell of a lot more than she'd expected. It felt as if a grown, fat man was sitting on her.

The demon's eyes widened with glee and a black, forked tongue slithered across its lips. It pulled its curved dagger from its belt, pressed its knees into her chest to lock down her squirming body, and lifted the dagger above its head with two hands.

"*Kraju d'menuni kash!*" it hissed. Then it jerked its arms further back an inch and lurched down with the blade.

Abby screamed and shut her eyes waiting for the knife to plunge into her body. A whizz of air stirred her hair making her flinch. She panted, waiting for the blow, but the demon groaned above her and fell to the side. Abby jerked up, scrambling away.

"Huh," she grunted.

An arrow was stuck in the demon's chest where its heart should be. Dark murky blood oozed around the wound. Black feathers were stuck in the end of the arrow. It looked handmade and very real. The demon didn't move any more.

Abby started to shake. She couldn't help it. She'd been in several scary situations in her life, especially since meeting Alrik, but this one took the cake. She stood up and her knee gave out. She could already feel it swelling from when she landed, but she locked it and gritted through the pain so she could turn around.

What she saw she could barely comprehend. A group of demons, not idummi, but tall, human-looking demons like Alrik surrounded her. They had various colored skin and hair just like Alrik too. They carried an array of swords, knives, axes, and one in the front held a black bow. He seemed to stand taller than the rest, though that may just be the command that surrounded his presence. He strode towards her. His lips were moving and garbled sounds came out, but she didn't understand any of them. She recognized the sounds of Demonish being spoken between the men.

His gaze traced up and down her then he glanced back and commanded something to his group. The others vanished in a flash of movement. Then he spoke once more.

Her thighs started trembling, and she flexed her thigh to try to keep her leg from giving out. Hot fire started burning in her muscle. It jerked and she grimaced as her muscle rolled and her knee burned tight. It felt a good two sizes bigger than it should be.

The strange man with the bow said something else to her, his eyes intense. Too bad she didn't speak Demonish.

With a curse, her knee gave out and she couldn't keep from crying out. She landed on her side, her hands going to her upper thigh to apply pressure there. It helped to ease the pain some but not by much.

The demon came towards her. He had skin like the pale moon and hair as black as Alrik's. His eyes were what really caught her attention though, they were green. No, that was too plain sounding. It didn't do them justice. They were the most beautiful green eyes she'd ever seen. Like the green in a photo of a tree in Hawaii that'd been colored and highlighted by some designer's hand to enhance it. It was brighter than the brightest grass or leaf even down here in the rift where colors were more vibrant. And, they were on a face that stared down at her with such intensity that it stole her breath away.

The demon stopped before her with his hand held out and whispering foreign words. She felt his magic travel over her body an instant before darkness took her.

Eleven

"What are you going to do with the woman?"

That same question had been plaguing Aidan since he caught her. He and his men didn't know what to make of her. She wasn't demon, nor vampire or shapeshifter, yet she traveled with none other than King Alrik Demuzi. That left them with human.

Just what the king wanted of them, they didn't know. If the king thought he could garner any kind of support from Aiden and his men then he couldn't wait to show him just how wrong he was. Few were hated more than the king of the shahoulin—a treacherous, evil bastard that deserved no less than a slow, painful death. Aidan just hoped some good might come out of this chance meeting.

His eyes once again fell to the unconscious woman. She was beautiful, captivating. Then again, he hadn't laid eyes on a woman in a very long time so maybe his sense of what was attractive or not was tainted. Maybe she actually looked more like a hag.

His eyes wouldn't let him believe it. She looked young, fresh, had a mane of shiny brown hair, and a body perfect for loving.

"That's a good question, Conrad, and one I don't have the answer to right now."

Conrad nodded and his gaze, just like the rest of the men's, fell to the woman. Aidan had ordered her to be laid upon some bedding near the fireplace until she woke. Her demon companion didn't have it so nicely. A smile tugged at Aidan's lips.

"How fares the king?" Aidan asked.

Conrad grinned with pleasure. "He's below in the dungeon bellowing his brains out to be freed. I don't think he much takes to captivity."

Aidan ground his jaw. "Now he has a taste of what he'd bestowed upon us."

"And it feels good," Conrad said.

Aidan laughed, his chest feeling lighter. "Yes, yes it does."

Conrad fell silent for a moment, and then hesitantly said, "You don't plan to let her go, do you?"

He could almost hear the twinge of hope in his fellow soldier's voice. "No, certainly not." He and his men had been without a woman for a very, very long time. He wouldn't let his fortune idly walk away now. The question then was what to do with her. There was only one of her and twenty-one of them. The men might share for a while but it wouldn't take long for possessiveness to flare. That, Aidan could do without. The last thing he needed amongst his men was rivalry over a single female.

It'd be inevitable if he didn't plan this carefully. "I'm thinking a challenge."

Conrad's grin faltered then transformed into a wide smile. "Excellent idea."

Aidan nodded. "There will still be some problems. Whomever doesn't win will feel it surely. This will create tension among us." Especially since Aidan planned to keep her for himself. He wanted to be the first to feel the naked skin of a woman pressed against him, the first to slide hard between her welcoming thighs. His cock hardened at the thought.

Conrad nodded grimly. "True enough. Mayhap if she's shared at some point, it could give all the men a chance to relieve themselves."

In thought, the idea worked out wonderfully. However, in Aidan's past a woman didn't exactly like to be shared without her approval. The thought of force did not sit well with Aidan. He knew all about being forced to do things he didn't like, and he wouldn't do that to a lovely woman.

"We don't want to lose her favor, Conrad. We do that and she won't accept any of us. No, we have to find a way around that." He knew by looking at her that the thought of taking on more than one man at a time wouldn't appeal to her. She had an innocent sexual allure to her. He wondered if she even realized it.

Conrad sighed and took a seat beside Aidan. "I hadn't thought of that. What will we do then?"

Aidan thought on it for a long while. His gaze moved from the flames licking at the wood to the prone woman lying in front of the fireplace. "I think we'll go ahead with the challenge. Whoever wins will keep her but in a few weeks' time we'll hold another challenge with the previous winner not participating. This will eventually allow everyone a chance to win her."

"What if she refuses to accommodate the winner?"

Anger flared in Aidan. "Then we'll make her." He wouldn't physically force her, but there were other ways. An idea struck him—maybe even pleasurable ways. A seduction. The pressure in his groin grew nearly unbearable.

A commotion started around the great hall's fire jerking Aidan out of his sultry thoughts. He went to his men. They wore expressions ranging from excited to wary. He didn't blame them. Having a woman here could prove a change for either the better or the worse.

One of his men, Drekk, caught him coming towards and nodded to the woman. "She's waking, sir."

A flash of excitement flickered in Aidan. He couldn't help it; he was just as excited as the rest of them. "Make room," he ordered. His men parted around the woman and Aidan came through to see her eyelashes fluttering open.

Greed filled him just looking upon her. What he would do to keep her for himself...

The woman sat straight up, her gaze darting around the men hovering around her. She started breathing fast in fear, pushing a pair of gorgeous breasts up tight against the snug, strange shirt she wore.

He stopped in front of her and her gaze flew to his. He watched recognition hit her eyes. Good, she remembered him from before.

"Who are you?"

She spoke strangely and he and his men looked at her in confusion. This wouldn't do.

Aidan turned to his men. "Get Gabrick here now."

No sooner than he made the order did Gabrick push his way through the crowd. The older demon had the greatest magical abilities among all of them. It was largely due in part to his abilities that they were able to keep their small castle invisible to the prying eyes of the world. They used to be out in the open, but in the past year idummi attacks had become more frequent. So, they'd pooled their magic and spells together to cast a protective spell over the castle. If all of them left for too long the spell would eventually fade and reveal their home.

"Can you make it so we can understand her and her us, Gabrick?"

The man nodded slowly, his eyes devouring the woman. A spark of possessiveness straightened Aidan's spine, but he ignored it. It wouldn't do getting revved up in front of his men over the woman, even though he planned to keep her for himself.

"It sounds like a strange version of the English human's spoke long ago. Let me see if this works."

Gabrick opened his palms and spoke a chant in Demonish. The spell weaved words of understanding, learning, and listening around his brain. Warmth surrounded Aidan and his men and then like a switch being thrown, the woman's words rang clear.

"What the hell is going on here? Who are you? Where's Alrik?"

All the men paused at the woman's words. She had a soft, pretty voice. A woman's voice. He could have groaned at the sound. Something that hadn't gifted his ears in so long.

Aidan took a step closer and once again captured the woman's gaze. "You speak to the king by his first name? Just what are you to him?"

The woman froze, her eyes narrowing in suspicion. "Tell me who you are first."

"Leave us," Aidan ordered in Demonish. His men did so, but slowly. After they had some space, Aidan knelt down by the woman. "I am Aidan and these are my men. We are outcasts from the shahoulin kingdom."

"Are you their king?"

"We have no king here." The very thought made Aidan's gut clench. Yes, he led his men but he was no king. His word wasn't law here and they all wanted it that way. The rulers had ruined their lives. They chose a more democratic approach with Aidan acting as a tentative leader. At any time, they could overthrow him if they chose and he'd easily step aside.

"What do you want with me?"

Aidan looked away as an image of her body naked and what it would look like flashed in his mind. "That's a harder question to answer. Why don't we start simpler? Why are you with the king?"

She smirked, the corner of her full mouth curving up. The sight transformed her face into something captivating. "He isn't the king anymore."

Aidan nearly gave a double take. "What say you?"

She shrugged. "He's no longer the king. He said we were coming this way to find some rogue demons, I take it that's you. He said we needed some supplies."

Aidan stood and stared off into the fire. The king wasn't the king anymore and he thought to find help from those he'd marked as outcasts after wrongfully imprisoning them?

"He's mad," Aidan muttered.

"True enough."

Aidan felt a smile cover his lips. Not only was she beautiful but humorous and wise as well. She'd make a fine companion for him and his men.

"Your name, woman."

She bit her lip as if unsure whether to tell or not. Eventually she sighed in defeat. "Abbigail."

He rolled the name around in his mouth. He liked the rounded sound of it, feminine. It fit her. "Abbigail, it is a pleasure to meet you. I am Aidan." Aidan and Abbigail. The sounds rang well together.

He held his hand out to her and she hesitantly gave it to him. Her hand was soft compared to his own and much smaller. He hadn't held a woman's hand in so long he'd forgotten what it felt like, the slight weight and the soft texture. He ran his thumb over it and pressed a kiss to her fingers. Her eyes flashed with surprise while something dark and hungry stirred inside him. He'd wanted to wait until he announced the challenge, but now he knew he couldn't wait. He needed her for himself, needed to see her flashing blue eyes at him, smiling up at him as he thrust between her soft thighs.

Turning his back to her, he faced his men. In Demonish he spoke. "We will have a challenge for her."

The men tensed. Hesitance, eagerness, and hope flashed among their faces.

"The winner will keep her but will not force her into any deeds she doesn't wish to do. After three weeks, we will have another challenge. The previous winner will not be allowed to participate so that everyone will eventually have a chance to win. Every three weeks we will hold the challenge again."

Aidan studied his men finding half of them approving, almost eager, and the others angrier at his command.

"What's a challenge?" came a soft voice from behind him.

Aidan froze. He turned back to her but words clogged his throat. He didn't know what to say. He tried to recall his previous interactions with women and the only thing he could think was that she wouldn't welcome this.

"What's going on here?" she asked again, her voice getting hard.

Aidan ground his jaw. To hell with it. She was here and she'd have to deal with the consequences. "We are keeping you. The winner of the challenge will win you, Abbigail."

She gasped and started backing up, her gaze darting amongst the men as if they might jump at her at any moment. "No, you can't do that."

"Yes, I can. I'm sorry but we have been too long without a woman. We will not let this chance slip by us."

"But, but I'll tell you anything you need to know."

He didn't say it aloud, but he thought it. You'll tell us everything you know anyway, Abbigail. "And what do you know, Abbigail?"

She hesitated and he could see her mind working as she thought about it. She crossed her arms across her chest. She had no idea, but half the men in the room groaned as the action pushed her breasts more fully into view.

"Take me to see Alrik first."

Aidan stalked to her. She didn't back down but she looked behind her as if she wanted to. He didn't stop until they nearly touched. "Why would you want to see him?" Anger and jealousy burned inside him.

"I-I need to talk to him," she stuttered.

"About what, Abbigail?"

She started breathing faster. It was torture seeing those breasts rise and fall. If he but leaned down he could pull a breast into his mouth. His mouth watered at the idea. So entranced was he that he missed part of what she said.

"...see if he's okay."

Aidan stared her in the eyes as he contemplated it. Then he nodded. "Come with me."

His men stared at him as if he had lost his mind as he led Abbigail away. He only gave them a swift shake of his head. He had his ulterior motives.

§

Abby followed the big warrior with silvery skin and dark hair. He looked similar to the demons yet somehow different. He reminded her of a vampire. Tall, elegant in nature, but with a warlike ferocity hidden underneath a layer of control, such characteristics were typical amongst vampires. He didn't have the bulk to his body as the others had and was slightly taller, though he was just as gorgeous to look at. Maybe even better. However, that didn't make him trustworthy. She had Alrik as proof of that.

Aidan led her down a stone stairwell. It rounded in a tight circle. The air became heavier and torches held by sconces on the wall lit the way down a long hallway at the end of the stairs. It was cold down here and one look at the metal bars lining either side of the hall and she knew it was a dungeon. Yet as she scanned the cages, she saw they were all empty. It was too early to tell if this bode well for her or not. Maybe they wouldn't imprison her. They could do far worse to her than lock her in a cage, she reminded herself.

At the end of the hall stood a heavy looking wooden door with a rounded metal hatch. She knew who was behind that even before Aidan opened the door.

"Abbigail! Where is she!" came a roar.

She'd recognize that voice anywhere. It made her heart jump and her feet walk faster. She reached the door before the man Aidan did. He eyed her strangely as if trying to figure her out. Well, she had news for him; she didn't trust him either. Maybe this was just the break she'd been looking for. She'd just have to wait and see. But first, she had to see him to make sure that he was alive and well. It felt like a driving need inside her to make sure with her own eyes that he wasn't injured.

"I'll kill you all!" His voice rang down the corridor.

Aidan stopped by the door and waited until she met his eyes to speak. "Just what is he to you?"

Her throat closed up. What was he? Friend, not so much. Lover, nope. Enemy, that was closer.

"He-he's just a friend okay. Let me see him, please." She hated to beg but she'd do it if she had to.

Watching her closely, Aidan grabbed the latch and pulled the door open. Abby all but ran inside. Her stomach dropped at what she saw.

An even larger cage stood in this room as if that was its sole purpose. Alrik clung to the metal bars of the cage. Heavy metal shackles bound his wrists and ankles to a large metal loop on the wall behind him giving him only so much space to walk. Blood smudged the metal from where they'd dug into his wrists.

Abby couldn't hide her reaction, she ran to him. Her hands closed around his on the bars and for some reason tears welled in her eyes. "Alrik."

She closed her eyes to hide her growing weakness for him and listened to the sound of his heavy breathing.

"What have they done to you?" he said. Anger, no, fury laced his words. He was seething. The look in his eyes was something she'd never seen before. He was not in control. He had gone past that point and had snapped. The look made her shiver and sent a bolt of fear into her belly even though she knew he wouldn't hurt her.

Abby looked up at his gorgeous face. Blood covered his lips making them bulge, and his left eye was so swollen the skin around it had turned a dark purple. "Did they beat you?" She couldn't keep the sound of hysteria out of her voice.

A tic pulsed at the line of his bearded jaw. "I'm fine. What have they done to you?"

"Well, nothing really. Alrik, they said something about a challenge and I don't know what they're talking about."

She felt his hands curl tighter around the bars beneath her hands. His gaze darkened with fury and he pinned that lethal look at Aidan. "She is mine."

"That remains to be seen."

Abby turned sideways so she could watch them both.

"She's here with me right now. That shows you everything you need to know."

Aidan shrugged. "Shows she has a kind heart, that is all. The men will appreciate that all the more."

"Alrik, what's a challenge?" What do I do? she wanted to say.

Alrik pulled himself into the bars with a bicep curl then his dark gaze locked on hers. "They will fight over you. Whoever wins gets to keep you, use you however they want. They will take your body, Abbigail. These men are savages."

"Not without your wish, I assure you," Aidan added hastily.

Abby's head started spinning. "What? Use me?" She knew what he meant but still trying to believe that it was happening to her was an entirely different thing.

"Yes, Abby. Use you as a man does a woman. Let me out of here, Aidan, or I swear—"

"You swear what? You'll break through the bars? I doubt it. They've held stronger men than you." Aidan stalked like a predator to the cage. "Let me ask you, king, how does it feel to be on the other side of the bars?"

Alrik roared. Abby barely had time to move to the side before he lashed through the cage, his arms swiping hard for Aidan. Aidan ducked easily to the side, a satisfied smile on his lips. The chains didn't let him reach far but if Aidan hadn't moved he would have caught him.

"It doesn't feel good, does it?" taunted Aidan.

Suddenly, Aidan grabbed her arm and started pulling her away. She fought it, digging her feet in. Spinning back around she grabbed onto the bars one last time. She met Alrik's worried gaze. "What do I do?"

"I will kill them all."

The way he said it, with such a dead finality, sent a chill down her spine. He meant it. He would find a way to get out of there and he would kill every last one of them.

"I don't want you to kill anyone." His gaze flickered with surprise then he stared off beyond her shoulder at Aidan. "If anyone touches her, I'll slaughter every one of you. There will be no mercy." He didn't say it in a threatening way but in a casual 'this is how it's going to be' way. That made it scarier.

Aidan didn't give him a chance to say anything else; he latched onto her waist and pulled her kicking and screaming from the room. She screamed loud enough for the whole castle to hear, but no matter how loud or how hard she kicked, he didn't let her go. She stared into Alrik's eyes as the door slammed shut, blocking him out. She'd never felt this raw feeling before, like she was being peeled away from something so necessary to her.

Aidan set her down and she whirled on him, enraged. Her hand shot out and caught his cheek with a hard slap. His head jerked to the side. She flinched at the cracking sound and took a step back as panic engulfed her.

She'd just hit her captor. No way in her mind could this bode well for her. Aidan's head slowly turned back to her. Something hot and earthy filled his eyes, startling her. When he stepped towards her, she flinched and threw her hands up in front of her face to catch a blow. But it never came. Something else did.

Her hands were jerked down in a rough grip, and then her body thrust up against his. His mouth came down a second later and ravaged hers. She tried to process it, but her mind struggled to keep up with all that had happened. All she knew was that he was kissing her like a man dying for his last touch. It was hard and swift and when he pulled away, they were both panting.

"I will win you at the challenge."

It was a promise if she'd ever heard one.

She shook her head in denial but he only jerked her back upstairs. She followed him like a zombie, which worked for her because it gave her a minute to process all that had happened in such a short span of time.

After they made it back upstairs, they forced her to sit at a table with food and drink shoved in front of her. She ate and drank like a zombie...little bites and sips. She just tuned out all the demons around her watching her with hungry eyes.

Her mind ran over that kiss and all she could think was—he didn't kiss like Alrik did.

THE FALLEN KING

Twelve

After picking at her food, Aidan and two other big men, one with golden blonde hair cut at his shoulders and another with dark red hair that fell down to his chest, showed her to her room. They locked her inside with a resounding click.

While the thought of being locked inside a strange room scared her, it also gave her some courage to sleep. Just not a good sleep. She woke throughout the night, her gaze sweeping the room for strange men only to fall back asleep when she found none. It felt strange to sleep without Alrik near. Her gut churned with worry over him. Had they beaten him? How was he? A part of her actually wanted him to break down the bars and come grab her, just minus the slaughtering part.

When the door unlocked the next morning, she followed the golden haired demon and the redheaded demon solemnly downstairs. She felt like she was walking her last steps to the death chamber. Only, they wouldn't kill her. No, they wanted to use her. Her hands were slick with sweat and she wiped them repeatedly down her pants. They led her down a different hallway this time and into a room big enough to be a ballroom. It looked like it could hold many long tables but it was devoid of anything--save many demons standing around the sides of the room. Their gazes were on her immediately, traveling over her body in a way that made her skin crawl. She wanted Alrik so badly she felt physically ill with it. Her stomach clenched and she swore if she but bent over she'd vomit.

Aidan waited at the front of the room. He looked every bit the commander standing tall, his chin up. His eyes smoldered at her. The two guards let go of her in front of him then took positions on either side of the room with the others.

"What's going on?" she asked. She had a feeling she knew but she had to hear it.

"Today we will hold a challenge for the rights of the human, Abbigail," Aidan announced in a loud, ringing voice. The demons murmured to each other.

An excited energy floated in the air. The men wore no shirts. They stretched their arms and bounced on their feet in anticipation. They actually wanted to do this.

A part of her hoped that maybe they wouldn't really want to participate in the events. Maybe they'd realize how crazy this was or that she wasn't all that attractive. Maybe.

As a simultaneous roar whooped from the men, her hopes were quickly dashed.

"Abbigail," her gaze went to Aidan. He was speaking to her and no one else. "Today we will fight but not to the death." That didn't relieve her in the least. "The winner will become your new master."

She shook her head in denial. "I won't do it. I won't touch any of you."

Anger flashed in his eyes. "You must."

She crossed her arms and took a step back. "Unless you plan to force me, I won't take any of you. Ever. And I'll fight every single moment of it." She said it with every bit of energy inside her.

Her words must have registered because unease flickered in his gaze. "And just what would it take for you to accept us?"

Her eyebrows rose. He gave her an option? She thought quickly. Then it hit her. "If you win me will you let me go? I don't belong here. I want to go home." She left out the part about Alrik kidnapping her. For some reason she didn't want to say anything that might make him look bad. Right now, he was the better choice by a long shot.

He slowly shook his head and her hopes crashed to the floor. He wouldn't let her go. "I can't do that," he said almost gently, "we need you. More than you could ever know." Her breath caught. Maybe if things were different, if she was someone different meeting him under different circumstances, she could like him. But he wasn't Alrik and he would never free her.

"Then let Alrik fight in the challenge." The words burst from her mouth before she thought twice about it.

Aidan jerked in surprise, and then he laughed low and deep. "Never."

"That's my choice. Let him have his chance. Without him, I wouldn't even be here. Let him have his chance to win me."

He ground his jaw, irritation creasing his forehead. "Why should I do that?"

It hurt to say it. Her body physically rebelled at the idea. "Because if you do then I'll willingly let the winner take me." Her voice nearly broke saying it. It was a huge promise to make.

His eyes flared, lips flattened as he contemplated it.

A demon standing on the side stepped forward. "What is taking so long? I wish to start this and claim my prize!"

"Silence!" commanded Aidan.

Other demons started speaking out until the entire room filled with an aggressive, hostile energy. Aidan eyed his men, his jaw working hard, and then he looked back down at her.

"I will do this for you under one condition."

Her breath caught. "What's that?"

He didn't answer, just grabbed her hand, and pulled her towards a door behind him. To the room he shouted, "Give us a minute. She needs to be convinced." That didn't sound good.

She had a feeling he was lying but didn't say anything. The door shut behind them, muting out the bellows of rage and anger shouted after them. Aidan led her deep into the castle until they came upon another door. Inside he locked it with a piece of wood barring the door by two metal rungs.

He turned to her and she balled her hands into fists. "And what exactly do you want?"

He let out an uneasy laugh. He reached for her and though she flinched, he grabbed her shoulders. His eyes bore into hers. She had no choice but to look back at him. "You swear to follow through with your promise?"

"Yes," she said though her voice wavered.

He released her and walked in an agitated circle, running his hand through his shaggy black hair. "I am not like the others."

She'd noticed but didn't say so.

He faced her, his eyes locking on hers. "I am not a demon."

One of her eyebrow's rose. "Then what are you?"

The corner of his mouth quirked up but it wasn't quite a smile; more a sad, mocking look. "I am a vampire."

She swallowed hard. Her suspicions had proven right. She didn't feel particularly good about being right on this. "Okay."

"I haven't drunk from a fresh source...in so long."

She heard the longing and the agony in his voice. It pulled at her heartstrings. Maybe she was too nice for her own good because it didn't bode well for her to feel anything positive for her captor.

Shoot, she'd already royally screwed that up with Alrik. She felt way more for him than a captive ever should about her captor.

"What do you normally drink?"

His smile turned bitter but his gaze roamed over her face with hunger before settling on her neck. Even hidden by her hair she felt his gaze scorch her. "Blood of animals. The men know what I am. You give me this and I'll let the fallen king participate in the challenge."

She tensed but her heart started racing. "Give you what exactly?"

His voice almost gentled. He tucked her hair behind her ear pushing it over her shoulder to reveal her neck. A body part so common had never felt so vulnerable until now. His gaze found her neck and she swore he could see her pulse pounding wildly. "Your vein this once," he said, his voice thick. "Give me this and I'll abide your wish."

Abby squirmed under his stare. Let him drink from her in order to have Alrik participate in the challenge? It could work to her advantage—if he won. If he didn't—she'd be screwed, royally.

"Okay," she agreed.

His mouth parted in surprise. A look that could almost be described as gentle hunger came over him as he stepped into her, wrapping an arm around her waist and pulling her flush against him. He cupped her cheek forcing her to meet his gaze. They were so close, the moment so intimate she felt as though she was standing naked in his arms. This moment

felt more intimate than their kiss did. She felt bared
down to her bones.

"You won't hurt me?"

He shook his head slowly and for some reason
she believed him. Maybe it was the sincerity in his
eyes or just her instincts but in this she trusted him.

Gulping, she nodded and tilted her head to the
side. "Then do it."

His breathing turned heavy and loud. His lips
touched her throat and she jumped, her eyelids
squeezing tight. His tongue darted out to lick a
warm wet path up her neck. She shivered, unable to
stifle it. The sensation was pleasant, might have
been nice if coming from someone else. Someone
like Alrik.

His hands were gentle on her as he wrapped
himself around her as if trying to get as close as
physically possible. He cupped her jaw, tilting her
head back. She felt so exposed and weak in his
grasp. His lips pressed a soft kiss to her neck. His
warm breath sent a shiver racing down her spine.

Panting, she waited for him to make his move.
But he seemed to be savoring the moment, taking
his time. His tongue passed over her and then two
hard points pressed against her. She heard him
inhale her scent.

She stiffened just as he struck. A fleeting
moment of pain as her skin broke then a warmth
built in her beginning at the bite then radiating
outwards to all points of her body. She could feel
the sucking sensation working at her neck and it was
more erotic than she could ever have guessed. But it

was all wrong, coming from the wrong man. She didn't want to like anything he did to her.

Moisture flooded between her thighs and her hands flew to his shoulders to hold on. Her lips parted and he groaned a deep, vibrating sound that shivered over her skin. Time seemed to speed up because he broke away too soon. Her hands still held him. She didn't want to let him go. Her eyes were slow to open but when she looked at him, she saw barely restrained desire lurking in his eyes.

"If I don't stop now, I'll take your body right here."

She shivered, the idea now actually sounding quite good. His bite had done all that? She was practically a quivering puddle of need. Wet and needy, nipples hard and wanting to be touched. She pressed fingertips to the wound and looked at them only to find no blood. She gazed at him in question.

"My saliva heals the wound after I feed." His voice was much deeper, a sexy rumble.

Abby swallowed hard and nodded fast. "Okay, it's done. Let's get out of here." She had to because right now what her body craved and what she wanted was two entirely different things. Moreover, a nagging guilt filled her as if she'd done something wrong. Like she'd cheated on Alrik... She shook her head to rid the negative thought. They'd never done more than share a kiss, she reminded herself.

Aidan's dark gaze bore into hers as if he could read her thoughts. "I'll win this and then we'll finish this," he promised.

She almost believed him. Almost.

Because she knew Alrik would win and she hadn't wanted anything so badly in a long, long time. The sooner he won, the sooner she could feel his mouth on hers. She wanted him, craved him, and needed him to appease the hunger stirring deep inside her. She froze, realizing her own thoughts. What in the world was wrong with her?

Aidan scowled. "You think of another now. Who? The king," he spat the word as if it tasted disgusting.

Abby didn't dare say anything.

Jaw clenched tight, Aidan grabbed her hand and led her back into the hall. The men were even more restless now.

Aidan made her sit in a throne-like chair at the front of the hall. "Stay here." To the room he said, "Bring the fallen king up here."

The men didn't move and all conversation ceased. The blonde-haired demon who'd escorted her from her room this morning stepped forward. Disbelief marred his handsome face. "What say you?"

"The woman says she'll not accept any of us under any condition unless he's allowed to fight for a chance. So be it."

"This is ridiculous," cut another demon.

Aidan's body stiffened in a lethal way as if trying to keep from physically launching at the man. "We are not rapists. We have her promise and she'll abide by it. Besides," now she could hear the taunting laughter in his voice, "we finally have our chance to beat the king once and for all. And fairly."

Some of the demons started nodding and smiling. Another came forward. "I agree. Let him fight us. He won't beat us. Too long has he sat upon a throne while we've battled. He won't win against us."

Others started murmuring their agreement and then the matter was settled.

Four guards split to go retrieve Alrik. Abby fidgeted in her seat feeling strangely nervous at the thought of seeing him again. A minute later Alrik came in. Each of the four guards struggled to keep hold of him. He lurched and jerked against them and the guards barely seemed to keep hold of him. She wanted to smile but kept her lips in check.

As soon as he entered the room, his gaze found hers. Fury burned in his eyes. She flinched thinking he knew what she'd done with Aidan then remembered it wasn't aimed at her. Still, she had to fight the urge not to rub at the spot where she'd been bitten.

Aidan strode back towards her. He dared to rest his hand on her shoulder as if they were friends...or lovers. "We've reached an agreement, fallen king Alrik. You will fight in the challenge with us. Winner takes the human Abbigail."

She could see the change come over Alrik. His body suddenly relaxed and an eager glint came to his eyes. A slow, cruel smile split his lips. "As you wish," he said.

Abby shivered at the promise in his voice, but apparently nobody else heard the threat or if they did they weren't bothered by it.

An hour later, Abbigail sat glued to the edge of
her seat, her hands squeezing tight to the seat, and
her entire body leaning forward at the action. She'd
never seen anything like this. She'd thought the
challenge would be orderly, regulated. Perhaps one
on one and the winner proceeds to the neck round.

No, no, no. She was wrong, very wrong.

At the order "go" from Aidan, the men set
loose amongst each other. Magic bursts flared,
flashed, and scorched as punches, kicks and elbows
were thrown. Blood splattered the floor making it
look like someone had taken a bucket of fake blood
and thrown it on the floor to make it look like a fake
crime scene. Or even a real one. She'd seen a few
that were this bloody. But to see the crime, so to
speak, take place was...utterly riveting.

She didn't know why but she couldn't take her
eyes off the sight of tall, strong, healthy men beating
the crap out of each other. They fought as if their
lives were on the line. Ignoring the fact that their
lives weren't on the line and they were fighting over
her, Abby barely blinked. Time kept passing and
those who were hurt and didn't get up were dragged
out of the makeshift 'arena' by others who'd been
taken out.

Not only was it terrifying to see such brutal
violence—the men held nothing back—they
pummeled each other with all their mighty strength
and called up deadly spells. Screams and grunts
echoed in the hall. This bizarre excitement must
have been what it felt like to sit in a gladiator arena.
It was awful watching bones break and blood spurt

but it was thrilling at the same time. Her heart felt like it could beat right out of her chest at any moment. After a while, she stopped wincing at every awful sound and bloody spurt and grew used to it.

And, Alrik was winning.

She couldn't stop the swell of pride in her chest. Her man was winning!

Her gaze had barely left him the entire fight. Most ganged up on him at first, but he'd taken down many. He was surprisingly swift and lethal using a combination of spells, elbows, and knees to his advantage. He used the hardest of his bones and was probably responsible for most of the blood on the floor. The men eventually stopped targeting him as they turned on each other, each desperate for the prize. She stifled a nasty shiver at that thought.

Yet, on the opposite side of the arena, slowly working his way in was Aidan. He moved so fast she barely saw him. It was the vampirism that made him fast and agile. One man with short black hair stood against him, legs parted, knees bent, his fists clenched and a stoic expression on his face. They were at a face off.

Aidan swept behind him in a haze so fast she barely saw it. Really all she made out was the black blur of his long hair. He made it behind the demon and kicked out both the demon's knees, but as the demon collapsed to the ground, he spun around fast, and with a scissor kick took Aidan down with him.

The fight turned brutal then, as if it already wasn't. The men grappled hand to hand. Necks straining as one choked the other, knees and chests shifting each trying to gain the upper hand and toss the other below him. They flipped and rolled. Aidan came out on top. The demon squeezed tree-trunk sized legs around his waist and she sucked in a breath as if her own oxygen was being squeezed from her. Aidan's face turned red, his nostrils flared.

Finally, he slid his hands up and through the grip on his neck, grabbed the demon's wrists and bent them backwards. The demon below him howled at the cracking sound. Even Abby flinched as his wrists flopped uselessly. Aidan stood, ready to move on to another foe as the demon was dragged off by the other losers.

This was way too exciting. Just what was wrong with her? She shouldn't enjoy these grown, handsome, scary men fighting for her, but she totally did. Sick as it was, this was the coolest thing she'd ever witnessed in her life.

The fighting continued and no surprise to her, but Alrik and Aidan were down to the last five. Three demons stood between them but she knew where this was going. Judging by the demon's quieting around the arena as they watched, they knew it too. They halted their jeers and cheers to watch the fight.

Alrik spoke deep and low, fast. Black skeletal fingers grew out of the ground and climbed up the demon launching at him. The demon screamed, his eyes widening with terror at the black, bony arms. They were attached to nobody yet seemed to slow him down. He fought them, grabbing them and throwing them to the ground but they kept coming. Alrik must have known the man had just lost because he turned and engaged the next demon, this time using pure strength with teeth-jarring kicks and crunching punches.

Abby's gaze darted from one fight to the other. Aidan fought against the other demon. The demon was good and held his own against Aidan's moves— he'd made it this far for a reason.

Alrik seemed to be slowing down, his movements not as fast as they'd been when he started. Not that she could blame him, after an hour of full-on war she'd be exhausted let alone still able to fight.

The demon Alrik had fought fell to the ground screaming as the black hands covered every inch of him. Finally, he screamed, "I'm out!"

At once the hands stopped then slithered back into the ground through some invisible force.

Now only four were left. She knew this would happen the second this all started. It would come down to Alrik and Aidan, two strong and passionate men.

Abby bit on her fingernails, tearing them as anxiety built.

Then suddenly something completely different happened. Aidan said something; it was too soft and faraway for her to hear, but all the fighting stopped.

Huh?

The two demons and Aidan shifted, turning towards Alrik. Abby stood, her eyes flaring at what she saw. Those cheating bastards!

All three turned on Alrik and jumped. She screamed as he went down to the ground, the floor shaking with a boom. She could hardly see what was happening through the flurry of fists, jabbed knees, and head-butts. She just saw it was all happening to Alrik.

Before she knew what she was about, she ran down the stairs and flew to the mass of fighting men. The sound of flesh hitting flesh grew louder. She heard shouts coming at her and knew they'd try to stop her, but she couldn't stop. They were killing him.

Heart in her throat, she ran as hard as she could. Without any real plan, she reached the group. Aidan must have sensed her, or heard one of the demon's yell something for he pulled back. Little did he know he just made himself a target. Abby jumped.

His arms came around her in a protective way to shield her from hitting the floor, which meant he landed on bottom. Good. She wouldn't be surprised if her eyes glowed red right now with how angry she was. She was pissed the fuck off.

They were lousy, no good cheaters!

She sat on Aidan chest and leaned down low to hiss in his face. His eyes darted to her mouth. He didn't look scared. He looked...pleased. She planned to rectify that in two seconds.

With a quick move, she grabbed his long hair in her hand and slammed his head back down. Then she did it again and again. She put every ounce of strength inside her into it and when she pulled back, breathing hard, she saw his eyes closed but the pulse still beating at his neck. Unconscious, but not dead.

Her head slowly turned to her left. Alrik lay on the ground, clenching his ribs and looking like he was fighting the urge to curl into a ball. His face was busted from his eyes to his nose to his mouth. Yet, she swore she saw his lips lifting into a smile.

The two other demons stood now looking warily between her and Aidan.

"Get her off the field so we can finish this," her next target said. He planted his foot on Alrik's neck and pushed hard. She heard Alrik's gasps for air a second before he pressed his hand back against the foot. Abby shook with rage. She felt close to how Carrie felt in that Stephen King movie after pig's blood had dropped on her. She'd reached the last straw.

All at once she called her magic. Her skin warmed, fingertips turned hot, and she swiped one hand at the two demons towering over her demon. They flew back as if a missile hurled into them.

She didn't stop there. Demons charged in after her but she could have been floating above them on a cloud with how much power surged inside her. There was no trying to conjure her magic or learn how to utilize it. She just did it.

Her hands pressed out in a 'stop' motion and all the demons, every single one of them, froze in mid-step. She didn't realize that what she'd just done was incredible and took so much power to do. All she focused on was getting Alrik and her out of here.

She held her hand out to Alrik and he looked at her with an odd look on his face. Still, he took her hand but wouldn't let her pull him up. Instead, he jumped up and somehow managed not to sway. His knees started to buckle so she wrapped one arm around his waist to help steady him. He looked at her with that strange look again...almost like she was the crazy one. As if.

Then, without further ado, she and Alrik walked out of the arena with her power keeping the men in check. She didn't even look back. She had everything she wanted right in her arms--a crazy ass demon who wanted her to commit murder. It wasn't normal, it might not even be right, but she wanted him something fierce.

In the great hall, she let Alrik go so he could grab a sack of supplies. With a harsh groan, he slung the bag over his back, grabbed his two swords lying in a pile of weapons, and then grabbed her hand. Warmth swelled inside her, but this time not from the magic still coursing through her body like wine.

Hand in hand, they walked out of there.

Abby couldn't hide the goofy smile on her face. Looking up at Alrik, she blasted him with that happy smile. He blinked and she swore his lips twitched though she couldn't be sure with all the swelling and blood caked around his mouth.

"I win this round."

This time she couldn't mistake the sound of his laughter; deep, low, and sexy. She laughed with him and together they left the castle and headed south once more.

THE FALLEN KING

Thirteen

"Let's stop here for the night."

Alrik hid his pained wince by turning his head to the side. He didn't want to appear weak to her. His body felt like it'd been pummeled with hammers. It took every bit of his willpower not to collapse to the ground and pass out. But he couldn't do that. She'd done the impossible back in the rogue demons' castle and gotten them out of there. The magical power she'd shown was incredible. For the first time since stealing her, he finally knew she could kill his mother if she harnessed her power. If anyone could do it, it was the human witch Abbigail.

"Here, sit down," she said, her face drawn in worry.

He shot a dark look at her command but she only rolled her eyes. If she thought that helping them out of a tight spot one time would put her in charge she was sorely mistaken. Although, something did change back there. Maybe it'd been between them the whole time, but when she stood up for him with her eyes glowing, her body ready to fight, he'd felt...good. He'd even felt proud of her.

"Don't think just because you helped out back there that you can order me around, Abbigail."

She got in his face or tried to the best she could considering he had at least a foot of height on her. Suddenly her hands shot up to his hair and she brought his face down. So surprised was he at the action that he didn't pull back. He just stood there stunned waiting to see what she would do. Her gaze softened searching over his face, and then she leaned in, wrapping her body against his with a sigh.

The ache in his chest became too much to bear. Not even he had the strength to turn away from her when she was in his arms.

Alrik leaned down and crushed his lips against hers. The pressure hurt his lips but he couldn't have passed up the moment for anything in the world.

His heart felt too tight in his chest as if it were expanding. Why didn't she pull away? He'd kissed her once before but he'd hardly left her any choice. Besides, she had been so surprised by the first kiss that she just accepted it. But not now; now she knew better and still her wet tongue darted out to lick at his lips. He'd seen the desire in her eyes before. She actually wanted him.

Her lips were soft and warm beneath his. A breathy sigh fell across his lips as she licked her tongue across his bottom lip.

Even as his cock leaped to attention, he pulled back suddenly, his hand wiping his mouth. This couldn't happen for too many reasons to count.

She watched the motion and hurt flashed in her eyes. "You don't have to wipe my kiss off you! I'm not that disgusting." She turned around and stalked away.

He took a step towards her then stopped himself. He started to call her back and explain himself but didn't. He ended the kiss because he'd been sitting in a dungeon so he surely smelled foul, and blood still covered his mouth where his lips had cracked from the beating. He didn't need her licking at that filth.

But he said none of those things. "I'll be at the lake."

She went deeper into the woods until he lost sight of her. Funny but he didn't worry at all that she'd try to leave him, not after she'd rescued him. They had a bond now, and it wouldn't easily break. Still, his gut tightened until he heard her reply.

"Fine!" came the snappy retort.

Alrik chuckled then grabbed his ribs as they jostled with the action. He hadn't told her but they didn't travel as far south as he'd have liked to. If Aidan and the other rogues wanted to, they could probably reach them within a matter of hours. But he'd needed to stop before he fell on his face.

They'd managed to find an open path of grass with tall vibrant green trees scattered on either side. Down the path over boulders and loose rocks rested a dark lake. He couldn't remember the name of this lake or if it was a fallout from Deco lake. It'd been too long since he had a geography lesson.

Down at the water he pulled off his shirt. He moved slowly because as he lifted his arms his muscles tightened, burning. He panted at the pain. The wind blew, splashing ankle-high waves into the rocky shore. He didn't sit down to pull off his boots because he wasn't quite sure he'd be able to get back up if he did. So, he toed them off then dropped his pants. They needed to be washed but they'd have to wait for another day. His energy level was running on fumes as it was. Every time he closed his eyes it became harder and harder to open them again. He left the clothes and slowly treaded into the water.

The frigid temperature hit him like a punch to the gut. His whole body tensed as goose bumps popped up over his skin. Cupping the cool water, he washed idly, his body performing the motions out of practice, but his mind was somewhere else. Or, he should say, on someone else.

Abbigail. His Abbigail.

She was his, too. She could have tried to escape or coax Aidan or one of his men for help, or even told them that he'd stolen her from her home. Yet she'd kept silent. Not a word of his doing or their plans had been whispered about.

He'd seen the way the men had looked at her. If he had been free he would have slaughtered every single one of them for looking at her like that...like they wanted between her legs. Only one man would be moving between her thighs.

And soon.

Shit. Had he really just decided that?

Damn right, his body answered. He would have her…soon.

Alrik ducked under the water and floated below letting the cold water cool his boiling blood. He would be the only one. Yes, his cock filled with blood, engorging into a hard rod even in the cold water. If he closed his eyes and concentrated hard enough he could almost feel her lips against his, imagine what she'd feel like wrapped around his cock—wet and tight—a hungry little muscle for him to plunder. He shivered at the thought. He wanted her hands and legs clinging to him, holding on to him as he sent her screaming his name in passion.

Alrik dove back to the surface and sucked in a harsh breath. His cock throbbed. With a groan, he wrapped a fist around it. Damn, he was hard as stone. He trailed his hand up and down the hard rod but the pleasure wasn't there at his own hand. If it were her hand…that'd be a different story.

His mind filled with erotic images: Abbigail kneeling before him with her mouth sucking his cock, her legs spread wide with his head buried in her pussy, and her curvy body riding his cock with her luscious breasts swaying in his face.

His hand moved up and down his shaft, breath stuttering from his lips before he realized what he was doing.

"Alrik?"

He spun around guiltily, his hands thrown up in the air at the soft voice. Slowly, his arms lowered back down but his jaw was much slower to close.

Abbigail stood naked at the water's edge, water lapping at her small feet. Her breasts were bare, full with small delicious pink nipples he wanted to suck on. Her waist dipped in then flared out wide to a set of hips meant for a man to hold. The light caressed her smooth legs making them shine. Her legs were strong but not overly muscular or long.

Abbigail was a petite thing. A curvaceous woman meant to be held as he fucked her. His cock throbbed, blood pumping hard to the organ. He must tread carefully here for he would surely blow it if he kept gazing at her nakedness.

"What are you doing?" he asked, voice dry.

She swiped hair back from her face, gave a tentative smile, and then came forward.

The water reached her knees before she squealed and jumped two steps back. "It's so cold!"

It was but if she thought to get in here with him while he had an erection the size of a tower that had no intention of going away, then he needed to keep her out. "It only gets colder as you get in. Go back to the camp, Abbigail." Even to his own ears his voice sounded huskier. If she noticed it, she didn't say so.

She stood straight at his words, a look in her eyes...a look with strength and desire floating under the surface. She took a deep breath and slowly waded in...towards him.

He flexed his abs in response. The pain it sent to his ribs did nothing to weaken his erection. His gaze fell from her face to her soft breasts glistening, bobbing in the water. His lips parted at the sight; his mouth suddenly dry as dirt.

"What are you doing, Abbigail?"

She was only a few feet away. He could see her shoulders trembling. Damn. She was cold. He didn't like that. Before he thought twice about it or tried to deny what he wanted, he reached forward and pulled her into his body. Heat flared between them creating a unique polarizing sensation in the water from hot where their bodies touched and cold where the water licked at them.

Abbigail gasped and as quick as a snake wrapped her arm around his neck pulling herself closer. They buoyed in the water, legs slowly kicking to keep afloat. She had yet to discover his erection but it was only a matter of time. If she touched him...he didn't know if he'd be able to not push himself inside of her, test her tightness, and see how wet he could make her. She was naked, her pussy bare and close, and within reach. It was almost too much. Alrik bit hard on the inside of his cheek to distract himself.

"I wanted to make sure you didn't need any help. And, I brought the soap." She held up the yellow bar he'd managed not to see before. He watched her with wary eyes. She reached behind him to lather her hands then started rubbing her fingers in his hair. Her touch was gentle, seductive. When she reached his scalp, his cock pulsed. Each gentle tug in his hair felt like a stroke of his cock.

"You don't know what you're doing, Abbigail," he warned.

THE FALLEN KING

"I think I do," she whispered, her voice so close to his lips.

Their eyes met and locked together. With his eyes he tried to tell her that if she wanted to back out now was the time. After he touched her, really touched her, he wouldn't be able to stop.

With her fingers moving so gently through his hair, washing him, and her eyes gazing at him with such gentleness, as if she cared, something changed. A wall dropped around his heart. It couldn't be a good thing because the wall he'd erected had only dropped once and the person who it dropped for was now dead because of him. Still, he felt that wall shifting, moving, and dropping.

He snaked his arms around her waist, pulled her breasts into his chest. The soft globes flattened against him and hard peaks rubbed against him. For some reason, he felt the urge to tell her the truth. He didn't want their last angry words to be hanging between them.

The words spilled from him. "I wasn't wiping your taste from my lips."

Her hands stilled in his hair. "What?" He heard the passion, thick and husky, in her voice.

"I was afraid you'd taste the blood on me. I don't want you to taste that."

Her eyes widened with a feminine softness, and then she rubbed her wet naked thigh on the outside of his.

He couldn't wait anymore.

185

§

Nothing had ever felt more right. There were times in life where Abbigail had been in just the right situation to have something good happen to her, and when that something good happened, a euphoric giddiness filled her. She could hardly stop smiling. Right now in Alrik's arms, she felt that same feeling.

Alrik wasn't just some coincidental event. He was a flesh and blood demon who was trying so very hard to resist her. She could see the war in his eyes, the way his gaze darted to the shoreline and around them as if trying to search for a reason to get away from her. He wanted her. He wanted her as badly as she did him. She was done fighting it.

At first, it'd been anger that made her stomp down to the riverfront. She was gonna give him a little piece of her mind, but when she'd watched him, naked, vulnerable and wearing a grimace on his beautiful mouth from the pain she knew she couldn't do it. No way, it didn't feel right. She knew exactly what she did want to do.

She dropped her clothes among his on the ground then, and before she knew it she was in his arms with his hard chest pressed tightly against hers. She shivered at the touch. Her nipples took in every single touch of them and shot spikes of pleasure to her needy center. She wanted to rub her chest against him to alleviate the burning wet, pulsating heat inside her. Her hands were soapy, entwined in the soft strands of his hair.

"You've made your decision, Abbigail. There is no taking it back."

Her heart stuttered at his words. She'd been playing it so casual as if she got naked in front of men all the time and just threw herself at them. When in fact her heart raced wildly and her body shook with need. He was so much bigger up close and naked. The man had a powerful, strong body. A warrior's body that needed a woman's touch. And she was going to give him what he needed.

She licked her dry lips a second before he groaned and crushed his mouth onto hers.

Yes, yes! she wanted to scream.

His kiss drove her mad. His kiss consumed her body and mind. Her hands tangled in his hair to keep him from moving. Their lips meshed and when his tongue slid along her lips, she parted them so he could enter. The kiss turned consuming, their breaths mingling, tongues exploring tastes. His was masculine, heady...sexy.

They fought for the kiss, heads turning left then right to get the better angle. He was trying to outmatch her, but she refused to roll over for him. Well, unless he asked her too.

Their tongues twined, wet lips fusing and sucking. A deep groan growled from his chest and reverberated all the way down her spine. She squirmed in his arms needing more. The kiss wasn't enough. His touch made her wet and ache to have him between her thighs. She needed to be touched.

She slid her hands out of his hair and down his chest. Her hands had a mind of their own. She had to feel him everywhere. Finally, she had her hands on him. His skin was hot, smooth, and firm at his chest. But that's not what she wanted to feel. Tongues rolling together, she slid her hands down low, leaning back just enough to slip her hands down his hard chest, over the hard rolls of muscles. His stomach twitched under her touch and a sense of power flared inside her.

She could do this. She could make this big, bad demon unravel beneath her very fingertips. With that thought, she reached down to encircle his shaft.

He tore his mouth away on a growl; she moaned. Her fingers didn't even touch around his thickness.

Their eyes locked and she said the first thing that came to her mind. "You're big."

His hands slid down and squeezed her ass, his touch not gentle but hard and possessive.

"Oh God," she moaned. She loved his rough touch. Would he be rough in all ways?

Then she was thrust away from him.

"What's wrong?" she breathed. Fire burned in her veins. She waded towards him but he shook his head stopping her.

He ducked under the water and she saw the soap bubbles float up to the surface. Then he burst to the surface, swam towards her so fast she could only gasp as his shoulder hit her stomach and he lifted her over his shoulder and carried her back to shore.

"Oh!" Yes, she liked this, she thought. They needed a hard surface. A soft moan left her as she trailed her hands up and down his strong back. Muscles rippled under her touch. He was so solid and built. She wanted to feel his heavy weight on top of her, wanted to feel his big cock thrusting inside her. Reaching even further, she cupped his tight ass.

He growled, the sound like a warning and then she was flipped around and her back hit the grass. He stood above her, his gaze devouring her. It was the look in his eyes that made her heart feel so full. He looked at her as if he'd never seen a more beautiful woman in his life…like he'd never wanted one so badly. Surely he had, she was hardly model worthy with her plain brown hair and simple figure, but under his gaze she felt like the goddess Aphrodite.

He dropped to his knees in front of her. Of their own will, her legs spread open bearing herself to his gaze. His eyes dropped to the neediest part of her, and if possible, his gaze burned brighter. His tongue darted out to lick his lips and she squirmed.

"You light me on fire," he said in a hoarse voice.

Abbigail shivered but not from being cold. "Then touch me."

Alrik in all his dark beauty bent over her, his hands cupping her thighs, his gaze locked on that center part of her. The first touch of his lips to her thigh sent her muscles tightening. She squirmed and wriggled, her thighs fidgeting but his grip only tightened, trapping her for his touch. He pressed kisses up her thigh, so close to the hot center of her. A soft moan escaped her. Her pussy was on fire, her bud swollen and throbbing to be touched. Instead of touching her there, he moved to her other thigh and pressed kisses up it.

"Beautiful Abbigail," he murmured huskily.

His words made her heart jump. He never said things like this to her. They softened her heart, and melted her.

Her nipples pulled into aching hard points. They were so hard they hurt. She cupped them, pinching her own nipples to ease the ache, but Alrik caught her hands and with a growl, shoved them away to cup her breasts himself. Rough hands squeezed and plumped her, and then finally his fingers found her hard nipples and pulled. Pleasure mixed with just a hint of pain and a flood of moisture filled her sex.

"Alrik!"

She lifted her weak neck to look at him. He looked like a man lost, his eyes hazy with passion, and his chest moving hard to breathe. Then, in a jerky move, he moved back between her legs, kept his hands pawing at her breasts, and then she felt it. The first fluttery touch so soft she almost missed it. Her entire body tensed, waiting for it.

It came again. The soft pass of his tongue over her. The hunger in his gaze belied the slow and gentle movements. The difference threw her, left her confused and yearning. She didn't want soft and gentle, she needed hard and firm. As if sensing her turmoil he gave her the opposite. Soft and wet his tongue passed in long swipes against her flesh, sucking her lips, then gentle nudging her bundle of nerves. She quivered. If not for his arms keeping her down she would have jolted up to hold his head to her.

"Please," she begged, barely recognizing her own voice. She wanted to tell him that she didn't need all this foreplay. She was already so close to coming, she just needed his cock inside her and she'd explode.

Then his tongue dipped across her in earnest. He narrowed in on her bud and flicked it gently, swirling slowly around her neediest part. Where he touched her became the focal point of all feelings. One hand traveled down over her stomach. His fingers spread out on her stomach making her realize his hand was big enough to almost cover her and then his hand massaged her inner thigh while his tongue tortured her.

"Faster," she panted.

Just a little bit more and she'd fly apart. Just faster, a little harder, and all the pent-up energy boiling inside her would spill over.

But he slowed down his movements instead. His tongue twirled around her lazily, torturing her. A finger trailed over her wet slit, pushing slowly inside. Her breath caught as a new fullness filled her. Then he pressed deep, all the way in and she moaned, her head whipping side to side. Her hands curled into the grass and she yanked out chunks.

Sweat beaded on her skin. Warmth filled her chest and face, flushing her.

Then something magical happened. His finger curled inside her and stroked something raw and erotic while his mouth latched onto her bud and sucked hard. He had known exactly what he was doing this whole time.

Her body arched off the ground as a strangled cry tore from her throat. He brought her up to peak hard and fast. Her cries rang in her ears as her body swept up to a great peak and shattered. Her body clung to his finger, massaging it; her hips jerked and shook against his talented mouth.

He gentled his movements, slowly thrusting his finger in and out and languidly licking at her as he brought her back down to earth.

The pleasure faded slowly like it didn't want to leave. It lingered. She tried to open her eyes but it took several tries before she could actually do it. Her whole body felt relaxed and lethargic. Still, she was ready to have him inside her. She lifted up on her elbows and looked down at his dark head between her legs.

"Alrik..."

His eyes flicked up to connect with hers but he still licked at her as if he had all the time in the world. Then he pulled his finger out from her and she watched with a soft moan as he sucked her wetness from his finger.

"Your body burns for me, Abbigail."

He lifted up onto his knees and his head fell back as if he was looking up at the stars. She licked her lips at the sight of all that strong muscle, then her eyes locked on his cock, hard and erect standing straight out from his hips. Her sex quivered at the sight. She wanted him to fill her up. Sitting up, she reached forward and grasped him in her hand.

His head jerked forward and he looked lost for a moment, and then his lips crashed down on hers. The kiss was fierce and hurried, their tongues whipping at each other. She couldn't keep from stroking him, from squeezing his girth, and wetting her palm with the liquid at the tip. Pulling back, she looked into his lost eyes.

"I want this inside me." She squeezed his cock for emphasis.

His eyes darkened, smoldered. "Are you sure about that?" She stroked him up and down, loving the way he shuddered under her touch.

She gulped and spoke honestly. "I don't know if I've ever been more sure about anything."

That was answer enough for him because one second she was sitting before him, cupping his erection, and the next she was flat on her back, his heavy weight pressing her into the ground. She spread her legs wide to fit his hips and still it was a tight fit. His shaft explored her entrance making her breath catch.

This was so different from anything she'd ever done before. They were eye to eye. Her hands swept up into his long hair to hold him and he fisted his hands in the ground by her head. She felt completely caged in, safe, and her heart pounded from it. The heavy weight of him covered her in a primitive way.

His cock bumped her, slipping inside slowly. She couldn't hide her surprise. He didn't plunder her as she'd thought he would. Instead, he slowly filled her up and spread her open. It was a tight fit, but she couldn't complain at the feeling. Her moans were testament to that. And when he thrust that final way in, they both stared into each other's eyes.

"Abbigail," he groaned, lines creasing his forehead. She could feel the restraint in his body, in the way his arms trembled and his eyes warred with him to thrust and take.

"Alrik," she answered. Then she leaned up and caught his mouth.

They were connected in all ways—bodies pressed tightly together, lips locked, sexes joined, and only then did he move. He pulled his hips back, his cock dragging through her wet, tight flesh causing a symphony of erotic sensations flaring through her body. Then he plummeted back in on a groan that she kissed away.

Something moved in her heart at his movements. He wasn't fucking her, wasn't just taking from her. He was seeing to her pleasure first. Even if she'd wanted to, there was no way to keep her heart from leaping in her chest at the close connection. This wasn't fucking. She just couldn't dare think what it was instead.

He moved faster, his rhythm building, their kiss never breaking. He felt so good inside her; so full, thick, and hard. Nothing had ever felt so good. She didn't want it to end. Every time he filled her he pushed her closer, his hips grinding against her bundle of nerves. She lifted her hips into him, accepting him, taking him.

He breathed raggedly. His muscles flexed so hard and tight she could feel his muscles trembling from the effort.

Finally, she tore her mouth away to breathe and he buried his face in her neck panting. Then he let himself go.

He pounded into her, moved hard and fast just the way she needed...almost to the point of overwhelming her. Her nails scraped down his back at the feelings racing through her.

They were wrapped in the moment together, bodies fighting to obtain release, breaths scattering in the wind. When his rhythm faltered, she knew he was close. She arched her hips into him at each thrust, her breath catching as her pleasure mounted. Then he filled her on a hard thrust, and she was torn apart by the seams. She screamed, heard his name leave her lips, heard his groan as he slid deep and spurted inside her, shaking like a leaf in her hands.

The moment faded slowly. Her breathing slowed. Their temperatures returned to normal, but she didn't want to let him go. He felt so good in her arms. She hugged him to her, felt his lips kiss her neck, and then he pulled away, and slipped out of her. She winced at the action knowing she'd be sore after that, but it was worth it.

He dropped to the ground beside her and she didn't hesitate to crawl over him, tossing an arm and leg over him, and burying her face in his neck. She loved his scent, so masculine and raw. She'd never really noticed it until now. Now things were different though. He pressed a kiss to her temple and she let sleep take her knowing she was safe in his arms.

Fourteen

The next morning Abby woke up feeling refreshed and excited. She couldn't hide her grin seeing Alrik still asleep beneath her. It was a small victory, but a good one to have finally woken up before him. Quietly, she pulled on her clothes, pressed a soft kiss to his lips, and then darted into the woods. She needed some time to think and her belly growled like a grizzly bear. For once, she was going to bring the food to him.

Now that the fog of lust had faded she had no idea where they stood. She really wanted to find out though. Now that they'd crossed that particular boundary, she wanted to discover what else was there. She liked him. The thought had her laughing, but it was true. She did. She really liked him. She liked that he could be sweet with her. She liked how tender he'd been when he touched her. She liked his strength and the way he'd fought to win that challenge for her—which she had no doubt he would have won if they hadn't cheated.

Yes, she really liked him. She liked a crazy ass demon who wanted her to commit murder. The scenario might sound irrational, but she'd seen too many things since coming to the rift for it not to be true—idummi demons, alien plants, a deadly thunderstorm, and a randy vampire who wanted to take more than a bite out of her.

A shiver raced down her spine. Even through it all, Alrik had proven himself responsible by caring for her, and she hadn't missed that look in his eyes last night. Did she know what it meant yet, no, but she wasn't going to stop thinking about it until she figured it out. He'd looked at her like...like he'd finally found something he'd been looking for.

Her heart flip-flopped, pulling tight like too much air filled her chest. She rolled her eyes at her own ridiculousness. What she needed was a good smack upside her head to get her thoughts back in line.

"Don't go stroking your ego, Abby," she muttered.

So he wasn't a "bang" a girl kind of guy, maybe he was that tender with all the women he'd been with.

So maybe what they had wasn't quite special. Damn but she didn't believe that. Not after what she'd seen in his eyes, and it hadn't just been in his eyes but in the way he'd kissed her , touched her, and held her. She'd had casual sex before, but what they'd shared last night didn't feel like that. He'd touched her as if she mattered.

Whether it was because of the incredible sex or just because she felt spry this morning, she found herself wanting to do something special for him. Those futhorc animals were all over the rift so she headed into the trees keeping her steps soft and quiet as she hunted.

She'd even use her magic to practice on it. Today she wanted to try something more powerful. After the spell she casted on the rogue demons she had a newfound confidence in her abilities. If she could do that then she could take down a little animal for breakfast.

Her new found-again powers worked at a thought and a feeling. If she concentrated hard enough she could slow an animal's movements, block them with an invisible barrier, or whatever else she could conjure up with her mind. What she couldn't do was call forth the dead like Alrik did in that castle. There'd been a dark, black energy around him like cigarette smoke. The black bony hands had worked to slow down and take down the demon coming for him, but she couldn't help but wonder how he became so accustomed to such dark magic.

Light rose sharply in the sky by the time she bagged a futhorc and headed back to the lake. She had a big smile on her face that didn't seem to want to go anywhere and she embraced it. She hadn't felt this good since...before Alrik took her and even then her life had been heading towards a boring routine of working five days a week for eight hours or more a day. Not necessarily an ideal way to live, but such was life. The daily grind was a necessary evil. After all, she couldn't live without making money.

Just as she neared the path that sloped down to the lake, a mighty roar blared. There was no mistaking the voice behind that awful sound. It wasn't the first time she heard him yell like that. The demon had a yell that could launch an army into war.

Heart galloping, she sprinted down the slope, fear gripping her. Something was wrong. He needed her. She skidded over the grass and rocks kicking up dirt and sliding across them before coming to a hard stop. It took her a second to comprehend what she saw.

He was fine.

He was dressed. No idummi demons or rogue demons attacked him, no wild storm had been summoned to drown him, and yet he looked beyond pissed off. His teeth flashed in a snarl, his hands were fisted loosely at his sides, and his legs were spread as if he was ready to attack.

"Where the hell have you been?" he growled.

Abby stiffened at his harsh tone, her jaw clenching as anger built inside her. This was what she got? After the fear-gripping moment she just had?

"I woke up before you and thought it'd be nice if I went and got breakfast for once." She could feel the ugly, bitchy attitude sneaking up inside her and hated it. Things shouldn't be like this the first morning after sharing something so shattering. A feeling close to grief, heavy and loaded, filled her heart.

"That was stupid. Anything could have happened to you out there and I wouldn't have been there to stop it!" His sincerity didn't help her to feel any better.

His reasoning may have been to protect her but that wasn't how she saw it. She tossed the dead animal at his feet, her appetite gone. "You know what, I'm a grown woman and I happen to be able to survive just a bit on my own. I don't need you for everything." Asshole, she added silently. That loaded feeling kept getting heavier and heavier in her chest like a balloon swelling. If it grew any fuller, her heart would start tearing in slow agonizing rips.

She knew this feeling and she hated it because it meant she wanted to cry, that she'd let him get to her on a deeper level. He was able to hurt her now. Fucking great.

He looked down at the dead futhorc and, if anything, looked more pissed. The muscle over his right eye twitched; a muscle popped in his jaw. What the fuck was wrong with him?

She'd heard of the 'awkward next day' after having sex with someone for the first time, but this wasn't how it usually played out, or so she assumed. She didn't make a habit of sleeping around, and she really didn't stay the night with the man if she did. Yeah, talk about awkward. The thought hadn't even crossed her mind that things might be awkward between her and Alrik, especially not over something so simple. Sure, she didn't know where they stood, but things didn't have to be like this.

"I'm very aware that you're a grown woman, Abbigail."

The way he said it, reminded her intimately of how he'd felt thrusting inside her last night. A blush colored her cheeks and she could do nothing to hide it.

Crossing her arms, she glared at him to hide the hurt burning inside her. Anger was so much easier to deal with because being angry was easy. Being hurt was more intense, because then she'd have to analyze why he'd hurt her feelings and what that meant to her, what he meant to her, and she wasn't going there.

Nope, not at all.

"We'll practice new spells and then get moving."

"I already did. How do you think I managed that?" She nodded to the dead animal. She'd managed to make the small animal's heart stop beating in an instant. It had been painless and swift for the creature. However, if she tried the spell again it wouldn't work. Already, she could feel that her power had dwindled from the effort that spell had taken. She would need some time to recharge her batteries, so to speak.

Alrik frowned. Ignoring the way his lips looked would have been the smart thing to do but yeah, right. Impossible. They only reminded her of how he kissed her so hungrily as if he couldn't get enough of her. Well, apparently that all changed today. He had had quite enough of her. Asshole.

His eyes closed and a shudder wracked over him. "Control your anger, woman. I can feel it."

Every single time he told her what to do, she wanted to grab fistfuls of her hair and pull as hard as she could. He managed to make her want to act like a child, stomping her feet in the dirt, screaming, and crying her frustrations. She really wanted to do all those things but she couldn't. Adults had to fight in a big-kid way.

So, she glared at him.

Her fingers bit into her biceps causing little flickers of pain to snap in her brain. She knew she wasn't really that mad, just fucking hurt. Which, of course, was worse. She hated this. She didn't want to fight with him after what happened last night. What they'd done hadn't just been sex and it certainly hadn't been fucking. They'd been as close as two people could get. They'd shared something special. Oh jeez, she rolled her eyes at her own sappiness. Now she was just being ridiculous.

"And if I don't?" she taunted. Okay, perhaps taunting was a bit childish.

He stalked towards her like a predator. Her first instinct told her to step back but she kept her ground, her chin tilting up. What would he do to her? It's not like he'd hurt her.

She wasn't afraid of him but that didn't mean he didn't unnerve the hell out of her. He stopped in front of her but she was ready to hold her own for whatever he dished out—maybe another tongue lashing or maybe he'd resort back to calling her witch. Only this time with a 'b' at the front.

However, he didn't do any of those things. What he did do surprised the hell out of her...and scared her even more.

Strong hands grabbed her shoulders, pulling her roughly towards him, and then he leaned down and spoke in measured, slow tones. But, something was off in his voice. It sounded distorted. All she could think was that it sounded 'demonic'. Harsh, slightly garbled, and dangerous.

"I am very close to losing myself right now, Abbigail. Control...your...anger."

Abby's anger fled in a flash. Something wasn't right.

In fact, something was very wrong with him right now. His eyes started to glow amber. A dark, icy energy emanated from his body. It reminded her of her own magic but whereas hers was warmth and good, his felt like the cold hand of death. She'd made him this angry? She wanted to ask why, but one look at the toll it was taking on him kept her mouth shut.

Moving slowly, she leaned into him and wrapped her arms around his waist. His body thrummed with cold energy, nearly vibrating her with its crackling power. She rested her cheek against his chest, forcing all the negative energy and thoughts to disappear. Under her ear, she listened to the thundering beat of his heart—it was too loud, too fast.

The temperature dropped. A shiver started in her chest and worked its way to her fingers and toes in a matter of seconds. It truly was the cold of death.

Anger started to stride back up at the thought of this curse on him, but she shoved it back down ruthlessly. He needed her right now. And she could do this, she could bring him back down from whatever precipice he teetered at. She didn't understand it, didn't even get it, but she'd help him because she knew if it was her struggling, he'd help her in a heartbeat.

"Let it go, Alrik. Just let go of whatever holds you. Hold me instead." His heartbeat thudded hard, once, at her words. As if his heart skipped a beat.

She held her breath, closed her eyes and simply held him. Puffy white clouds formed at her mouth as she breathed. Time passed slowly. She couldn't begin to know just how much, minutes maybe. An eternity.

What felt hours passed and then an arm came around her, she could feel it trembling and she hoped it wasn't from the effort it took not to hurt her. Happiness burst inside her. She wanted to cheer for him. She didn't know what was in this haunted demon's mind, but after seeing him like this she'd find out.

His chest stopped pumping so hard, his heartbeat slowed to a normal *dum, dum, dum*. When his other arm wrapped around her waist, she sighed and pressed a kiss over his heart.

The cold started to recede. Her shivering died down, but her nose still felt cold and it surely looked bright red about now.

Still hesitant, she slowly looked up. His eyes would show her what she needed to know. That would be the final tell. But when she looked up, his eyes were pressed closed, a look of intense pain on his face.

"Alrik...what's wrong?" she asked in her softest voice.

The muscles along his forehead and mouth twitched and jerked as if they were being zapped with electrical impulses.

"Look at me, baby," she coaxed.

She clenched her fingers in his shirt. She wanted to cry. Just seeing the agony written all over his face made her hurt inside. He was grappling with something but she didn't know what. It was all inside him with that black, evil energy clouding around him like noxious gas. She wanted to wipe it all away with a snap of her fingers.

His throat bobbed as he swallowed then slowly he opened his eyes. The all black recesses looked darker. How there were different shades of black she wasn't sure, but his eyes hadn't been that black before. A shiver passed over her.

"Alrik, honey?"

As if finally hearing her voice, his head slowly turned down to her. The tarry ink of his eyes looked like a river of oil, no whites, no distinguishing pupil, just darkness. He blinked once, twice, again. Before her very eyes, she watched the darkness fade—not completely—but enough to transform the black color back to what she was used to—something close to a deep shade of blue or the darkest form of gray.

Her stupid heart raced and she recognized the awful feeling inside her for what it was—fear. For the first time since being kidnapped by him, Abby saw the control the curse could have over him. In this instance, he'd been able to control it. What would happen if he didn't?

Reaching up, she cupped his cheek. A wet tear escaped her eye and she quickly stood on tiptoe to press a kiss to his lips so he wouldn't see it. Gasping, she jerked back from him.

His skin felt like ice.

A sob threatened to break from her throat but she held it back. What in the world was going on with him?

Gradually, slowly, he cocked his head, arms tightening around her, and his head dipped catching her lips. Warmth grew between them like the heat of the sun touching snow.

He reached, cupped her bottom in one big hand, and lifted her up against him with a growl. A surprised moan bubbled out of her. At this level their hips aligned and she could feel his cock, hard and ready pressing into her. The swift mood change had her struggling to keep up but she went with the flow, taking his kiss and giving it back.

His tongue dipped inside her mouth then retreated slowly, tasting her. As if some thread snapped, he dropped her to her feet in the next second and stormed away from her. He snatched his swords off the ground and slid them into the holster on his back. The man couldn't even dress without keeping those sheathes on.

His eyes didn't meet hers. "Let's practice. I want you to try making fire now." His voice sounded normal and not like the distorted demonic tone from before.

Abby was frozen in place, confused. So was this how they were going to play? Just act like nothing completely freaking bizarre had just happened? She didn't think so.

"Wait, wait, wait, don't you think you could explain what the heck just happened here?"

He started gathering up sticks and breaking them into pieces for a fire.

He didn't look at her, and didn't say a word

"You know, I don't really take silent treatment so well."

Alrik tossed some dried leaves on top of the pile of sticks and glared at her. "What do you care what happens to me?"

Her heart softened, eyes rounded. "I do care." The admission felt like something so much more powerful that what she'd actually said.

He shook his head. "I told you already. It's the curse."

Abby sat down on a boulder sticking out the ground near the water. "I'll try to start a fire and you are going to tell me all about it." She made sure her voice left no room for argument. Besides, she knew something was off. They'd fought before but he hadn't nearly hulked out like that. Well, maybe hulking out wasn't quite the best term for it. He hadn't been close to smashing the ground with his fists so much as...using dark magic. A nasty shudder passed over her.

Concentrating hard, she stared at the twigs and broken branches willing fire to spark and engulf it. Her temperature warmed almost as if she was already sitting near the warm flames.

"My mother cursed me with rage to control me. I never saw it, never felt the change overcome me. I'd actually," he paused and rubbed a hand over the back his neck, "embraced it. It felt amazing to have that kind of power."

Inside she stiffened her breath catching.

"Why would she do that?" she asked softly. Maybe it helped that she wasn't looking straight at him and focused on her task of creating fire, but she wanted to jump up and down cheering because he was opening up to her.

"I don't know exactly. She hated me, maybe. She was always a bitter, unhappy woman. After my father died, I became king since Telal abandoned us to live above the rift." He made a derisive snort that told her just how he felt about his brother.

A burning sensation tingled along her fingertips like holding your hand too close to fire. Her breaths came faster and she reached closer to the wood imagining and feeling all the power inside her thrust up and out to the wood, burning it.

A spark caught—just a small explosion like a firework popping. Abby let out a happy squeal at her little victory while Alrik simply nodded once at her.

"Keep trying."

Well, she supposed it was better than "that's not good enough."

She tried again.

"So you don't get along with your brother I take it?" She remembered Telal from news reports. Governments across the world bought his weapons. He made things from knives to automatic rifles. Of course, his golden skin and blue hair made him stick out just a little in the human world.

He made a strangled sound, almost like a laugh and choke mixing. "No! He betrayed us to the vampires, to that bastard Tobius en Kulev. They brought war on us and shut us inside this rift like a bunch of caged animals. He had to create an entire army to do it. They called themselves the Atal Warriors. It took nearly a hundred years for them to break us, but they finally did. Nothing's been the same since... Telal should have been king. He is the eldest. It was his duty." His lip curled with disgust. "But he betrayed us to Tobius, and let his own people get slaughtered."

Abby had to look at him. A haunted look shadowed his eyes. "Why would he do that?" she asked gently. She wanted to know it all, everything about him and his people.

"Tobius en Kulev started it. He wanted war with us so he could cage us down here like animals. He used excuses to rally people. He preached how dangerous we were to all...to humans, vampires, and shapeshifters. Finally, he instilled enough fear that though only a few demons had ever hurt anyone in such a way, enough people rallied against us. The shapeshifters stayed out of it and the humans didn't have the skill required to war with us, so that left the vampires. He created the Atal Warriors—a vampire organization trained to kill us." He shook his head solemnly. "My father died in the battle. It lasted a long time. We would not give up, but always being besieged such as we were—it was only a matter of time before we fell.

One hundred years we fought but they kept coming. Father fell, Telal betrayed us and went to the surface, and we were left locked inside the rift. The Atal Warriors killed any who dared to leave instantly. That was their new job, you see, to guard the rift from us," he hissed.

"So all that happened because of your brother?"

He nodded his jaw clenching. "And Tobius' grudge against us. Rumors spread that his hate for demons came because of a woman. Some woman he loved ran off with a demon." He shook his head. "Not that I could blame her. A demon would make a much better mate than a vampire." Suddenly a grin flashed across his face. "No matter, the vampire got what he deserved. I started training a special team of warriors. We planned it carefully. I spent years on the plan. Then one night we set it in motion. My team ported to the earthen-realm, destroyed the Atal Warriors there, and then tracked down Tobius all in a night. They were the best trackers, the best fighters. They slaughtered him and brought me back his head as proof.

I kept the head on a pike out front of the castle for nearly five years after that. It wasn't just for me but for everyone who remembered his cruelty." A strange look flickered over his eyes. He held his hand out and stared at it as if seeing something weird. "It was after that I started to change. I never realized it though. I'd look in the mirror and knew my skin had changed, but I never questioned it." That hand curled into a fist. "Such was the curse that gripped me."

Still, the thing with his mother rubbed her the wrong way. "But why did your mom curse you? I mean, what could she get out it?"

He was silent for a moment, his head cast down over the futhorc he skinned. She got the impression that he was thinking about it as if he hadn't yet. "Power."

"But she was a queen. I assume that means you come from a big fancy castle, get to rule over people, and the usual aristocratic deal, yeah?"

His hands stilled on the animal with knife in hand. "Power over a person is much stronger than ruling a kingdom. It was more than that. She had every bit of control over me, my feelings, even my actions. She would give me this potion. Stupidly, I'd drink the nasty liquid. She said it'd calm me down and it always did, but little did I know that it also kept me ensnared under her toxic spell." He stabbed the knife into the animal and cut in a jabbing motion as he tore the skin off it.

Abby flinched and looked away. Maybe talking to him while he had a knife in his hand wasn't such a good idea after all.

"But why did your brother betray you like that?"

Pain flashed in his eyes. He must have loved his brother very much. "Before he ripped the kingdom from my hands and banished me, he told me. I spent so long blaming him that it's been hard not to even if it was his fault the war started. He claims that Tobius made a pact with him. Telal wanted to start a group of trained warriors to protect our kingdom from idummi and other demonic attacks. They did happen frequently back then. He wanted the vampires and us to form an alliance and work together...or so he told me. However he was blinded by Tobius' hatred for us and Tobius didn't waste the opportunity to destroy us."

Abby froze at the sound of his voice. He sounded so sad talking about it. It broke another piece inside her.

"Keep practicing on the fire."

Abby faced the makeshift pit again and called for the power inside her. She could feel her magical abilities growing. It was like learning a new instrument. It took time and practice but she was getting better at it. Already she could call the magic forth much quicker and the time between casting a new spell was faster. Soon she'd have enough power to summon a portal to earth.

Oh God. Abby looked over at Alrik. His shoulders were hunched and his eyes downcast in thought. Could she really leave him? He said he couldn't defeat his mother and she knew him well enough to know he wouldn't just walk away from this. Obviously, the curse had become his life. He had a dispute to end and there'd be no stopping until he finished it.

The first thought that popped in her mind was no. She couldn't do it. No way could she leave him down here with rogue demons, idummi creatures, and a queen bitch who wanted to kill him. A wild thought sprung making her stomach flutter. Maybe he could come with her. Maybe she could convince him to let this all go and come home with her.

Her lip curled as logic set in. Just what would he do up there, become a banker? Yeah, right. The man was a king, a fighter, a magician. Not exactly the kind of guy you put behind a desk for eight hours a day. Nothing about Alrik fit in with her normal-day world.

"You're not focusing." He came to her and settled behind her on the rock. Warmth and muscle pressed into her back as he surrounded her, wrapping his arms around hers. Strong fingers clasped her wrists, holding them out towards the round circle of twigs. His voice was deep, low, and near her ear. "Feel the fire inside you, deep in your soul. Call on it and shoot it out from your body. Let it warm you, guide you. I know you can do it."

Abby relaxed against him, trusting him with her weight. His voice, deep and lolling, sucked her into a trance. Everything that was happening went to the back of her mind—the wind blowing, the leaves rustling and swaying in the breeze. Even the light above and sound of lapping water over rocks faded leaving only them. Alrik and her.

At his request power surged up inside her as if obeying a master. Warmth heated her like a blanket. It pressed up from deep in her belly, spread to her chest and out through her arms, and then shot from her fingertips. The invisible force showed no color, no sound, but in her witch's eye she watched the vibrant billowing reds, oranges, and blues spew from her fingertips. The fiery power arched through the air and reached the fire. One spark flared while another burst. Then in a small explosion, the wood caught flame all at once, crackling and radiating heat.

Abby was slow to come out of the trance she was in. When she did she felt no heat at her back but her smile grew and grew at the sight of the fire.

"I did it! Alrik, I did it!" She jumped and performed a fist pump at her own awesomeness. It almost didn't seem real. She headed for the fire and felt the real heat of it. She couldn't stop smiling. She did this. She actually made fire just with her powers.

Then it dawned on her—a strange feeling. It was like one of those times where you realize that something is off belatedly. In this case, Abby turned around slowly.

She saw Alrik facing the lake, then as her gaze passed him, and her own eyes widened. Her lips parted and a scream tore from her throat.

Fifteen

"You have got to be kidding me," Alrik muttered.

Alrik's gaze locked on the giant beast lumbering out of the water. The middle of the lake rippled and bubbled like boiling water. With a mighty splash, the water exploded out at once from the rippling circle, raining heavy water droplets around it. A grisly creature started to appear. First a head, a mighty, round glob of flesh the color of sick green and cream mixed together. The flesh looked lopsided and pliable like putty. The creature's eyes came into view. They were yellow orbs that instantly narrowed on them.

The creature slowly lifted up to its incredible height. Water cascaded down the jaheera demon's torso like a waterfall; water churned and swished around the demon's legs making noise like a boat crashing into waves. It kept lifting itself up until it towered over the lake like a colossal monster.

It stood as if they'd disturbed it from a deep sleep. However, Alrik knew that water was not deep enough to house such a creature, and he knew just what kind of creature this was. These kinds of creatures did not dwell idly in lakes.

Abbigail's terrified scream notified him, and the rest of the rift, that she just saw the jaheera demon too. Alrik planted his hands on his hips and considered things for a moment. Well, he tried to but that woman had a pair of lungs on her like no other. No one could think over that noise. Turning to her, he shushed her. She snapped out of her scream and blinked at him, then her eyes widened and jaw dropped. She looked cute like that, even as she looked at him as if he was crazy.

"Silence, woman, I'm thinking."

"You're thinking right now? At a time like this! There's a freaking giant thing coming out of the water like some kind of Cthulhu monster. I really, seriously think it's about time we got the hell out of here, Alrik!"

Damn her. He leveled his gaze with her and once more said, "Krishnoe. Silence, please."

Her jaw worked side to side but she quieted down and stepped up beside him. When her hands shot out to latch onto his arm, he had to stifle a smile. Her touch made him stand a little taller knowing she needed him, wanted him, to protect her.

His gaze fell back to the lake. This was curious, indeed.

A jaheera demon spawning now? They came from a layer in the rift deep below where he and Abbigail stood. A place where no light or goodness shined through. It was where they belonged and stayed. The only times the jaheera parted from their ancient home was for a bigger purpose. There was no question who'd sent this jaheera demon to them now.

"That's a jaheera demon. They come from the rift far beneath us," he informed Abbigail, "but they never come up here. They can't. They are bound to their rift by ancient shahoulin magic."

"Then why's it up here right now? And why the hell aren't we running?"

"The jaheera are said to be quite slow. It's almost pathetic really. Once in an age they were the largest creatures down here, they consumed all beasts and grew in magical power and strength. However, their power was their downfall. My people, the shahoulin, locked the jaheera in magical cages beneath this rift when they turned to harm us. It would take a mighty power to break one from that cage."

"Your mother," Abby said.

"Oh, absolutely." Again, he loved her intelligence. She knew hardly anything of his world yet she caught on quickly.

"What did you mean when you said they have power? What kind of power?"

He shrugged. "I'm not sure. I've never actually seen one before and I've never fought one. It's said they can cast magic like you and I, that they have old, dark magic. Obviously they are quite physically strong."

"Being the size of a small mountain I'd think so."

All too quickly, the demon finished rising to its massive height. It looked so tall that if it reached its arm up it'd touch the hazy clouds above. The demon's torso and head showed while the rest still stood below the water line. Water lapped at its disgusting body and Alrik could just make out greenish hue swirling in the water around the demon as its toxic skin contaminated the lake.

Alrik hadn't been alarmed at first. The demon was some distance away, and besides, they were slow. They had to be for such big beasts, but he quickly learned he was wrong, very wrong.

The demon opened its jagged mouth and let out a horrendous, ear-piercing bellow that shook the trees and jolted the earth with a rumbling quake. He and Abbigail turned away at the sound. She punched her hands over her ears. The awful noise tried to puncture his eardrums.

Then the demon started moving towards him. One stocky limb lifted above the surface, kicked forward then drove through the water with loud booming steps that sloshed the water like a hurricane.

Alrik took a step back, his arm swiping at Abbigail's and pushed her behind him. He'd been wrong. It didn't move slowly at all. The beast moved its massive body fluidly. In what must have been two or three steps it arrived at the lake's shore.

"Dear God," Abby gasped. Her fists squeezed his arm in warning.

Alrik agreed. Just as he latched onto her hand and prepared to run, the demon opened its mouth and from between ragged, yellowed teeth spewed noxious green spittle. The wet spray was accompanied by a bellow of sound that spewed the green substance against the trees and ground.

Alrik had only a moment to see the green spittle sizzle and smoke against what it touched, before he grabbed Abbigail and ran for it.

They sprinted hard up the slope. Again, from behind them, he heard the bellow and the wet spewing sounds of the demon's toxic spit falling on the forest around them. Water sloshed as the demon came on shore. The odor of burning trees and grass mixed with something he didn't recognize, but his instincts told him not to let the green spit touch him.

Just ahead of them trees bowed as the green liquid touched them. They withered down as if acid had been poured on them until nothing was left but a stump of a tree popping and sizzling up in smoke.

"We got to move!" Alrik roared, for the first time since seeing the jaheera feeling real panic.

"I knew I was right," Abbigail sputtered.

Trees crashed to the ground in front of them. They raced and weaved through them, jumping over boulders and sliding down rocky slopes.

"Don't touch it!" he yelled, jumping over a fallen branch with smoking green leaves.

"You don't have to tell me that!" she yelled right back.

That's his girl.

Heavy, pounding footsteps came at them like cracks of thunder. The ground shook with each booming strike. The demon was following them, crashing through the forest like a wrecking ball. Horrible sounds followed them—the sounds of trees slamming to the forest floor, groaning at their death.

All he needed was a good place to slip into and hide for a few seconds, then he could stow Abbigail away and fight the demon. His heart raced nearing panic levels. He'd been wrong, too cocky.

If they were still kids, his brother would have slapped him upside his head for not being more cautious. Oh well, what was done was done. Now he had to protect her. He refused to let the thought of failure even enter his mind. No way will he let anything happen to her.

He'd die first.

A long valley lay before them filled with bright yellow grass waist tall. In the distance, deep in the south, he could just make out a tendril of smoke in the air. It was so far away it could just be his eyes playing with him, or maybe it was just a tree swaying in the wind. Whether the smoke bode well or not for them, he charged towards it with every ounce of strength inside him. Even if he had to pull her along, he'd get them to safety.

"You're doing great," he called to Abbigail. It might be a strange time for it, but he was so proud of her. The woman had a lot of fight in her.

Suddenly, the ground shuddered beneath them. They had to stop or else be thrown to the ground as the earth swayed beneath their feet. Abby slammed into his back. They wobbled side to side as the ground shook with a jerking, quaking action as if it was trying to bubble up beneath their feet.

"What's going on?" Abby asked. He didn't like the fear in her voice.

Up ahead, the ground split open in a nasty snarl and a loud hiss. The earth parted to reveal an open lip in the field. A black, cavernous slit formed in the massive crack in the ground, and in a rush, it split from one side of the field to the other, completely blocking their way.

"The jaheera is conjuring up magic." It split the field completely in half, blocking their only real exist.

"Is the fissure real?"

Alrik couldn't be sure. "It could be an illusion or it could be very real." He glanced back behind them and saw that at the very least they had put some distance between them and the demon. Alrik grabbed her hand again and headed for the crack.

The first thing he noticed was the grisly smell…like rotting flesh that had been sitting in stagnant water. A gag rolled up in his throat that he barely managed to control. Abbigail wasn't so lucky. She turned around and her body wretched up the contents of her stomach. Her hand squeezed his hard and he returned the gesture to offer his support.

He was close enough now to see that the crack was real. Either that or a really good illusion. Still, he had to be sure. Quickly picking up a small rock, he threw it. If it was an illusion it might stop in midair as if hitting a wall or it might land on top of the black crack as if it was a solid surface. If it were real, it would fall into the crack.

He slung the rock and watched it. Abby stood up, wiping her mouth on the sleeve of her shoulder. His poor woman looked pale and perspiration covered her forehead. God damn, he needed to get her out of here.

He was so busy watching her that he didn't see what happened to the rock. Abby squeezed his hand, her expression turning into one of panic.

"It's real. It went into the chasm!"

Thundering steps boomed closer. "Come on!" Alrik grabbed her hand and started to run, but Abby didn't move with him.

She stood there, shaking her head.

"Don't give up on me. We can beat this!"

She laughed and looked at the miles of expanse the crack had sundered, then back at the giant beast barreling towards them. "There's nowhere for us to go. We have to do something."

Alrik twitched. He didn't like this. He didn't have any time to think! "Fine, you start running east. I'll hold the demon at bay."

She cocked her head, fear gripping her beautiful eyes. He hated the look. Nothing would make him happier than to wipe it away forever. "What do you mean? We can't separate now. We're stronger together."

With a flourishing move, he pulled his swords out from his sheath and twirled them once. "I'm going to kill it."

"But you're the size of a small bush compared to that thing! You can't just expect to stab it and beat it."

Alrik shook inside. He could feel his temperature drop as anger rose. No, not now.

His eyes squeezed shut. He tried sucking in quick breaths but it was useless. She was royally pissing me off. Not with her life on the line.

His eyes shot open and when he leveled his gaze on hers, she took a fearful step back. "Your eyes are doing that thing again..."

"For once you are going to do what I tell you to do. Run east. Find a place to hide and stay there. I'll come for you." His voice was a distorted growl. It wasn't just anger coursing through him but fear, fear for her life.

"And if you don't?" she asked softly.

His hands tightened over the sword handles. The icy anger felt so good that he shivered, embracing it even as he knew what it'd do to him. "I said I'll come for you," he said clear and hard. She flinched at his tone, a flash of pain swept over her eyes. He hated it. He hated that he caused her to hurt, yet that hate only morphed inside him like shapeshifting animal, turning into vile, ugly anger. "Get out of here now." His arms shook with the need to lash out and hit something, to feel the spray of blood on his face, and the crushing of bones beneath his fists.

He didn't know if he could control himself or if he could keep himself from lashing out at her if she said or did the wrong thing in those tense moments. Not now, not when the rage gripped him in its bitter hold. He didn't know what he'd do if he hurt her. Not when he was so close to finally getting what he wanted.

"Go now!" he yelled.

She jumped at his yell, swallowed hard, and then took off running along the heading east. Alrik whipped the blades in his hands, loosening his wrists as he squared off against the demon. He had an advantage now—a boiling mass of rage itching to be let out. And, he couldn't wait to feel the rush.

Alrik let out a battle cry worthy of waking the gods. The demon slowed its thundering steps at the sound as if nervous for the first time. Then he charged forward, blades pointed behind him, ready to whip, slash, gouge, and cut.

The demon stopped at once, its great head turning east to track Abbigail. Alrik saw black. She was his and nothing would touch her. His vision shifted, distorted, and then changed so he only saw in blacks and greys. Around the demon became a foggy grey color like a stormy day while the demon stood out in stark, oily black.

Yes, his rage screamed inside him. Yes! Kill, hurt, maim!

With his rage out and free, his heart pounded violently. His mind was freer than it'd ever been. No thoughts of consequences, logic, or worry bothered him. All he needed, all he wanted, was to shed blood. He took the curse his mother had placed on him and embraced it with open arms.

Swirling smoke billowed out from the demon as if a fire surrounded it. Alrik knew what it was—a spell being cast. He could see it through the curse's eye. Before it could finish the spell, Alrik sprinted past the demon's leg, slashing with both blades.

In a quick burst he chanted, "*Kahlab'du shtow zhenyul garrah'deen fuh!*"

His spell created more smoke but only grey smoke compared to the demon's black. The demon's spell stopped as Alrik's spell blocked the demons from finishing.

Blood surged through Alrik's veins. The rush was better than the best sex, the best anything in the world. He sidestepped then jumped and rolled out of the way as the demon lifted one mighty foot and stomped it into the ground leaving a large cavernous dip where his foot hit. The slam on the ground jerked Alrik from his feet sending him tumbling to the ground before he could get in an attack.

But he leapt back up, then raced along the demon's other ankle, at the back of it he slashed his swords in a non-stop X pattern, crisscrossing and cutting skin into little chunks that plopped to the ground. Dark green blood, black and inky in his vision dripped to the ground with a sizzling hiss.

The demon let out a horrendous cry as its leg gave out. It went crashing down to one knee. Then its great arms swung around and around, trying desperately to catch Alrik. Alrik ran and ducked, rolling under the sweeping appendages but he couldn't escape them all and one slammed into him like battering ram. His swords fell from his hands as he went soaring through the air.

He landed hard on his back to the sound of cracking bones in his shoulder. At once pain flared on the left side of his body, but the rage inside him tampered it down so he barely noticed it. He started to get up but his leg wasn't acting right. He tried to put pressure on it but it only jolted forward, not letting him stand. He wobbled as he braced himself on one foot.

The demon shrieked again.

Then he heard soft footsteps coming from behind him.

Fear gripped him deep in his gut. His head spun around and he watched Abbigail charging towards him with the look of a mighty, determined warrior on her face. Her hands were outstretched. Even in his rage, he saw the bright orange glow of magic bursting from her fingertips as if it couldn't be contained. The bolts shot straight for the demon.

"You will not hurt him!"

He jerked at her words. That couldn't be what she said. That'd mean she somehow cared for him. She didn't. He'd stolen her, planned to use her to his own means, to her own death. An imminent death she still knew nothing about. No way did she come back for him. His heart cracked in his chest. A real physical ache that made him want to bellow his pain for the world to hear.

The demon started falling. Flesh charred along its entire upper body that released a disgusting, stomach-churning smell. Even if he couldn't move he had to help her. Alrik dropped to his knees, ready to cast his own lethal spell when he froze.

Time slowed for long, endless seconds, and all he could do was watch.

The demon opened its mouth and let out a roaring bellow—green, goopy spittle sprayed from it like from a hose. Alrik couldn't run, he couldn't hide, he was too close...and so was Abbigail.

With a power from somewhere deep inside him, from desperateness, he used the strength in his good leg to jump up and catch Abbigail. She grunted as he slammed her to the ground, covering every inch of her body with his.

The acid spittle landed on his back and legs like fiery poison. He shouted brief and hard as his body started jerking from tiny convulsions as the noxious spray ate through his clothing as if it was nothing and burned into his skin.

Abby's wide eyes turned up to his, and then she pushed him off her. Where she got the strength, he had no idea. He couldn't focus on anything but the pain. Even worse as his back hit the ground the acid was only shoved deeper into his skin.

His rage started to fade. It was too much; he struggled and tried to fight the urge to pass out.

Abbigail stood and shot more power out one more time at the demon.

It bellowed and choked as green acidic spittle dripped down its chin and torso, sizzling its own skin. Then it collapsed to the ground with an earth-shattering thump.

The last thing he saw before his shaking body took him under was Abbigail leaning over him, her mouth moving. He tried to focus, tried to hear, but he heard nothing but a high-pitched ringing from faraway in the distance. Just as she leaned over him, his body shut down.

Sixteen

"Alrik!"

He wouldn't move. Abby couldn't stop shaking. His chest rose and fell but was he okay?

The demon was dead, and if it somehow decided to get back up again, she swore she'd summon more power than a god could to destroy it with how pissed off and terrified she was now. Alrik was hurt. Not a paper cut hurt or an 'ouch I slipped and skinned my knee hurt'. No, she could smell, see, and hear his flesh burning where that green acid touched it.

"What do I do? What do I do?"

She could smell the demon carcass each time the wind blew. Her stomach rolled with nausea at the rancid odor. She needed to get them out of there. They needed to get somewhere safe so she could flip him over and see to his wounds.

Abby stood and looked over Alrik for a moment while chewing furiously on her cuticle. She needed to move him. The demon had to be at least two-hundred pounds though. This wouldn't be easy, but she had to do it—for him. He saved her life.

Her chest tightened at the thought and she forced it away. She couldn't think like that, couldn't let herself think with her made her decision. She needed to check his wounds.

Kneeling beside him, she grabbed his side and pushed. He barely moved.

"Holy hell you're heavy," she muttered. Switching tactics, she turned around and used her back and legs to push against him. Finally, she felt him move. After he finally budged just enough, she pushed hard with her legs and got his left side up in the air.

A deep groan sounded from his chest. Abby dug her ankles deep and pushed the last of the way. His heavy body thumped to the ground, this time with his back in the air. A nice row of perspiration had worked up over her forehead. Abby wiped it off with her shoulder then turned to assess the damage.

She sucked in a breath at what she saw. His shirt lay in tatters around his back. His pants had deteriorated where the acid hit him and it seemed that's where the bulk of it went. Where his pants had covered his thighs and calves were now gaping holes dotted like Swiss cheese.

She pulled back the fabric and gasped. His skin had bubbled up. It was a harsh red and swollen. Her gut told her she had to do something. But what?

"Alrik, you need to wake up." She hated the sorrow in her own voice, but she couldn't hide it. The tears were barely at bay as it was.

Taking deep breaths, she looked up at the sky. After a minute, she got her breathing under control, and had stopped sweating. She needed to inspect the wounds even if it grossed her out.

"Time to put your big kid pants on, Abby. You do this kind of stuff for a living, remember?" Yes, but not to people she cared about.

Slightly more relaxed than before, Abby set to work. She lifted Alrik's shirt up as gently as she could. Apparently, that wasn't gentle enough because he groaned in his sleep as she did it. "I'm sorry," Abby kept whispering to him until finally she got the shirt up around the uppermost part of his chest.

Her hand flew to her mouth at what she saw. The vile green acid had mostly hit the lower part of his back. The green goop had burned into his skin making swollen bubbles of flesh stick out from him.

Abby sat back on her heels.

She was useless.

Utterly useless.

She was in a world where different rules applied and in this case, she knew nothing about healing a demon's acid burns from another, bigger, and crazier demon.

Her instincts wanted her to clean off any excess acid with water. She laughed at that. The lake was at least a mile away. The dead jaheera had crashed between her and the lake, and on top of it all, she had no way of transporting the water. No bucket, no cup, no hose, nothing. She couldn't do anything but wait for him to wake up because she didn't want anything more than for him to wake up.

He needed to be all right. He had to be.

She scrubbed a hand over her face and growled in frustration. Why did things have to be like this? She shouldn't care for him. However, she did. She should run, right now! Run away and try to go home. As if she even could.

Well you haven't tried, taunted logic.

Abby flew to a stand, conjured her magic forth and tried to create a portal home. That's all she had to do—envision her little house she rented that she was so proud of. She could see the little strap of lawn she had out front and could see the front door hanging open like she'd last seen it with Mike standing there. Her body grew warmer and warmer, she could almost feel it happen, but it was as if little shocks exploded from her fingertips but didn't quite catch like they should.

"See, I can't do it," she said, pacing beside Alrik. Even if she wanted to, which admittedly at this very second she didn't, she couldn't go home yet. She wasn't powerful enough. Nevertheless, the sparks from her fingertips, the supreme warmth, told her just how close she was. If she kept growing it could just be a matter of days, maybe a week tops.

Abby looked down at Alrik. His face was turned towards her and his long hair shadowed his cheek.

Could she really leave him? After he saved her life, and after they made love together? Even after knowing she had these...strong feelings for him?

Kneeling down, Abby pushed his hair back from his face. Oh, God, she realized.

She didn't know.

She just didn't know if she could do it.

What would happen to him if she did? Would he continue after the queen and get himself killed? Would he come after her and try to steal her away again? She wouldn't be so easy to grab this time. She'd be prepared for it.

She didn't have any answers, but she did know that he wouldn't give up. That was the only thing she knew for certain.

Abby lay down next to Alrik and listened to his steady breathing in and out. She felt exhausted even though she'd only woken up a matter of hours ago.

She laughed. Was it really just this morning that she woke before Alrik?

Her muscles relaxed, thoughts quieted then slowed. The beautiful night sky above was a lovely view to watch. It was so peaceful here. You never heard the rumble of cars, the plowing of heavy machinery, nor had a view filled with paved concrete that covered up the beauty of the earth. None of that was here, and she didn't miss it. Not one bit.

Alrik jerked beside her. She turned towards him, running her hand softly over his hair, one of the few places she could still touch with him lying in this position.

He mumbled something in his sleep.

She could barely hear the whisper of sound.

"What was that?" Abby whispered, unsure if he could even hear her. His eyes were still closed and sleep still claimed him.

His upper body jolted as if he was being shocked. He cried out; a heavy, grief-stricken sound that tore straight through her and froze her in place.

"Arianna."

This time she heard it. He'd said a name, a woman's name. He hadn't said her name. He'd said someone else's.

A funny feeling filled her chest right under her sternum. Abby rubbed it. Just who was Arianna? And why did he sound like he was dying when he said her name?

Her stomach moaned with queasiness. Why did she suddenly feel like her heart had just been ripped out?

She would just ask him about it when he woke up. She laughed aloud at the thought. Maybe Arianna was his mother's name or something. A humorless laugh escaped her. No, he wouldn't have sounded sad talking about his mother like that. Whoever Arianna was, she could hear how much he cared about her.

The pressure in her chest grew nearly unbearable.

She needed a good slap in the face. Who was she kidding beside herself?

Everything would be okay. It was as if even the smaller, smarter part inside of her couldn't believe that.

But she had to. For her and Alrik's sake.

§

Abby must have fallen asleep. She hadn't even realized it. It'd just happened. However, she was pretty sure that when she dozed off it wasn't with a sword pointed to her throat.

Abby's eyes rounded as she looked down at the razor-sharp blade tucked gently under her chin. Her eyes traced up the long, slightly curved blade to a hand the color of dark cream then up over a ragged, white tunic to a handsome, striking face adorned with golden yellow hair that hung in braids down to his shoulders. It was also a face she recognized.

"Remove your blade!"

Shit. She also recognized that voice.

Blondie stepped back, sheathing his sword with practiced ease allowing Abby to sit up. What she saw made her stomach sink.

"Fuck."

The rogues had followed them. With a quick look, she made sure Alrik was fine. He was still out like a light but his chest moved steadily up and down.

Leaning down, she kept her eyes on the one man who watched her with unnerving intensity, and spoke into Alrik's ear. "We have company, babe," she whispered. Whether he could hear her somewhere in there or not she didn't know but tried anyway. "Aidan and his men are here. If you want to wake up, now would be the time to do it."

He didn't move. Not even a sigh or nod of his head. At least that was better than hearing the mysterious name Arianna. Whoever she was. She hated how petty she was being, but she wanted to know every little detail about this person, their life, and why Alrik said her name with so much...pain. A pulse of pain swept through her. Why did he affect her so much? Why did she even care? She shouldn't.

Putting on a tight smile Abby stood. She needed to be on even ground with Aidan, the vampire leader of the rogue demons. Gosh, wasn't that a heck of a title?

"Aidan," she said with a nod.

Aidan arched a black eyebrow and looked behind him at the rotting carcass of the jaheera demon. "My, haven't we been busy?"

"Nah, happens all the time." She grinned at her own joke and crossed her arms to try to look more intimidating. She felt anything but confident right now. What she actually felt was raw, hurt... a bit like crying.

He'd brought all of his men. There were at least twenty of them. Some wandered around the demon carcass, others sat by a fire eating great hunks of meat, and a few watched her, Alrik, and Aidan with curious glances. Great, she needed this complication like a hole in the head.

After the fight with the jaheera there was no way she could conjure up the kind of barrier spell she'd done in Aidan's castle if they needed to escape. No way. And even if she could, how was she supposed to move Alrik? The man slept like the dead. She couldn't lift him, couldn't drag him...and couldn't leave him. She was royally screwed if they tried to steal her or hurt them, she added. Yes, that'd be equally as bad if not worse. All she could do was hope they stayed on their best behavior and left them in peace.

Aidan didn't smile back at her. He strode forward, his brow creasing with worry. When he neared, he spoke in a low voice. "What happened here, Abbigail?"

Abby fought not to lose her nonchalant attitude, but it finally won out and she dropped it, settling with crossing her arms instead. "We were attacked. We took it down. Simple, I guess." It didn't feel simple, though. Not in the least.

Aidan looked back at the demon. His mouth floundered open and closed as if trying to find the right words and then he laughed humorlessly. "Maybe you don't understand or maybe it is I who doesn't understand, but that is a jaheera demon. I personally have never seen one until now, but several of the men have. They say it has been ages since these demons came onto this rift." He caught her gaze and leaned in, crossing into her private space. "They say these creatures are caged by magic in the nether-rift. So, tell me, Abbigail, human witch, just what is it doing here and why is it after you?"

Abby didn't like where this was going. On the sly, she prodded Alrik with her foot but he didn't stir. He needed to be answering these questions not her.

"Um, well, it's not after me. It's after him so you'll just have to wait until he wakes up to get your answer." She lifted her chin to finalize her words.

One black eyebrow rose at her. She glared at it. "Abbigail, you are lying."

"No, I'm not."

Now his other eyebrow rose to match, turning his expression into one of unbelievability.

"Abbigail, when you lie your voice goes higher, you speak faster, and you swallow hard."

Abby snorted. "That's not true." But, a blush started coloring her cheeks. With humiliation, she realized she did just speak fast and her voice sounded like a little girls.

How did he know this about her? She didn't even know him.

Blondie, who hovered near the demon carcass nodded, then called out, "It's true! You do!"

Abby set her lethal glare on him too. How could he hear from that far away?

Suddenly all the demons around them nodded at her, and then resumed what they were doing.

"I told you," Aidan said, a smile to his voice. "Now, tell me the truth."

"Well, it wasn't necessarily a lie. I mean it wasn't after me, per se. It was after him." She poked Alrik's hip with her foot, this time a bit harder. He still didn't come jolting awake like she'd hoped.

Aidan nodded grimly at Alrik. "He was touched by the beast's acid spray. His skin is infected. It'll leave a nasty scar." He said it so casually as if he just relayed his favorite kind of food, or, blood, rather.

Abby frowned, her teeth worrying her bottom lip. "I don't know what to do. Can you help me?"

He looked completely taken aback by her question. His eyes rounded, brows flew up, and then he caught himself and resumed his stoic expression.

"Help you? In return for what?" His gaze darkened and the look he gave her was so raw, earthly, and male that she could hardly suppress a shiver. The look reminded her of their intimate moment with his warm mouth on her neck. Damn. Just thinking about it made her blush, not from pleasure, but with guilt. She felt like a teenager again not wanting her mother, or in this case, Alrik, to learn what she'd done.

"I'll hook you up on a date with my best friend."

He blinked, shook his head, half-laughing, and cocked his head at her. "What?"

"My friend. She has a thing for vampires, I swear." Okay, that was an exaggeration. She tolerated them well enough as a shapeshifter. "She's beautiful, fit, and happy." Okay, that was pushing it. She was strong-willed, perky, and very determined. She was beautiful, though. That wasn't a lie. "She's a lot of fun too!" That also wasn't a lie, though it might depend on one's version of 'fun.' Jenna preferred extreme everything. The shapeshifter thrived on chaos and in creating chaos. That was her 'fun'.

Aidan slowly shook his head. "You are confusing me now. Let's get back to the topic at hand. What will you give me in return for healing him? It must be a great gift for I hate this man. We all loathe him and the rest of his kind. To do this for you, to stop the infection, I'd need a great boon."

"Your kind? But, you're all demons. Well, I mean, you're not but, yeeeah."

His mouth twitched. "His kind is haute. Aristocrats, the high-blooded royalty, who sit upon their dais and cast judgment on all others. That's who he is. What he is. And that's what we hate." He stepped closer a dark look glowing in his eyes. "Now, tell me. What will you give me if I let my men heal him?"

Damn. Abby looked around as if she might happen upon some extravagant gift she could give him, like a diamond ring maybe or a beautiful woman willing to be bitten. That didn't happen. Finally, she shrugged and went for honesty.

"Listen, I don't have anything to give you, but if you're ever up on earth and I'm there, give me a call. I'll hook you up with my beautiful friend Jenna. That's all I can offer you." She knew she was playing dangerously but she had to. It didn't make her feel good to have to blow him off, he seemed like a nice...vampire guy and all, but she had Alrik. Well, and that whole situation was a mess of a disaster as it stood.

His mouth twitched with anger. He glanced at Alrik and scowled. "It's him, isn't it? You love him?"

Her reaction was instantaneous. "Whoa, whoa, whoa! Love is a big word." Abby threw her hands up and took a step back. Fear clutched her stomach with an icy grasp. Why did she feel so panicked at the mention of love? "I care...a bit about him. That's it."

He shook his head and then stalked away from her. She had the sense she'd hurt him. "You're lying to yourself," he called back to her.

Abby took a seat next to Alrik and cupped his dark hand between hers. She hadn't been lying. She didn't love him, but that didn't mean she didn't care a bit.

Just a bit.

The man kidnapped her after all. That surely took a few points off anything she might feel for him.

"Will you help him or not? He saved my life." She called out to him, letting him know with her desperation that the power rested in his hands to help her, gift or no gift.

Aidan stopped walking. Slowly he turned around and watched her, his jaw working. She could see the thoughts running through his eyes: anger, disappointment, and frustration. She could only hope that whatever decision he made bode well for her.

He didn't say anything for a long time. Or, at least, it felt like a long time. For minutes he watched her, watched Alrik, and the whole time she saw him weighing the consequences of whichever decision he'd make. The man was smart and she respected that.

"I'll help him but only for you."

His words stunned her. She looked away unable to hold his gaze. The small amount of time she'd been around him had influenced him that much? It was too much for her. Nobody should feel so greatly, do so much for someone after being around him or her for only a matter of hours.

Then, it hit her. Of course! She wanted to smack herself upside the forehead. The man, er, vampire, hadn't been around a woman in ages. He'd said so himself. Surely if their roles were reversed, she'd lie, beg, steal, and do anything to get a piece of a man. He didn't actually care about her. This was all an act because he really wanted in her pants, badly.

Aidan shouted a gruff order at his men. Three demons came over, one carrying a brown satchel slung over his back. They pulled Alrik's shirt up and his pants down. No underwear for the fallen king of demons.

Don't look at his butt, she told herself.

As soon as the thought 'butt' entered her mind, her eyes betrayed her. Heat suffused her cheeks. He had a great ass. Firm, tight, and sculpted. She knew first hand just how firm. She swallowed hard, and then felt that feeling of being watched.

She looked up and nearly cursed. The three demons were grinning at her—busted. No way could she feign a lie about why she was checking out his ass.

With a casual shrug she didn't feel, she walked away to watch them work.

They worked over Alrik like a trained medic team. One pulled out a bundle of herbs wrapped with a thin length of rope, the next grabbed a flask made from what looked like deer hide sewn into a pouch shape, and the last pressed against the sores along Alrik's back with his fingers.

Alrik might be sleeping but he let out a pained groan as the demon pushed on him. She took a step forward, ready to draw blood but then he relaxed his grip. Abby pressed a hand over her heart. The pumping organ felt as though it'd jump through her chest.

"Don't hurt him." The words slipped out. She hadn't even known she was going to say it.

The demons looked at her, unsmiling, then muttered to each other about ridiculous 'witches' and 'kings' and a 'waste of a good woman'.

She watched every move they made as they worked. If they decided to try anything crazy or weird, she'd be ready to attack in a second, but they never did.

An herb mixture was combined with water into a pulp-like concoction that they pressed over Alrik's wounds. She swore she heard a fizzling sound when it touched the infected flesh. After the pesto-looking mixture covered each of the bubbled wounds, the demons stood and started to walk away.

"Wait, what happens next?"

The tallest of the three, a man with beautiful dark skin like mahogany and long, wild braided hair spoke up. "We watch him. The herbs will heal him but it takes time."

"Okay, thank you."

The man shook his head, a frown on his mouth. "Don't thank us, thank Aidan. We wouldn't have helped this man if it meant saving our own lives."

Abby snorted in disbelief. "You hate him that much?"

The man stared at Alrik's prone, unmoving form. Hate and rage swirled in his eyes, barely leashed. "Yes, that much."

She didn't get it. What could he have done that'd make these people hate him so much? He'd kidnapped her but things hadn't been that bad. He never hurt her physically or emotionally since she'd known him. She'd rate him a pretty fair kidnapper overall.

"Why?" she asked. She had to know.

The man shook his head. "That's for him to tell you, not me."

With that, he turned and walked away.

Abby watched over Alrik as night grew heavy and the demon's fires burned brighter. A strange, dark colored tattoo covered his side. It must have been painted before he was cursed because the colors and design could barely be made out. Damn she hated this. She couldn't stop thinking about what the demon said. What could he have done that was so terrible that these demons shunned themselves to leave their kingdom?

She wanted to defend him and stand up for him, but she didn't know what she'd say because she still didn't really know much about him. That actually hurt, probably much more than it should.

She didn't talk to anyone for the rest of the night, not even when Aidan tried to draw her into conversation. Too much was on her mind. The woman's name Alrik spoke last night, the hate these demon's had for him, and the jaheera demon attacking them. It was all too much to take. A part of her wanted to forget all of this. She wished it'd never happened, but a part of her rebelled at the thought. Then that'd mean she'd never have met Alrik. She forced herself to stop thinking about him, about everything. It was exhausting work.

When her eyelids grew tired she didn't sleep by Alrik's side but by herself.

Seventeen

A big hand covered her mouth, stifling her air supply.

Abbigail jerked awake on a startled scream. Only her eyes focused on a dark, handsome face above hers. Her heart leaped at seeing him awake for the first time since the jaheera attack. Slowly, he pulled his hand away and pressed his cheek to hers, his lips to her ear. One arm curled around her waist, pulling her into his heat. Instantly, her body relaxed against his and soaked up his warm touch.

"Speak quietly, they are still sleeping," he whispered.

Blinking the sleep away, she realized it was still dark out. She could hear the crackling of the fire, the wind blowing tree leaves, and a few deep snores coming from the demons.

"What's going on?" she whispered back.

He looked over his shoulder then pressed his lips to her ear. God, she didn't want to like it, but seeing him alive and well, feeling his strength and heat wrapped around her sent a raw shiver down her body. Nothing could have stopped her from reaching around his back and holding him.

His muscles stiffened under her touch. She stilled too. For some reason, things felt different now. He didn't know about everything that had happened since he'd been passed out. He had no idea she heard him say that name that haunted her dreams before he woke her.

Touching him almost felt like touching a stranger. That was until his head turned and his lips dipped to press a kiss to her neck. Her breath caught at the soft touch, her body becoming aware of him in a way that was impossible to ignore. Before she knew what he was about to do, he tilted her head and his lips caught hers in a devastating kiss. All doubts fled. This was real, not some petty, jealous idea she'd conjured up to fill her mind. This man in her arms, kissing her with hunger and passion, was real.

He kissed her slowly, leisurely as if he was sampling from her. Firm lips captured hers. Wet and smooth his tongue slid inside, curling against hers. It felt like so much more. Kisses never felt like this like the world stopped turning just because of it, like the pleasure shared between them was the only thing that mattered in her life.

Then he broke the kiss, shattering the foggy haze he'd pulled over her brain. His lips were wet, and his breathing louder; she couldn't stop staring up at him. He looked like some kind of fertility god people used to worship—sexy, strong, and vibrating with health.

His lips pressed against her ear again to whisper. His voice was deep, soft, and low. "We have to get out of here right now."

"Do you—"

"Quiet," he whispered in her ear, once again checking behind his shoulder. "I want you to get up and follow me."

"Wait!"

Alrik cast her a lethal glare. "Whatever you need to say will wait until we are far away from Aidan and his men."

They were beginning to sound like two students trying desperately hard to have a conversation during class and not get caught by the teacher. In her world, she'd always been caught.

Her hands kneaded the strong warm muscles in his back. They did need to talk, like right now because she was so done playing around with him. She wanted answers about everything and she wasn't going to practice magic again until he told her. She wasn't stupid. She'd wait, but not for much longer. Something much bigger was on the line for her now. Something, that if he broke, she knew would never fit back together right.

"Fine, but we need to talk."

The infamous four words, 'we need to talk', were apparently not unknown to Alrik because he jerked his gaze to hers and his eyes rounded wearily.

"Fine, just stay quiet and watch your step."

He stood without a sound, no knees cracking, no squishing the grass beneath his feet. Just a smooth, graceful move like a cat prowling. Abby wasn't so athletic. She took his outstretched hand and stood but having just woken up she wobbled on her feet. Her left ankle wasn't quite awake yet. It felt heavy and hot as blood rushed to it.

"My foot's asleep," she whispered.

Alrik's jaw clenched so hard, she could see the bone working as he ground it. With a shake of his head, he bent to the waist and lifted her into his arms. She almost squealed, but managed to clamp her lips shut just in time to meet his warning gaze. Strange, but some kind of feminine glee filled her. He was carrying her like Rhett Butler in Gone with the Wind, though decidedly less romantic since they were escaping from some demons and not going to a sexy bedroom to make passionate love. Yeah, she liked the other scenario better.

He managed to keep his steps surprisingly light and quiet. Abby clung to his broad shoulders keeping her chin tucked against his muscular shoulder and her gaze locked on the campground. She blinked then scanned the makeshift beds on the grass again.

She was counting them but came up three short. No, make that four, she amended. Aidan's pallet was bare as well.

"Um, Alrik—"

"Not now."

He started running with long barreling steps. The man was tall and strong, and boy could he move fast. Not once did his grip on her waver. She jerked her gaze forward just in time to see them nearing the massive black fissure the demon created before it died.

A cry started from the back of her throat before she could stop it.

Alrik jumped and they flew through the air in a mighty arch. Her stomach bottomed out as if she was flying downhill on a hurtling rollercoaster.

Icy fog covered her. At first she thought it was the temperature of the air just being cold that high up, but he couldn't jump that high. They hit the ground way too softly with his knees giving in a bit to take the hit.

"You used magic." That explained the icy feeling. How fitting that hers warmed and his chilled.

Alrik had just taken a step forward when a metallic sound filled the air like someone playing with a knife or...

As soon as the thought struck a blade slid in front of them to block them. The sharp point rested eerily close to their throats. Aidan appeared from behind her. Amazing, she'd never seen or heard him move. He had to be quiet even by demon's standards.

"Did you really think we'd just let you leave so easily?"

Alrik took a step back and Aidan let his blade fall. Maybe it was her ego talking but she figured he did it for her. He wouldn't hurt her. She just knew it deep down in her gut just like she knew Alrik would never either.

"Aidan, what do you want from me really? Do you seriously think you can keep me here if I don't want to be kept? We're not at your castle now. We're in the open, and I'm not trapped. It won't be easy to hold me now."

Anger flashed over Aidan's face. Abby flinched at the violent look and struggled until Alrik set her down. He pushed her behind him and she went happily since for the first time she felt real fear of the vampire.

"What do I want? What do we want? How about justice? You took me from my home. I don't even know who I am!" Aidan screamed. His fangs flashed, gaze turned violent, and cheeks flushed.

Abby's jaw dropped. Even as she tried to step away from them both, Alrik tagged her hand and held tight. He wouldn't let her go. What on earth were they talking about? How did he not know who he was, but knew he was taken from his home? Actually, better yet, why would Alrik do this?

Her mind spun with unanswered questions.

Aidan caught Abby's expression and nodded. "See, this is what he is," he said. "A monster. How did a vampire come to be here in the rift? Ask. Him."

Alrik didn't say anything seemingly content to keep his mouth shut. Well, Abby couldn't deal with it. She had to know. She needed to know not for Aidan but for herself because, though it pained her to admit it, she cared for him.

But did she care for a monster? Panic and pain threatened to erupt inside her, debilitating her. She stomped it all down because what she didn't need to do right now was freak out. She needed answers.

"Believe it or not, but I don't know all matters of your life except that you ended up a prisoner in front of the court where I meted out fair justice," Alrik said coolly.

Aidan visibly shook with rage, the silver of his blade distorting the reflection of the fire from camp into oblong, menacing shapes. "Fair justice? You call being stolen from my family fair justice?"

"I know nothing of that."

She could hear the edge of frustration creeping into Alrik's voice. A part of her was relieved to know that at least he hadn't done something that awful.

"I know nothing of who I am, and when everyone shunned me, when nobody helped me to explain why I was different or why I needed blood, you and yours left me to fend for myself. And when I did, you sent me to the dungeons to become a work slave.

You are nothing. You are a worthless pile of shit that doesn't belong on the bottom of this slave's boot. You were never a king, and never worthy to wear a crown. It was a farce and we all know it. Telal should have been king. He had a good heart. He was meant to rule."

Apprehension made her twitchy. She didn't like where this was going.

A steady tremble came from her hand. With a start, she looked down only to realize it wasn't her trembling, it was Alrik. His entire body was starting to tremble from some untamable emotion he was trying to keep hidden. Yet, he didn't open his mouth, didn't defend any of his actions. She wanted to shake him, yell at him, get in his face and make him defend his actions.

Slowly, as if it took all of his control to keep his words clear, Alrik spoke. "Telal made his decision. He betrayed us to Tobius en Kulev. If not for Telal, my father would still be here. I had nothing to do with how you came to be here, vampire."

Aidan smiled. The look sent a foul shudder down the back of her neck. "I was a young one when I was ripped from my home and taken to your kingdom. Yes, I remember you then. It's been a long time, hasn't it?"

Alrik's head jerked as if dodging some painful thought.

"Do you even remember yourself then? Your skin was still golden much as your brothers, your mothers...your fathers. Such a lie it was. At least one good thing has come about over these long, merciless years. You're ugliness has finally grown to show the world your true nature."

Alrik froze. He didn't flinch or jerk. He didn't curse or make a move in violence. No, he only froze in a way that scared her more than if he'd done all of those things.

Abby couldn't stand it. Her patience fled and her temper popped like a balloon filled with too much air.

Abby charged forward, as far as Alrik's grip let her, and got in Aidan's pale face. "You don't even know what the hell you're talking about. His mother cursed him. It filled him with some kind of rage that turned him into this. She's been controlling him this entire time."

Something flickered in Aidan's eyes—disbelief.

"Yeah, that's right. Why do you think he's here and not in his kingdom? Why do you think I'm here—a human witch?" She clenched her jaw and glared, ready to do it all night until she drove her point home.

"Tell me what happened." He directed his words to Abby but kept his eyes on Alrik. The anger slowly drained from his face.

Abby looked up at Alrik to find a strange, uncertain look in his eyes. He looked as if he didn't know what to do or say, almost childlike. She squeezed his hand and stepped into him.

"All I know is that he stole me from my home," she said.

Immediately, Aidan tensed. Before he could do something crazy like attack Alrik or offer to be her hero, she held up her hand.

"He brought me here and told me that a seer said the only way to defeat the queen is by me. A witch."

"What has happened with the queen?" Aidan tensed, and she could see the dark glint in his eyes.

He hated the queen maybe even more than Alrik did. She had to look away. Seeing so much anger and hate was unsettling.

She jabbed Alrik's side. When he didn't answer, she prodded him again, much harder. Finally, he shook his head. "I banished her after I discovered her black magic. Not only was she casting on me, one can only guess how often, but she fed me potions. I was completely in her grasp without realizing it." His eyes got a faraway look in them. "I should have. I was stupid and trusting. I should have known what was happening to me under my own roof."

"If you banished her then why are you still," Aidan looked Alrik up and down, "different. Why don't you look how you used to?"

"That is why I sought out the oldest of all seers. Since I banished her, I got worse. I couldn't sleep, didn't want to eat. The seer says she made the curse two-ways. A backup curse she placed on me, essentially, in case I ever did learn of it and try to kill her. It grips me now more than ever."

Aidan nodded towards Abby. "What does this have to do with her? Why a human? Why a witch?"

"The seer told me that I cannot kill her because the curse will not let me hurt her. He said the only one powerful enough to kill her is a human. A specific human. Abbigail Krenshaw." He squeezed her hand and she sent him a small reassuring smile.

"Supposedly, I'm really powerful or something," Abby said, trying to lighten the dark mood.

Aidan smiled wryly. "Seeing as you froze me and my men in place and escaped from us without too much trouble, I'd have to agree."

"Yeah, well, about that whole escape thing. You can't keep us here, Aidan." His pointed look gave her pause. "Okay, well I'm sure you could keep us here but what for? Just let us go. We have a queen to kill." Wow, she was talking about it as if she was actually going to go through with something so insane.

"What do you get out of this?" he asked her.

Abby put on a smile as she struggled to find an answer. Alrik looked down at her and something strange swirled in his eyes. It was a haunted look. A look that flashed at some hidden thought because instantly guilt and shame filled his gaze. The look sent the hairs on the back of her neck standing up. She did not like this. She didn't like this at all.

He was hiding something.

Something that had to do with her. Whatever it was, it wasn't good. Then she remembered. At first, she did think he'd kill her. There was no way he'd let her kill her mother and just walk away plain as day. Maybe he really did plan to kill her.

Intense, stomach-churning pain exploded inside her. Tears welled in her eyes. Her body suddenly felt so cold, except for where his hand still clutched hers. Maybe it was just her mind playing tricks on her but she swore he held her hand so much tighter than before as if he was clinging to her.

He saw the look on her face and knew. He knew that she knew.

Looking down, she stared at her lighter colored hand in his dark, cursed one. His touch had comforted her before. Now she felt only disgust. She sniffled, her nose starting to run.

Oh, God, why did it have to hurt so badly? Her heart felt like it'd exploded in her chest cavity like something hard was lodged inside her was trying to break her apart. She wanted to just run away and bury herself away crying until she turned numb. Just numb.

Stupid, Abbigail.

She understood now why she was reacting this way to that betraying look in his eyes. Those few moments where raw honestly had flashed in his eyes and told her something she wished she'd never found out.

She loved him.

It took effort, but she swallowed hard and pushed back the tears, delicately cleared her throat so the heavy emotion couldn't be heard and then tugged her hand—hard—until he let her go. Another lance of pain cut through her. Oh, she hated this, both wanting him to touch her and not touch her.

She managed to lift her heavy head to Aidan who watched her with an intense look. "What is it?" he asked.

"What do I get out of this?" she repeated. Damn but her voice was hoarse. It couldn't be more obvious that she was near the breaking point. "Apparently, I don't get anything out of this." Her lips twitched with a bittersweet smile. Alrik was hiding something from her. Something big judging by the guilt in his eyes. She didn't need to have witch's instincts to know whatever it was didn't bode well for her at all.

I trusted him! her mind wailed.

"Come with me and you will." Aidan's final plea didn't move her in any way except to make her feel worse. She didn't want to hurt him, but that's what she had to do. She could use his help but he wouldn't help her. He just wanted her for his own purposes too, and then what would happen when the other demon's got jealous of him having a woman? There'd be bloodshed and somehow she'd get hurt in the process.

"No, I'm not going with you either."

Disappointment flashed in Aidan's eyes, pulling her heartstrings.

Alrik tensed, his big shoulders bulging. "What do you mean 'either'?"

She tried to hold his gaze, but couldn't.

Aidan saved her from the pressing intensity radiating from Alrik. "You will let her make her own choice. If she doesn't want to help you any more then she doesn't have to. She can come with us."

No, no I can't, she wanted to say.

The atmosphere shifted, becoming tense like a string pulled taut. "I'm not leaving here without her, and I think it's time you took your leave Aidan," growled Alrik.

That icy energy was starting to pour out of Alrik. In her witch's eye, the one she'd managed to shut off for so many years, she could see it like a fog forming around him.

Some instinct inside her had her taking one step back then another as the two big men faced each other. It all felt so wrong. She didn't want them to fight. She didn't want to be the cause of any of it.

But that look in his eyes...

God, how could he?

What did he have planned?

How could she have been so blinded by him?

Well, she wasn't now. She'd woken from her stupid, romantic dreams. He was up to something and if it wasn't to kill her like her gut told her, then it was something else but it was just as bad. Maybe he meant to kill her and her mother? To leave no possible witnesses? Another horrible idea hit her. The thought nearly sent her to her knees. Maybe he'd already killed her mom.

Oh, God...

It was hard to breathe. She kept sucking in air but it wasn't enough, it didn't fill her lungs full like it should. Her mind whirled as if she was riding a carousel spinning out of control moving faster and faster. Blood pumped fast and hard in her head and throughout her body. She was too warm; too much was happening.

Alrik and Aidan were in each other's faces. Their lips moved but she couldn't make out what they were saying. So much anger. So much negativity. They shook with the rage. That icy cloud around Alrik grew and grew. She didn't want anything to do with this. She just wanted out. She just wanted to go back home to her rented little house with the cheap furniture.

She just wanted it to stop.

She didn't know who threw the first punch. The men were a blur of movement, but one of them struck first. All she saw, or, heard rather, was the sound of flesh being pummeled. She winced stumbling backwards as her stomach convulsed trying to make the contents in her stomach come back up.

"Stop it." Her voice was too quiet.

"Please, stop it," she tried again, a little louder.

Still, the men launched at each other, grunts and cracks, and those horrible sounds of flesh hitting flesh assaulting her senses as they did each other.

Her senses went on overload. She couldn't contain it anymore. She had to unleash the burning, fiery energy boiling up inside her. It had to be released—must go somewhere. The spinning of her mind had to stop. The pain in her heart and in her belly had to stop.

With a shout that could cause an avalanche, she screamed. "STOP IT!"

With her scream, something else happened. Something she didn't expect.

The men were thrown back as if struck by a wrecking ball. They flew high into the air and backwards. They had to have gone nearly half a mile. Abby shook, her knees knocking together, and her arms trembling with the force of what she'd just done. She'd never done anything like that.

She could hear the demons waking up behind her, asking questions, and moving around. There was no time to waste; with one final glance at Alrik she watched his body slam into the trunk of a tree. It was too far away to be certain, but she thought she heard a bone-snapping crunch. The tree shuddered and limbs broke and crashed around him.

She took a step toward him then caught herself. He'd be fine, she knew that. Besides, she needed to get away from him now, not run over there and try to nurse him back to health.

She just hoped he was hit hard enough to give her some time to run. With her heart breaking, she took off down the length of the fissure.

It took her a moment before she realized it.

That she was a blur of speed.

All that energy inside her still hadn't burned up. Her high emotions drove the magic in her blood.

The fire was still there, even as she trembled from the power of it, and she ran fast as light away from the one who broke her heart.

She had at least one thing to thank Alrik for ; he had helped to make her stronger. Now she could get away from him.

Eighteen

Alrik was dreaming, or not really. He drifted between two worlds of consciousness, one he is aware that he was waking up, and the other still lingering in the dream world.

As a young man he used to dream in vibrant colors of scenes that always seemed cut short and never made any real sense. All they served to do was make him feel good or bad when he woke up. In that way, his dreams used to set the tone for the day. But, he hadn't dreamt in a long time. Not since… His body jerked, fighting the thought but it came anyway, always unrelenting.

The last dream he'd had happened before Arianna's death—before his brother took back his kingdom.

Then he had dreamed of a fantasy for what happened could never be true. He had looked like his real self, golden-skinned like his brother Telal. They stood next to each other on the dais in the kingdom's hall. All the haute and prolitare stood in the crowd, most but not all with smiles upon their colored faces.

A somewhat familiar face was there. The succubus woman, Lily Bellum. She meant something special to his brother. That was evident from the way his brother's eyes watched her with reverence and in the way he kept her hand tucked in his.

As his mind started to drift out of the dream, a different memory took him. The bitter sounds of Telal weeping at her death. Alrik had felt the same way seeing his Arianna die in front of him. He'd been unable to heal her. Except while there'd been two deaths that night his Arianna couldn't be resuscitated. At least Telal got his woman back.

More strange thoughts came seemingly out of nowhere as his body drifted in the ether of sleep lightweight and floating in air.

Once upon a time, he could heal death from a person's soul. It would only work on a fresh corpse, but that kind of mighty power ran through his veins. Using that kind of power would zap him, incapacitate him for days maybe even longer, but once in his hands he held the power to heal. No longer did he have that.

It'd died with his heart many years ago.

That didn't mean he didn't try when Arianna fell before him, her white gown pooling around her body, and blood spilling from her lips.

He'd leaned over her graceful body and her last words had ringed in his red-hazed, raging mind for a long time to come: "Be good, Alrik".

He'd gone mad. He'd summoned all the magic inside him to heal her, to bring her back, but nothing happened. Not a lick of warmth had stirred inside him that accompanied a healing spell. Nothing but iciness encased him. Her breath never stuttered once, her heart didn't beat again, not even a single palpitation.

She was dead, and it was his fault.

Not that he quite saw it that way at the time. At the time, it was Telal who'd killed her, Telal who had stormed into his life only to ruin it again. Only later, after he'd been cast out banished from the kingdom by Telal, did he think. When one had nothing but his own thoughts as he wandered an endless land, his thoughts became him.

Oh, he'd thought over that terrible night again and again and again.

The more he walked the more he realized. His brother might have cast the final blow but if not for all of his own deeds, Arianna would still be alive and breathing.

He didn't come to such a discovery easily. Oh no, it'd taken months and months of trekking through the rift, searching for his mother, and cutting of idummi heads to realize it.

He got her killed. His actions, his deeds led her to that place to begin with. He was the reason she was dead. And, he was the reason he couldn't save her.

Yet even that wasn't the whole story. For it was the curse that bound him to think dark thoughts, to be dark inside that made him unable to heal with spellcasting. His mother's curse held the real blame. It was her fault ultimately, and he'd see her pay before he died.

His thoughts drifted as his numb body floated between sleep and aware. He drifted below the line of conscious once more allowing thoughts and colored pictures of the past to come over him.

It went back to the dream on the dais where he stood with his brother and his mate.

He was smiling at Telal.

Seeing that, even in a dream stunned him. It was as if he saw himself from another person's body. He watched his smiling, golden face with violet eyes and auburn hair shining with the glint of red in the light—colors he hadn't witnessed on himself in ages—as if he watched a stranger. For that's what he'd become to himself.

His gaze wandered to the woman standing next to him. She stood with her face hidden in the shadows. Unease flittered through him and he tried tugging on her hand to bring her into the light with him.

Telal made a joke and Alrik laughed. Their voices were muffled, faraway sounding to his dreaming mind. He couldn't make out the words, but he could feel the emotion of it. His chest warmed and his body felt as if he was floating as the laugh went through him.

His gaze moved back to the woman standing with him covered in shadows. A frown tugged his lips, and he tugged on the small, delicate hand trying to pull her into the light but she resisted. He wanted to see her. Needed to see her face.

No words left her lips but he sensed a hesitation, the "no" on her lips, though she never spoke. She started pulling away from him and sorrow clouded his heart, made him slow to grab for her when she pulled back. Then, she slipped into the shadows and was gone.

That dream had happened within a month of Arianna's death, and now he'd just had it again.

What did it mean?

Had it hinted at Arianna's impending death? He didn't know, but then why was he having the dream now? Did it have anything to do with Arianna at all? Maybe the dream had everything to do with Abbigail? If it did have to do with Arianna then that didn't make sense. Why did he look like his old self? Maybe the dream had just been a sign that she was the hope he'd been looking for because t she could have found a way to cure his curse. Then they would be standing hand in hand, mated, across from his brother and mate.

Too many questions and not enough answers.

He cursed himself, wishing he'd asked the seer. The seer would have the answer. He needed to know.

Some niggling thought kept coming up. Was it Abbigail and not Arianna pulling away from him this time? Even in sleep, his gut churned at the idea. If so, why would she? The very thought brought a sharp, tight pain into his chest and throat as if he was stuffed to full.

Yet the thought didn't sit right with him.

Alrik sighed. That dream had happened more than a year ago, before his life was completely ruined. He never had a repeat dream until that one. Why that dream? Why now? Those dreams didn't bare repeating since he could never forget it.

Damn if the dream didn't make him feel things he hadn't in so long. It made him want to share the mirth he'd found so briefly in his dream. He wanted to find it and share it with her. Not Arianna. He could see now that it wasn't meant to be. Even with her death staining his hands, he could see it. He did love her. He'd loved her for a very long time, but they'd had such a short time to grow together. In fact, Alrik wasn't so sure they did at all. Maybe if they'd had more time together.

Maybe...

But if he did love her then that couldn't explain what he felt for Abbigail Krenshaw. For that woman, that human, made him feel things so wildly different, so tremendous that he didn't know if he could always keep it contained.

Alrik started to rise back to consciousness, his dream and painful thoughts fading. But then, something pulled him back under and he dreamt once more.

This time he dreamt of something new. Something he'd never dreamt of before and it set forth a new drive in his heart.

Abbigail and he were at a strange place where the sky shined so bright he had to squint to see. White soft sand rested beneath their warm bodies, the substance finer than sugar. The heat made him so warm like he could never remember being, almost as if the beautiful light was baking him.

Abbigail looked stunning. Nude, her skin glistened in the bright light with splotches of sand on her legs and arms. She looked up at him with that brilliant smile on her face, and he couldn't stop smiling back and sharing in the moment with her. He reached over, his hand cupping her cheek as he leaned in to kiss her. In that moment he realized his skin was golden. Her beautiful eyes slowly closed and her lips curled with a smile that parted for him.

But his dream warm fuzzing feeling in his chest ended with a mighty blow.

Alrik came crashing back into reality as a mighty kick landed against his ribs. His eyes shot open, and before he thought twice, magic thrust from his fingertips. With a grunt the perpetrator slammed into a tree sending flakes of woodchips around him.

Alrik stood slowly, cradling his side with one hand. He surveyed the man he had pinned to the tree with invisible binds. Of course, he should have expected it. The vampire would not give up so easily.

"Trying to kill a man when he's down? I thought you were above such sleazy tactics, Aidan." Not thinking about why he did it, he released his magical hold on Aidan.

The vampire smiled, a flash of fang showed and then disappeared. "Just giving you a good old wake up call, king. Your woman has fled. I would have sought her out...but she made her choice. It isn't me she wants. Apparently it isn't you either."

Alrik saw Aidan's sickeningly happy smile and wanted to run his fist through it.

Memories surged back at once. Fucking hell.

Alrik jerked his gaze in the direction from where it all happened, where Abbigail had unleashed such power that it'd stunned him with its strength. She'd tossed him and the vampire as if they were mere pebbles not large, fully-grown supernatural men. And she'd done it over a long distance.

So, what the seer said was true. She really was powerful. For the first time he really believed she could do this. He'd seen her perform magic at the castle, then with the jaheera, and now this. In such a short time together, that only meant she was growing stronger and recovering faster. Soon, she'd be able to cast powerful magic more than once a day and not be spent.

She must be spent, exhausted and hungry now. That kind of spell casting came at a price. He knew, he'd casted his share of magic before. A physical need in his gut screamed at him to go after her, to feed her and take care of her. He would just have to convince her to stay with him. No, no.

He didn't know how much she'd realized, but she definitely had learned of his lie. Once again, it was all his fault. He hadn't been able to hide his eyes from her. She was too smart to miss the overpowering guilt he'd felt.

"Where did she go?"

"My men said she ran east along the fissure then disappeared. They tried to track her but couldn't. She might have used a spell to cloak herself. Or maybe she ported home."

Alrik froze. An overpowering sensation swept through him. The feeling that he had no control over this situation, over her, and was helpless to everything.

Dread grabbed him by the heart.

Home? She could make a portal and go home? A foul roiling emotion filled his stomach like a lead ball. His fists clenched into hard hammers ready to pound.

"She wouldn't leave."

"If she could do what we've seen her do, then I think she has enough power to go home and make sure you never touch her again. But, hey, that's just my opinion."

Suddenly Aidan found his neck in Alrik's hand and his head slammed into tree bark.

"Watch what you say to me," Alrik growled.

He had to go after her. He had to find her. He would because nothing would stop him. After he found her, they'd talk and then...everything would be okay. He'd explain...

Betrayal burned hot inside him like fire.

How could she just leave him? After he took her body...after she kissed him and looked up at him with soft, innocent eyes.

His hands shook with the need to release the high emotions riding inside him.

He needed to get her back. It was a physical ache burning inside him, a panicked throb that wouldn't ease until he had her safe in his arms. When he got her there, he was going to do more than hold on to her.

"Go, I'm done here with you. I must say I think I can move on now. Now that I've seen how far you've fallen," Aidan said, despite the fact that his throat was being squeezed with an iron fist. He sounded as if this wasn't concerning in the least.

Alrik tried to ignore the vampire's taunting words. He released his grip then stalked away, heading west. If it took every last one of his days to find her, he'd use them all for her.

"Who would have thought you could love after all?"

Alrik didn't stumble, but inside he did. His heart skipped a beat, his mind spun circles in his head. He didn't turn back around. "I don't love her." He said it as if to prove to himself he could. Yet, his voice wasn't strong with the words, his soul not in them.

"Then why are you putting her in danger? She may be powerful, but the queen could just as easily kill her before she could cast any magic. Surely, you know this! That you are putting her life at risk!"

Alrik was far enough away that the vampire's shouts faded with an echo.

He had to ignore them. He had to because he needed her. Whether she was willing to help or not.

Things had changed. This was more than just a quest to kill his mother and remove the curse.

Something had happened between them. Why else did he have this physical need in his gut pulling him towards her and needing to find her? To keep her for himself, always.

There was only one answer to the question to why he had this need.

Surprisingly, he knew the answer and it didn't scare him. Not in the least.

It might have in the past, but now he saw a spark of light at the end of the tunnel. That light was made from Abbigail Krenshaw. Now he felt up to the challenge; proud and ready to be the man he knew he could be.

A bit of warmth flared in his chest as if he stood near a fire. It ebbed and waved as he stalked the night, tracking her.

He loved her.

This changed everything.

Nineteen

She didn't want to cry.

Liar!

Abby sighed and poked her finger into the dirt moving it around.

Okay, she did.

Maybe.

Just a little.

She wasn't a crier, not really. Sure, she cried when she got that letter from her father, but she wasn't really a crier. She definitely wasn't a loud crier either. She didn't sob or boohoo around. Not that there was anything wrong with that, but she could never let herself do that. It was too embarrassing.

The worse was when she would watch a drama movie with Jenna where the climax comes and a loved one or a dog—the dogs are the worst—dies. Jenna, always the stalwart, watches without expression while Abby cornered in her chair trying to hide her face from the burning tears in her eyes.

Hell, she felt embarrassed crying even when she was alone in her house. It didn't matter how silly it was, she still felt that way.

She'd walked the whole day. Pain kept her moving like a zombie across unknown environments. A part of her expected to be jumped by idummi demons or maybe a wild plant monster or something, but nope. None of that happened. A whole day passed. She knew that because she'd left Alrik at night and that strange light, similar to the sun but not nearly as bright, came up and then went down again.

Everything hurt, even her eyes felt dry as a desert as if she'd been staring straight into a light bulb without blinking.

She only stopped because one of her legs had given out. Her knee bowed out and sent her crumpling the grassy ground. So she just stayed that way, cheeks in the grass, finger swirling in the dirt.

He would come after her.

How far away was he? God, she hated that she wanted to know but she did, badly. She didn't want to know out of fear of being caught but at the hope that she might see him.

Pathetic.

She'd been running on anger and high emotions. After the rogue demons started to follow her, she remembered to cloak herself. Surprisingly, it'd worked. Not even seconds after they started off in the wrong directions, talking amongst themselves and trying to figure what had happened to her. It was eerie watching as they started to run in the wrong direction, talking amongst themselves, and trying to figure out what had happened to her.

Abby had learned that little spell from her mom.

Back when she used to practice magic, her mom used to tell her stories. One story was about a witch who could cloak herself completely, turn herself invisible with only a thought and a burst of magic. A witch could even lose her scent, but that required a potion with special herbs that Abby would likely not find in the rift.

So, instead she'd cloaked her body. Did demons have a powerful sense of smell? Probably not, or at least, she hoped not. She was relying on the fact that aside from Alrik's incredible strength, which was far greater than a human's and his ability to wield magic, that he didn't have the nose of a hound. Still she couldn't be sure so she had just kept walking. After a while, even her stomach stopped its annoying growling.

Damn she was tired. Each time her eyelids drooped it became harder and harder to pull them back up. However, sleep never came. She tried to no avail. Something was wrong with her.

Yeah, it's called paranoia!

True enough. She was paranoid because she really didn't want to get caught. Not by Alrik, the vampire, or the demons. She just wanted to be left alone with no more thoughts and worries. She wanted to go home and get back to her job, if she still had one. She wanted to look up her half-sisters, the Bellums, and see if a friendship could be found there. Heck, she even wanted to tell her mom she was sorry and that she understood why she'd done what she did.

Abby curled up along a tree. While walking, she'd tried to find a hiding place but she'd found nothing but long rolling hills and mountains in the distance. There'd been nothing, nada. Of course that'd be her luck. She just knew that if Alrik had been with her he'd probably have found some secret cave that was perfectly safe and much warmer than out here in the open.

Whatever, this spot on the ground was just as good as any. Maybe if she just slept for a little while she'd feel better, the tightness in her throat and chest would ease.

The real question was: could she keep up the cloaking spell while sleeping? She had no clue, but she was about to find out.

Abby's eyes drifted closed.

Her thoughts refused to slow. Her mind didn't want to stop thinking about Alrik. Her heart wanted to keep reminding her of how badly it hurt.

Well I don't want to think about it, she wanted to scream.

Tears pooled in her eyes. She didn't want to think about how much it hurt to leave or how much it hurt to know he'd been hiding something huge from her. She sniffled and wiped the tears off her face.

As she did, a strange feeling came over her. One of those little sensations you got at the back of your neck when you were being watched. Her eyes popped opened, straining in the darkness as she kept her body still. Something was here. From her view, she saw nothing but more grass at the level of her head with great mighty trees flowering pretty red and pink flowers from above. She hadn't even lit a fire so she had no light.

That was the thing in this rift. No sun, and no moon. So when the daylight came out it wasn't nearly as bright as it should be and when it got dark it got really dark. No luminous moon lit the way for her. Her human eyes could only adjust so much and still they left her squinting hard into the night.

Nothing strange stood waiting for her. That left only one other option, which was the worse one.

Moving with agility that surged from a rush of adrenaline, Abby spun around and let a spell fly from her fingertips. The spell was weak, a cloud of fog at best.

Alrik stood there.

Her breath caught, lodged in her throat with so much emotion: happiness, anger, pain. Her chest squeezed tight like being wrapped in a painful bear hug.

With a flick of his wrist, he deflected her spell as if shooing away a fly. She must be weaker than she'd imagined if he could deflect her spell so easily.

Abby gazed up at him. She'd been away from him for little over a day and yet he looked taller than she remembered.

That's only because you're sitting on the ground below him, idiot.

Not true, she corrected. He also looked even stronger and more gorgeous than she remembered. His eyes looked brighter and not as dark as they'd been. They were inky black recesses that she could lose herself in but somehow they were lighter than before. How did he do that? How did his eyes change colors like that or was it just a trick of light? Maybe his dark black eyes had never changed at all.

"You thought to leave me?" he asked.

Anguish coated his words and the sound took her back. Out of all things she might have expected if he caught her, the sound of pain wasn't one. That sound grabbed her by the heart and squeezed until she gasped. God, she did love him.

So stupid, Abby.

Abbigail pushed herself to her knees then slowly stood. There, she felt more in control and more on level with him even though he still stood more than a foot and a half taller than she did.

"Yes." She had to swallow over the knot in her voice because it took her two tries to speak, and even then her voice came out throaty.

"Tell me why."

Her eyes traced to the grass. That was easier to look at.

She countered with her own question. "Who is Arianna?"

She watched him from the corner of her eyes and saw his eyes flare with surprise.

"How do you know that name?" he demanded.

Abby met his gaze as her own anger rose. How dare he take that tone with her. After she saved his butt nearly twice if you included the jaheera attack and she was.

He came towards her. Each step sent her heart beat pounding faster and faster. He kept coming until he grabbed her by the shoulders. "How do you know that name? Answer me!"

She looked up into his eyes. What she saw there broke down her anger. He looked panicked, uncertain. God, she hated seeing that look on his face. She wanted to help him, to make him feel better, and to maybe even make him happy. She didn't want things to be like this.

"You said her name in your sleep," Abby said, pain masking her voice. "Why don't you tell me who she is and then maybe you can explain why she sounds so important to you?"

Let it be his sister's name.

He released his grip on her and started building a fire.

Just like that. Back to work, and back to ignoring her questions.

"Alrik, I swear that if you don't start really answering my questions, I'm leaving."

His jaw clenched, and he slammed the wood in his arms down to the ground. She jumped at the violent action. "You threaten me now?" he growled.

"I don't see it that way, but I guess...in a way, yes, I am."

He shook his head in disbelief. With a rushed spell and a flick of his fingers, a spark caught and the wood started burning.

She almost thanked him for giving her heat and light. She could see his dark face so much better now.

He took a seat by the fire, set his swords on either side of him within easy reach, and then he pulled something out of his pocket and tossed it to her. She caught it without thinking and instantly groaned at what she saw. A hunk of meat. She tore into it with relish.

How did he do that?

Here she'd been contemplating, no, planning to leave him and he managed to stride back into her life and dominate it. He'd manage to give her heat, light, and food within five minutes. Damn, she didn't know if she loved or hated him right now.

"I was going to mate with her."

And…. just like that she felt like she'd been socked in the gut with a massive fist. Her stomach churned, threatening to spew up the little bite of food she'd taken. "What's mating?" She had a pretty clear idea from the word, but she had to be sure.

"I was going to bond myself to her. I had her previous engagement annulled so I could have her."

"What happened?" To her, she left off the question. Something had happened, something bad, she could feel it in the waves of tension surrounding him.

He let out a hallow laugh. "She died. What do you think happened? She died trying to save me. That damn woman!" He scrubbed a hand across his face, then threaded his fingers through his hair tugging on the hard locks.

She winced, half-expecting to see the strands snap under his harsh grip.

"You loved her," Abby said over the tight grip on her heart. Each word hurt to say. It hurt even more to think about. "She must have loved you to do what she did."

His eyes met hers and an odd look rolled over them. A flicker of doubt maybe? "I don't know if she did or not. She must have cared enough or she wouldn't have jumped in front of me to take the spell that would have killed me."

He didn't even sound certain. Abby's eyebrows flew up. "Who was casting the spell to try to kill you?" she asked gently.

"My brother."

"Oh," she said quickly, not knowing quite what to say to that.

He waved his hand at her shaking his head. "I don't blame him now. I did. I did for a long time especially after he dethroned me from the crown and banished me from my homeland. No, it was only once I was out in the endless wastes of this forsaken place that I was left to my thoughts. Maybe I did too much thinking, but it wasn't his fault.

I would have done the same thing in his place. Arianna was the only loose end. She should have been up above in her room. Stupid woman...what was she thinking? I couldn't even save her," his voice drifted off becoming soft and hoarse. "I should have but I couldn't." He sounded so lost she wanted to do or say anything to get that ragged look out of his voice.

"There's nothing you could have done, I'm sure."

Distaste twisted his lips into snarl. Suddenly he slammed his feet to the ground and stood in a rush, his hands balled tight at his sides. "I could have saved her! I could have fixed her!" His shout probably could have been heard halfway across the rift.

Abby swallowed hard. "How?" She kept her voice gentle and soft as if she was talking to a hurt animal.

He held his hand out in front of him watching it. Turning it over, he gazed at his palm with an eerie look in his eyes. A wild, crazed look came over him.

"The blood, the royal blood in my veins touches my magic. It heals." Slowly, he kept turning his hand over and over, over and over.

She could feel the chill of his magic emanating from his hand. "How can you heal?" Healing magic was a tremendous and rare gift, or at least among witches it was. It usually required a variety of tools at the witch's side: herbs, healing potions, and spells. Of course, what did she know? She stopped practicing a long time ago and both she and her mother considered themselves 'grey' witches—that left them somewhere in the middle on the magic scale.

Abby thought back, but couldn't remember ever meeting a 'white witch'. They must be rare. But in Alrik's case he was demon. She'd already learned that the magic differences between humans and demons were great. Even some of the rogue demons, well, all of them had magic powers. However, Aidan the vampire did not.

"How does your healing work?"

He laughed as if she said something funny.

That's it. She'd had enough of his moping. Abby stood and waited until his eyes met hers, then slowly walked up to him. He eyed her warily. With a quick move, she sat in front of him, right on his thighs with her back to his chest. He tensed beneath her, but as she leaned into his strong chest his body slowly relaxed. She could feel the tension leaving him.

"Spread your legs," she whispered. Heat flared inside her at her own daring.

But, he did. He spread his muscled, hard thighs letting her fit between his legs. Strong arms wrapped around her waist, pulling her further into his strong, warm chest. A soft sigh escaped her.

"You shouldn't have left me," he said in her ear. His voice was deep, husky. A shiver raced down her body.

"Why? It's not like you didn't find me anyway."

His cheek pressed up against hers, warming her cold one, and creating an ache inside her. An ache to turn her head so their lips would line up and he'd be kissing her. Her heartbeat picked up, rapping faster against her ribs. She was suddenly rather warm in his arms.

"You can't ever leave me, Abbigail."

The sincerity in his voice made her heart skip a beat. "What?"

He tightened his arms around her as if to prove a point. "The seer should have told me. I had no idea it'd be like this." His arms tightened more, nearly cutting off her air. "Do you know how hard it's been watching you crawl into a space inside me that even Arianna never touched?"

Her breath hitched. "What?" Her vocabulary had apparently diminished down to one word questions.

"I-I can't go through with it. I can't do it. I can't risk it." He sounded as if talking to himself.

"Alrik, what are you talking about?"

He shook his head, knocking hers in the process. "I can't do it. I can't put you in danger. If I did it, again...I could never live. Never, ever." He was whispering now, his voice hoarse.

Abby spun around in his arms, plastering her chest to his, her hands in his hair, bringing their lips close. She stared into his eyes. The raw pain she saw made her heart ache.

"What are you talking about?" He shook his head and she tightened her grip in his hair. "Answer me, honey, please." Something big was happening here, she just didn't know what exactly. But, she was finally going to find how what had guilt eating him up inside.

"I can't do it. You've made me care." Wetness formed at his eyes.

She couldn't have been more shocked if he struck her right now.

A single tear slid down his dark cheek. Yet his expression was stoic and distant, his eyes not meeting hers. "You've made me love again, and I can't do it. I can't put you in danger."

Her heart leapt flying high as a bird, but still the words were surrounded in agony. "Honey, what are you talking about?" She wrapped her legs around his waist, looped her arms around his shoulders. She pressed kisses to his cheeks and along his straight nose. "Please, just talk to me."

God, something huge was happening but she didn't know what to say or do to take the pain out of his voice. She wanted to focus but she was still floating on high after his subtle declaration.

He loves me.

One strong arm snaked around her waist and his hand slid up under her shirt. Her breath caught at the skin on skin contact. "Alrik?" She held him tighter as she pressed her face into his warm neck.

"She wins. I'll never be who I was. She's won. I can never lift this curse."

He sounded defeated, and she winced.

"Why not? Isn't that why I'm here?"

"Not now. I won't put you in danger. I won't risk it."

Abby squeezed her eyes shut. She supposed now was the time she'd get the other answer she wanted. Just what did he have planned for her after she killed his mother?

"You have to tell me what you're talking about, Alrik, because I don't get it. Why don't we just go and kill the old bitch?"

Tension filled his shoulders. She could feel them harden beneath her grip.

He pulled back forcing her to meet his eyes. A long moment dragged out between them and then he spoke and shattered her world. "If you kill her you'll die."

She blinked, swallowed, and tilted her head in confusion. "What?" Now she tensed. Her throat struggled to work.

"The seer says that you are the only one who can kill her, but if you do then you'll die with her."

"How?" she croaked.

"I don't know. He didn't say. So now do you see?" He grabbed her shoulders and shook her to make his point. His crazed eyes beseeched hers.

Oh, she saw a few things. All the pieces finally fit together, she just wished that maybe they didn't because she didn't like how the puzzle looked after it was put together. It wasn't a pretty one.

He would have let her die for him. He would have sent her to her death to remove his curse. Inside it felt like two hands were tearing her heart in half. One part of her understood. He hadn't know her then and neither of them felt about each other like they did now. However, the other part didn't care. The other more emotional part wept with white-hot pain in her heart that he'd see her die.

How could he?

Pain sat in her chest like a heavy weight. Pain at what he'd kept hidden from her after all that they shared and pain for him.

Fiery emotions tore at her. It shouldn't be like this. He didn't deserve to have to live with this curse. It wasn't his fault. If she didn't kill his mother then it would be her fault that he lived with this curse.

Then Abby might as well be the one who cursed him, because by not helping him she was making sure he stayed cursed. She'd be the reason why every time he looked in the mirror he saw somebody else's reflection. The only one who could fix him, who might have a shred of hope at saving him from the curse, was her.

But, she'd have to die to save him.

Tears pools in fill her eyes and slipped down her cheeks in streams. Only by the strength inside her did she manage not to burst into sobs like she wanted to. Never once had she sobbed and cried hard before but right now, she did. The burning pain in her needed release. It had to go somewhere.

She wanted to scream her rage to the heavens at the unfairness of it all.

However, she didn't do either of those things.

Instead, she embraced the demon in her arms, the demon she loved, and kissed him with every ounce of that beautiful love inside her.

The kiss was raw, wild, and a little unhinged. His lips moved against hers as if trying to memorize the feel of them. A soft sob escaped her at the thought.

Somehow it felt as if she was losing him. They went at each other like ravenous beasts...like people who didn't have much time left together.

Tongues stroked in hot, wet strokes, hands clung and teased. Both of them moved, reaching under each other's shirts and pulling them up and off.

With an irritated grunt, Alrik struggled over the clasp of her bra.

That one little action made her giggle. The hot poke of pain in her chest lessened as his strong fingers fumbled over the three little hooks. He didn't find it so funny and cursed in Demonish. Another fit of giggles swept over her that dried away her tears and left her feeling light as feather. As he finally got one hook open, then another she took the opportunity to run her hands over his round shoulders, and down the warm skin of his back. So strong and hard. She loved the way he felt, loved the dips and contours of his muscles.

"Fuck!" he cursed. Finally, the bra straps slid down her arms then he ripped away the offending material. Without missing a beat, he grabbed her by the waist and lifted her until one tender nipple was at mouth level, and then he sucked it hard.

She gasped, her hands threading in his hair for anchor. He suckled her. Warm lips tugged and tortured her sensitive peak. Raw heat kindled inside of her as wetness dampened between her legs in a flood. With that one masterful touch she was ready for him...more than ready.

"Alrik," she gasped.

His mouth released her breast with a wet pop, and then he opened that sexy mouth wide and latched onto her other breast. Oh my. Her eyes rolled back into her head and it turned into a struggle to keep the heavy weight of her head up.

Fuck it, she thought. It fell back, which worked out great because it pushed her nipple even further into his mouth and he didn't waste the opportunity. He scraped his wet tongue around and around her peak flicking across it until her core throbbed in time with the movement. Each possessive tug, every tender rub pulled an answering need from deep inside her.

That's it. She needed release. Too much pressure had built up inside her.

She shoved his shoulders hard. He didn't have to but he rolled back taking her with him, cradling her against his chest as he laid back.

She landed on top of him and rubbed her core against the immense erection in his pants. A breathy moan escaped her. Need drove her movements and made her unable to stop rubbing her tender clitoris against him over and again.

"Abbigail!" He said her name like a curse.

She couldn't stop moving, her hips undulated against him working them both into a fiery frenzy. Sitting up she traced her hands over his hard chest, and down the flats of his nipples. Her mouth soon followed, kissing and tasting his warm masculine essence. Hard muscles bulged in his abs teasing her to touch.

So, she did and followed the tempting path of hard muscle and satiny skin with her lips. His abs bucked under her touch. His erection pressed hard against his pants as if trying to escape.

She didn't know what was louder: her panting breaths or his deep grunts. Either way they created a sensual storm around them.

Her hand cupped his length, tracing over his hard cock, and squeezing him. The fabric of his jeans had to go. She needed to feel him hot and hard in her hand. She moaned just at the thought of how he'd soon be filling and thrusting inside of her. Her core beat with a pulse at the erotic vision.

"Abbigail," he said again, this time a warning.

She laughed softly and darted her tongue beneath the band of his pants. His entire body stilled.

Yes, she thought. You're mine now.

She wanted to see him under her control all that under brilliant strong man melting all because of the flick of her tongue. She wanted to see him, this strong and brilliant man, squirm and melt under her all from a flick of her tongue.

Abby curled her fingers into the band of his pants. Only a row of four buttons kept her from what she wanted, and from what pushed hard against the seam as if trying to escape. She hooked her fingers around the first button and opened it.

"I want you, woman," he growled, his voice making a shiver race down her stomach.

The tip of him poked through; hard, rounded, and wet at the tip. Her tongue darted out to wet her suddenly dry lips. Slowly she opened the next button and then the next until finally he sprung free, eager, and solid.

She curled her hand around the shaft loving the contrast of rocky hard strength and velvety soft skin. Her hands pumped up and down the dark shaft, but her eyes watched his expression. His lips parted, abs curled as he arched and thrust his hips into her grasp. He was a beautiful, sexy sight.

"Oh baby," she breathed at the sight.

"God damn you," he cursed.

Every instinct inside her told her to tear their pants off and sit on top of him until she felt him invading every inch of her.

But this was such a good, bittersweet torture that she couldn't. Not when she had the sexy dark demon undulating in the palm of her hand—literally.

So she licked up and down the length of his shaft, listening to the catch in his breath, the deep groans rumbling from his chest, and the way his hands gripped then released the grass at his sides.

As her tongue performed a particularly seductive move around the tip of him, he automatically reached for her head. Her heart stuttered in her chest as her breath caught. Would he curl his hands into her hair and push his cock into her mouth? The thought aroused her so much she flushed.

He reached for her but before he touched a strand on her head, he pulled back. His hands shook as if it took great effort to keep them at his sides. That made her grin and suck on the tip of him even harder.

His hips bucked forcing his cock deeper into her mouth.

She didn't want him to behave. Not now. Now she wanted him wild and unleashed. She wanted to feel every single sensation that he felt for her. She wanted their love to be a physical thing that could be felt in the air around them.

So, she swirled her tongue over the tip of him and sucked his cock into her mouth. His wet shaft glided smoothly into her mouth, filling her wide and deep. He was big, bigger than she'd ever had. Her lips spread taut around his shaft, nearly hurting but my God was it worth it. Her hand worked the bottom of his long shaft, fist pumping slow before gathering speed. His harsh breathing filled her ears as her mouth worked him up and down, sucking and licking, lips caressing his hard shaft.

It had all been worth it because his entire body jerked under her touch, hips twitching then pumping to fill her mouth as if he was fucking it. His chest rose and fell in hard pants like he'd just finished a hard mile-long sprint. Ecstasy tightened his features with raw beauty. She moaned around his shaft, actually wishing he'd come. Just come now and spend in her mouth. She wanted to give him that pleasure, wanted to taste all of him in a way she couldn't explain. As if she wanted to share everything with this man, take in all parts of him and give it back ten-fold.

"Dreenaru gina slinah!"

"Hmmm?" she hummed as she sucked him deep again, moving faster now with both mouth and hand. His cock grew harder, hotter. The vein pulsed beneath her fingertips as his thighs trembled, actually trembled at her touch. She felt like she had the power to move mountains.

"You are incredible," he said huskily, translating for her.

Yes, well, she felt incredible bringing him this kind of pleasure. Each grunt and groan from him, each thrust of his hips and hard roll of his packed abs sent a pulse straight to her clitoris. She ached. Squeezing her thighs together did nothing to ease her. Hot moisture escaped her at the action and rubbed along her swollen folds.

"Stop now, Abbigail. Take me inside you," he pleaded.

Yes! Her body screamed.

She wanted to stay and tease him but instead she listened to him, her body too tense to do otherwise. In a rush, she kicked off her shoes, socks, and tugged down her jeans. Her panties followed next, and then she tossed her leg over his wide, thick waist with the V of muscles cut above his hips bones.

God he was sexy.

His hands steadied her, caressing from her thighs up to her waist then around to her ass. She was open to him completely. As she arched over him, prodding his cock with her entrance, he took full advantage of her position. He squeezed and molded her breasts, tugged a hard nipple between two warm fingertips. His other hand slipped down her side and gave a quick squeeze to her hip before cupping her sex.

"You are so beautiful," he said.

A soft moan escaped her. Her heart melted and need poured from her. She tensed at his touch. She thought he might take to torturing her as she had him, but he didn't.

His fingers slid over her wet center to dip inside and tease her of something much bigger and harder to come.

"Alrik," she gasped. Her hips rocked against his fingers.

He moved much too slowly.

One hand tugged her tender nipple in time with his fingers thrusting lazily in and out of her. His touch created a spike of pleasure from her brain to her core that threatened to burst. Her breaths turned ragged as need built. She could come she was that close to climax. She just needed a push.

"Touch me," she begged, trying to watch him but she could barely manage to keep her eyes open.

"I am touching you." The corner of his mouth kicked up in a sensual way she wanted to bite.

She might have laughed if she could. "No, I mean touch me faster."

His palm suddenly pressed hard against her clitoris then his fingers curled inside her rubbing over a spot that instantly made her head fall back and her body tense.

Oh yes, right there, her body cried.

Everything that mattered, everything that she thought or felt centered on his hands and the pleasure he wrought from her.

"You make me feel more than I ever have," he said roughly. His palm circled over her clitoris rubbing in a steady rhythm.

How could he share such deep words at a time like this? She couldn't respond coherently let alone with the thought and care his words deserved.

So, she said the simplest and most honest thing she could think of. "I love you."

His fingers around her breast as he thrust his fingers inside her, curling them as his palm pressed against her and moved faster. Blissfully, wonderfully faster. Her sex clenched around him as her breaths caught. The erotic sensations were too much. Burning waves rose inside her. Her skin drew tight as hot steam built up inside her. He kept playing her, thrusting faster, pressing harder against her, and building her up to a tremendous peak.

Then, he drove her over.

She shouted a strangled cry of pleasure. She trusted him completely with her body and with her pleasure. She trusted him because she loved him. She could feel it in the wild palpitations of her heart slamming in her chest.

"Alrik, Alrik..."

His arms snaked around her waist and then her back pressed into the grass and his strong body cocooned hers. Hot lips pressed against hers wringing another kiss from her, this one sweet and filled with longing. She couldn't possibly float any higher, any lighter at that moment because right then everything in the world was right.

As her body floated back down to earth and her skin cooled, she rubbed her legs against his, wrapped her arms across his back, and simply cradled him to her. Time passed, she couldn't be sure how long and they just kissed letting the passion cool.

When he finally slipped his hips between her legs and slowly entered her , her breath caught and needy warmth fill her, she was ready. He took her slowly, his eyes loving hers, their lips kissing then tasting each other's necks and shoulders.

He wasn't fucking her.

He wasn't having sex with her.

He was making love to her.

She held him close as each thrust brushed her clitoris making her blood burn hotter and hotter. He took her slowly toward another heart-soaring peak. This time she knew he'd be right there with her though.

Her hips rocked against his until they made a perfect tempo together. He grew restless, breaths coming heavier as she entwined her legs with his, opening her core to him.

He groaned deep in his chest as if she was killing him.

"You are so beautiful," he said in her ear.

No, you are she wanted to say but didn't. She didn't want anything to ruin this.

One arm slid beneath her hips to pull her up.

A strangle moan escaped her at this new position. "It's too much," she whispered raggedly. Her thighs started to quiver, her core to pulse, and she knew she was so close. But, she didn't want to go without it.

"It's perfect."

He drove into her faster, harder. They were one with uneven breaths mingling and lips clinging to each other without really kissing. He was hard and moving inside her, pushing her closer and closer.

"I love you, Alrik." Her heart stuttered at saying the words aloud. But his response erased any doubts she had whatsoever.

The hand at her hip flexed against her. "You'd be scared at how much I love you."

His reply shocked her, but then he slid his tongue against hers and focused all his energy on making her scream. Which he did, two more times before finally burying himself deep and jetting into her.

"You're crazy," she said afterward.

Their sweat-slicked bodies had long dried. He'd wrapped her up in his arms like a precious bundle he didn't want to let go. She'd never cuddled before, couldn't stand it in fact. However, with Alrik she could easily get used to this.

"No, I'm not. I'm just feeling something I haven't ever felt before," he said.

His words shut her up and got her thinking. While this whole situation might be one big mess, she'd at least gotten one good thing out of it.

Abby pressed a kiss to Alrik's lips and he returned it.

Yeah, that was worth it.

Twenty

The soft, feminine voice hissed at him.

"Alllriiiik. Awaken, Allllrik."

He twitched, fighting the lulling sound. There was something about it he recognized but couldn't quite place. What made his hairs stand on end was the magic encompassing the words. The woman wasn't asking, she was commanding it with vast power behind her words.

As if in a daze, Alrik woke and stood. Abby turned on her side but he had no care for her.

"Come to me. Coooooome."

He started walking. The voice seemed to come from nowhere yet must have a distinct location. No matter, the spell slowly wrapped around his mind and body knew where to take him. He walked across the base of the mountain towards the south where the flickering of fire in distance looked so much closer.

As soon as he saw the fire, he knew that this wasn't a dream. He was being summoned. And his mother was waiting for him. It was her sick magic being forced into his body to answer to her will. He tried to fight it, but no amount of spells he tried to cast overcame her power.

Each step he took he tried to still it. Nothing worked. His body just kept moving. He dug his heels into the ground and desperately tried to turn away from the fire in the distance. He had to get back to Abby. She was alone and unprotected. His heart started hammering in his chest. Sweat beaded his temples and slicked down his face.

The path he walked ended on a ledge just past the mountain. He couldn't see down it yet but he knew it wasn't a cliff because he could just make out the other half of the valley sunken into the ground. The area felt warmer here. Sweat pooled and slid down his back and chest. Humid air suffocated him as he neared the ledge like a walking zombie.

Without even a moment to determine the drop off, he was sent rolling down the hill. He rolled like a log falling down and down. The grass was wet, mossy. The valley had a distinct moist smell. The trees were wide and not as tall as the other rift trees. They were bulkier and shorter. Their long branches hung like old arms out toward the ground with thousands of dark green leaves coloring them.

A fire roared nearby. He could hear its mighty crackling flame, and smell its woodsy stench. Except it didn't just smell of woods. Something was burning in that fire. Something that smelled so repulsive his stomach clenched to keep from heaving.

Wherever that fire was and who tended it was behind him, but he couldn't even turn his bloody head to look.

Like a robot, the spell commanded him to stand and come forward. Then he saw her. And her army.

Fuck!

Things were so much worse than he expected. She didn't have a small army of maybe a few dozen idummi under her control. She had more than a few hundred.

The idummi stood as his body waded through the crowd. They parted for him sneering and chomping their teeth at him. Rage boiled in his blood. He fought even harder against the magic binding him. He'd tear off every single one of the demon's heads and toss them into the fire pit right after he slaughtered his mother.

And there she was—his mother—in all her crowning horror.

She stood on a stone dais. It looked recently built, not aged as some of the temples and old buildings he'd seen along the rift. The corners were sharp and not worn down. The rock still shined as they had just been dug up. A set of six stairs were carved into either side of the dais. The whole thing looked so out of place in this marsh that he would have laughed if he could. Only his mother would require elegance and royalty while banished from home. She hadn't learned to hunt her own food or to live humbly as he had. No, she just weaved her spells until she had an army do it for her. Smart, really.

The fire roared off to his left. Massive stones formed a circle around the base and a mighty black cauldron was held above it by tall metal stakes coming from the ground. Idummi worked around it with their bony legs bent out at sharp angles. Their green skin shined sickly in the fire light. They tossed things into the black cauldron. A ladder stood up against one of the stakes and one idummi held a mighty pole that he used to stir the hellish concoction inside.

She had her minions create her favorite part of the castle—the throne. She even had a lavish chair on top of it. The frame looked elegant and intricate, worthy of royalty even in his eye. The wooden frame curled into spirals at the bottom of the four posts, and at the top two curled back. A rich green cushion decorated the wooden frame and she sat upon the edge of it, her bony, golden shoulders thrust back, and her body facing him with a mad gleam in her eye.

She stood as he neared.

"I see nothing has changed," said Alrik.

Even out here in the middle of nowhere in a damn marsh she wore a vibrant splash of color on her face. Her eyes were darkly lined in black to better show her violet eyes. The reminder of what his real eye color looked like didn't sit well with him. The fact that he had anything in common with her made him want to jump into the fire until he burned to a crisp.

Her long raven black hair sat in two heavy braids on each of her shoulders. Gold, silver, and red thread was weaved through the braids, and atop her head was a golden crown. It wasn't her royal crown. No way would they have let her leave with it when he banished her from the kingdom.

No, she'd forged her own. Two crescents of shimmery gold stood apart from each other. Small jagged points stood facing each other from opposite sides of her head. A middle piece with luminous diamonds and rubies flashed from the fire light, and atop the crescents and middle connector were two sheer points like horns of an animal. They arched up into the air.

Her red gown had gold flowers etched into the tight bodice and white fur lining the long, elegant sleeves and the bottom of the dress swept the ground as she stood.

"What do you want from me?"

He looked upon her cold beauty and golden skin with uncontained disgust.

A small smile played at the corner of her mouth. "Is that any kind of greeting to give your mother?"

"No. The better one would be to cut your fucking head off."

Her eyebrows rose. Good he surprised her. That made him feel better.

The smile died from her face. Even the life in her eyes seemed to die. She raised a hand and flexed her fingers in the air.

Alrik choked. An invisible forced grabbed at his throat and squeezed. He struggled, but couldn't move his legs or even his arms under her magic. His eyes squeezed shut as his muscles flexed hard against the choking, his bones grating, and throat bruising.

"Look at me!" his mother hissed like a serpent.

He took his time and slowly opened his eyes while inhaling air through his nostrils. Once they made eye contact, she held the spell for a moment longer then released him. She released all of him because he once again had control over his body. He rubbed at his throat still feeling the lingering invisible hands.

"You have been busy son. Visiting the last and most powerful seer. Seeking to murder me, your own mother," she said in a soft, mocking voice. She walked down the dais as if she was in the ballroom back home making a grand entrance. Idummi parted for her as she knelt and picked something up and then she tossed it at him.

Alrik felt his body jolt.

The seer's head landed near his feet—a bloody hunk of meat. His dark face was frozen in a look of terror, his eyes rolled up.

He couldn't say anything as rage boiled inside him.

Then with the seer's blood on her hands, she held her hand up as if awaiting a man to take and place a kiss upon it. Her other hand grabbed the long length of her gown and lifted it as she came near him.

"You've been very bad…I mean really, son, trying to kill your own mother?"

With a vicious snarl, he ran for her. The seer's words didn't matter. She was so close he could almost feel her blood coating his fingers.

Her trickling laughter taunted him as if she found him entertaining. He didn't even come close to reaching her before she tossed up her hand as if waving and he was blocked by an invisible wall. He knew spells and magic. He could fight back but as he thrust his own magic out to dispel the wall, nothing happened. More of her feminine laughter assaulted him.

Maybe, just maybe if he could get his hands on her then he could end her life the old fashioned way—by cutting her damned head off.

An idummi crept up between them. He bowed before his mother like a servant and spoke in a garbled, demonic voice. The idummi had their own demonic language and trying to speak in the shahoulin tongue of Alrik's people was hard for the creature.

"Master Demuzi, it is done."

His mother clapped, her wild eyes gleaming with madness. "Fantastic and here I thought things were starting to get boring. Bring it here."

The demon slinked off back toward the fire pit.

Alrik tensed. He'd thought things were bad enough before, but now a sinking feeling came over him.

His mother saw his look and smiled.

"What are you going to do?" Just asking the words was like trying to pull his teeth out one at a time.

She made a tsking sound and shook her head. "You'll just have to wait and see now won't you? Besides, you mustn't think I brought you all this way for nothing?"

"Salindra, what have you done?" he shouted. His body lunged toward her but the barrier spell kept him from doing more than leaning towards her. His palms twitched and fingers itched to scrape his fingers over her colored face until he saw blood.

Suddenly, the demons swarmed around him.

They bounced on their bony, lithe feet and stared at him with excited eyes. Alrik spun around finding more and more of them around him. The creatures didn't look as if a spell kept them here which only meant that his mother had actually gained their support without magical means. Just what could she offer these ruthless, cannibalistic demons to keep them loyal? He was afraid to find out.

Once again, he spun and faced his mother.

"Why?" he gritted out.

"Your father was strong. He kept our people in line, and well, he kept me from causing too much trouble. Of course, if I would have dared any of my games while he was king he would have had me imprisoned. But you, my son, were so new to the throne. Telal, my eldest, was supposed to take it, but he betrayed all of us to those vampires. Well, he'll get his as you will yours. You were so eager to please." She twirled in a circle with her arms spread out from her like a little girl dancing. "Eager to please me, the court members, and the commoners. It was sickening really watching you bow down to them like that."

"I wasn't bowing to them. I was helping them repair the damage from the war!" Alrik fought against the barrier spell separating them. He dug his body into it just hoping it would break. All he would need was one second and she'd be dead.

She rolled her eyes and made her face into a mocking sad expression. "Aw, poor Alrik. Where did my tough son go? Where did his kingliness go? Well, you were no fun so I fixed it. I fixed all of that. You were so regal and fun after I fixed you." She laughed a cruel sound. "And the best part was that you didn't even see it happening. I took your hair and bound it into a totem where I cursed you once a week for nearly a thousand years. I fooled you for a thousand years! When things started to get boring, I would give you my special "stress-relief concoction". Sure you would feel dazed and relaxed for a minute, but the rage would grow in your heart." She sighed in pleasure.

"I wonder how many innocent prisoners you sentenced to die or to become a slave because of that little potion. Fifty? Maybe more?" She laughed delightedly.

"It wasn't me. It was you and your black magic. Let this barrier go and fight me." Still, he couldn't believe that. He'd done those things. Every last horrible one of them.

Her shoulders shook she laughed so hard. "As if I don't know what you're thinking. As if I don't know that you'd sooner kill me than save that precious human of yours."

The change in topics sent him spiraling. "What? What are you talking about?" A part of him knew that she knew about Abbigail. Of course she would, but still to know what she was capable of and to know that Abby was alone not far from here sent fear unlike he'd ever known through him. It froze him to the bone.

"Why don't you bow for me?" she suggested. Her red colored lips twitched.

She didn't control him now so he stood as tall as his great height let him. "Never."

The idummi chattered and laughed around him as if he'd said something funny. She would have to make him bow before he did so of his own free will.

"What if I said I'd spare her life if you bowed?"

Alrik tensed. Something had changed. She wasn't taunting him, she was being serious. A cold knot of fear lodged in his gut, spreading out to wrap his heart in an icy fist.

Alrik bent one knee and placed it on the wet soggy ground, then the other. With fists clenched at his sides, he glared up at his mother.

"I bow."

The look in her eye became almost insane. Her eyes widened pupils dilating. "You care for this human. How odd indeed and what a sneer to poor, poor Arianna."

"How do you know about that?" He managed to keep his voice calm even as he wanted to scream and rage against her. She died after he banished Salindra.

"I know everything, son."

"You don't know everything." Now he laughed. He knew something great and powerful that she didn't. He had the most powerful witch at his disposal.

For a moment, unease flickered in her eye and then it vanished. "Hmm, we'll get to that later. Bring her forward."

The idummi jumped and squawked in their excitement. Alrik looked over his shoulder and felt his heart stop beating. Two idummi had Abbigail by her arms. Her eyes were locked on him. He could see the fear in her eyes. But, she kept her cool and walked rigidly along. One way or another, really bad things were going to happen this night.

If only he'd had more time. One sweet night with her was not enough. He needed years, maybe longer to learn everything about her, to touch and taste every inch of her body. He just needed time with her.

"Alrik, I'm sorry. They surprised me. They jumped me while I was sleeping."

"Krishnoe!" commanded his mother.

Abby's lips snapped shut but not on their own. His mother wielded magic to do all of her biddings.

God, what he would do to see that power stripped from her.

His mother strode toward him and placed her hand upon his shoulder. He tried to lift a hand to snap her wrist in half but her icy magic once again engulfed him. Even as he tried to turn his head to sink his teeth into her hand, she controlled that too.

"See the fallen king bowing before me like a coward. Is this the kind of man that makes your human blood hot?"

Alrik stiffened even as he waited to hear her answer. That's right, even now he was unsure of what she thought of him. She'd said the words but they were still so fresh and new in his head. She said she loved me. He was acting like a coward. He'd already willingly bowed to Salindra.

"He is not a coward, but you are," his Abbigail said.

Sharp fingernails the color of bright red blood cut into his shoulder. "What say you, human?"

Alrik might have grinned if he didn't know better. However, he did know better and his mother could kill Abbigail.

But Abbigail could kill her?

Alrik had no idea what chain of events was about to happen next, but nothing prepared him for what his mother had planned.

Twenty-one

Abby lifted her chin. "I said you're a coward. Why else did you need to possess Alrik to get him here, and why else did you send a horde of demons to get me, a mere human, when you could have done it yourself? You're scared. You're afraid of us."

Abby didn't know how to get them out of this but she'd do whatever it took. She'd save Alrik if it was the last thing she did.

Maybe if they'd acted sooner they'd be sleeping comfortably in her bed in her little rented house right now, and not in the grasp of an evil demon with tremendous powers and a horde of idummi following her. But, they couldn't go back. She couldn't change what had already happened. All she could do now was try to keep them both safe.

As she met Alrik's stricken eyes it only solidified her conviction. She would die for him.

Abby shifted her stance and spread her legs shoulder-width apart keeping her hands open at her sides. She was ready. Magic stirred inside her as she called it forth. It was subtle like a warm blanket settling over her and gradually warming her.

"Release him and let us both leave here and no one will get hurt," she said calmly.

The queen—an elegant and fantastical looking woman with gorgeous golden skin, a mane of hair worthy of a shampoo commercial, and violet eyes so piercing they might be beautiful if madness didn't linger there. The queen's jaw fell open at Abby's order, then it snapped shut so hard and fast she could hear the clink of teeth.

"How dare you, you loathsome little human? You are nothing!" The woman's hands shook as she clasped them together and took a loud seething breath. "You are nothing compared to me. To even dare so…you will pay."

That didn't sound good. Abby's stomach clenched. She wasn't worried about herself. It was Alrik.

"Bring me my potion!" the queen screamed, her voice shrill. Her eyes glowed with uncontained madness. Even her movements weren't graceful as if she was becoming unhinged.

An idummi stepped forward, his ugly face smiling to reveal sharp pointed teeth yellowed from neglect. He held a tall glass in his hand. It reminded her of a vase that one might put a single flower within. Inside the container was a vile looking substance. It looked murky brown like thick muddy water, but that wasn't what made her run for Alrik. What made her run for him was the look in the queen's eyes and the aura of magic surrounding the potion. Something evil had been put into that potion.

She'd nearly made it to him. The muscles in his neck and back strained as he fought invisible bonds holding him down.

The queen smirked and gave Abby a look that clearly said: I know something you don't.

"Alrik!" Abby shouted.

There was no time to decide what kind of magic to use, to know which spell might be best. She just went for it. With a slash of her hand, she cut his invisible bonds. He tore free and lunged for his mother.

Abby panicked, fear guiding her actions. She wanted to scream at him to run away with her. They could only make an escape together. It didn't help that his precious swords were back at camp lying next to where he'd been sleeping. What could he do without his weapons?

"Abbigail get out of here!" he bellowed and charged through a path of idummi standing between him and his mother.

The idummi didn't draw blades but attempted to tackle his midriff and slam him to the ground. Abby ran after him. No way could she leave him.

"Not without you!" she called back.

Alrik's icy magic shot out from his hands. Demons went slamming back as if a tidal force threw them.

Idummi surrounded Abby. She let out a sound unlike she'd ever made before. Her knees bent and her body tensed for battle. The roar she let out was one made from many waging war in the history of the world. Hers mixed alongside Alrik's and together they fought their opponents. They sought blood on their hands. They fought for justice and love.

Abby cast spells as if she'd been doing it her whole life. Demons went soaring through the air. Four swarmed her from her left and she turned to them letting out a fiery spell that encased the demons in searing hot flames. Their chaotic screams were barely heard over the rumble of adrenaline in her ears.

She'd turned into a violent creature that reacted to the threat and took action without any thought or remorse. She would protect herself and she would save Alrik's life—she loved him more than anything.

More demons lunged at her from behind as they tried to grab her. She barely ducked away from one when another grabbed her. The green creatures were strong for something so boney and withered looking. It easily pinned her arms at her sides effectively keeping her from throwing out spells.

Abby fought to catch her breath. A demon on either side of her kept her in their clutches. Their claws nearly cut into her. Their grip was so tight she could feel her skin pinching and blood bursting to the surface. Nothing they could do would make her flinch. She stayed strong and didn't show any pain. No weakness.

Alrik was slammed to the ground by demons. He landed hard, his head cracking against the ground. Demons surrounded him turning him onto his back. They grabbed his arms and legs and spread them out from his body in an "x" position.

"What are you doing?"

The queen still had that smirk on her face. Abby wanted to beat it off of her. Not a trace of fear could be seen in her eyes.

That nagging feeling came back in full force. The queen had something up her sleeve and it had to be an ace.

Dead carcasses littered the ground. Abby had only done some of that damage. She eyed the dead demons and could have laughed at how many more Alrik had managed to take out in that same amount of time. Her chest puffed up with pride. Her man was a warrior.

The demons hauled her forward. They stopped just as she reached Alrik's feet, literally.

"Hey honey," she said softly to him.

Apparently now was not a good time for sweetness for his glare nearly singed the hairs off her head. "You should have listened to me." Anger laced his words and burned bright in his eyes.

She suddenly started blinking fast to keep any possible extra moisture at bay. "Yes, well, I won't leave you. I told you that."

His chest strained against the arms holding him, but his eyes held hers and in them she saw a cold, dead fear.

He'd already marked her for as good as dead in his eyes. That hurt like a punch to the solar plexus.

Well, damn him and his mother. She would show them both. She'd find a way, somehow, to save him and she wouldn't die in the process. Abby felt something chilling, and altogether calculating, slither over her skin. A strange acceptance settled inside her. She'd already killed idummi. She'd killed an animal to eat. She'd created flames at the flick of her fingertips and had stopped nearly two dozen of Aidan's men from coming after her with a single spell.

Abby stood tall and let her power radiate around her in a golden halo from her body. Only those with magical powers could see the "magic" in others. So as Abby finally stood accepting her fate, whatever it might be, Alrik and his mother gazed upon her with wonder.

She was a witch. She was powerful. And she was ready to defend her mate.

Abby's gaze slowly reached the queen's. She had the satisfaction of watching the queen do a double take.

"Quite the little warrior, aren't you? Humans always were so…barbaric."

Abby smiled and took her words as the compliment they were. Her people, humans, had fought long and hard for everything they ever wanted or needed. They fought and killed for food, they worked through blood and sweat to build homes and cities. In times of trouble, they had the capability to come together through differences and hardships. They were fighters. They were barbaric.

Right now Abby could feel her ancestors grinning through her smile with pride.

The queen snapped. "Hold his mouth open!"

Alrik's eyes flared wide with panic. While she thought he'd been fighting his captors before, now he really did. He tossed each of the demons holding his arms off as if they were children, but even more came at him piling on top of his body. Abby struggled against the hands holding her.

The demon carrying the tall glass with that murky substance inside knelt beside Alrik.

"Don't do it!" Abby shouted.

She fought hard against the demons. Their tight grips tore through her skin. Another grabbed her waist as she fought; her feet slid kicking up dirt as she struggled. Whatever was in the glass was a vile, evil spell. She could feel its dark energy like a pit from hell. And they were going to pour it down his throat.

She tried to think quickly. What did she do? Did she fight demons holding her and use even more magic? Magic that she needed to defeat his mother?

It didn't matter what she did.

"Don't drink it!" Abby shouted.

"Like he has a choice," his mother sneered.

Two demons crawled next to Alrik. Their knobby, long fingers curled into his mouth. Abby gagged at the sight.

"Don't touch him," she said her voice much softer now, weaker. They were going to lose this one. She could already feel it. Still she fought against the hands holding her no matter how useless. The second she got her arms free she'd kill them all. They'd regret touching him this way.

The demons wrenched his mouth open while the one with the glass poured the concoction down Alrik's throat. He wasn't gentle about it. The foul liquid spilled over Alrik's cheeks and dribbled down his chin. He made awful gurgling sounds as he choked and struggled not to swallow the liquid.

All at once, Alrik's body stopped fighting. His eyes closed. A hard shudder traveled through his body as if he'd been zapped with electricity.

Abby stopped struggling. The deed was done. All that was left was to figure out just what that potion did.

"Step away from him," ordered the queen.

The demons backed up with slow cautious steps. Not even they looked sure what might happen.

Alrik's teeth clenched, gnashing together. His brow furrowed and grunts of pain sounded from between his teeth. He sounded like a rabid animal. Abby once heard a dog fight when she was a kid. Alrik sounded like that. Snarling and growling with aggression.

Then screams tore from his throat. Bone chilling screams. A sound she could never forget. His eyes popped open—black pools spiraling like water spinning down a drain.

"What are you doing to him!" screamed Abby.

It happened so quickly she had to blink to be sure.

He stopped moving. Completely stopped.

His dark swirling eyes gazed up at the sky unblinking and glassy. His body lay frozen like the dead. Only the subtle rise and fall of his chest gave away any sign of life.

"Alrik…"Abby said hesitantly. "Baby?" A piece of her heart broke off like a shard of glass.

"Alrik, Alrik," the queen mocked in a child-like voice.

"You bitch!" Abby lunged for the queen. The queen stumbled back a step before she threw a barrier between them with a flick of her wrist. Abby seethed but at least got some satisfaction at the fear in the queen's eyes.

"You want to know what I've done to him? Then I'll show you. Rise, Alrik."

Alrik slid to his feet. His body moved in a boneless way like a puppet being controlled. One second he was lying down unmoving and in the next moment he was standing perfectly at attention.

A trickle of unease slithered over Abby.

"Mistress," he said.

She must still have the effects of the spell Aidan's man put on her for she knew he just spoke in demonic and yet she'd understood his guttural, garbled words.

"Do you know who this woman is?" the queen asked him.

Alrik turned slowly to face her. He stood with his shoulders back, strong chest thrust forward, eyes seeing her without any recognition whatsoever. No love was there, no fear, worry, or panic, only passivity. As if he didn't know who she was.

"She is Abbigail Krenshaw. A human with skills in witchcraft." He paused his dark eyes blinked once. "There is part succubus blood inside her."

His mother "hmmed" and "ahhed" as he relayed the information. "Half succubus? That is interesting. Does that give her," she waved an agitated hand in the air, "any special skills I should know about?"

Alrik took a deep, lung-filling breath as if breathing her soul into his body. "Only longevity and the alluring beauty only found in succubi."

Now was so not the time to blush, yet Abby felt her cheeks flame anyway.

"Alrik, what's going on?" she said softly.

He didn't even look at her just gazed forward like a robot. Another chunk of her heart broke away and with it nearly tore a sob from her throat. Oh God, how did she fix this? How could she help him now?

He was gone. Completely gone. Not a sign of life in him.

The queen smiled with glee. Satisfaction gleamed in her eyes. "Isn't it beautiful? Let's see just how strong the spell is. I've used only the best ingredients for it. The freshest, most powerful of blood I could find…seer blood."

"Alrik, kill that demon." She pointed to one of the green, yellow-eyed monsters standing nearby.

The creature squawked and started shuffling around, unsure if she really meant it or not.

Alrik didn't hesitate. His body turned, eyes locked on the creature, and then he took four long steps that landed him directly in front of it. In two swift moves he acted. His big hands squeezed the demons head and then jerked it hard to the right. With repulsive snap, the body crumpled to the ground in a heap.

Abby swallowed but the knot in her throat wouldn't go away.

The queen clapped, laughing like a giddy child as she bounced on her feet. "Wonderful! Perfect! My ultimate creation! Now, kill her!"

"What?" Abby said, her stunned question unable to be contained. "Oh fuck, oh fuck, oh fuck!" she said getting louder and louder.

Alrik turned towards her with every tall demonic inch of him then strode for her with long determined steps.

"Alrik stop this!" she demanded trying to put some authority in her voice. That didn't sway him. The demon's holding her released her. She started backing up. "Baby, I love you! Don't do this!"

Demons stood in his path. Alrik kept walking straight for her, batting the demons away with sweeping arms if they were bugs. As he neared her, the demons holding her arms at her sides ran. Abby couldn't fault them for their fear because she spun around and ran.

§

The queen let her go. Abby figured it was probably a great power trip for her...to know that Alrik would follow her for however long it took until he killed her.

Abby ran hard, from him. As she did, she tried to think. She needed a spell that would negate the one controlling him.

His hard barreling steps boomed after her. Her lungs started burning as she ran up the hard slope. Her legs muscles burned, but she pushed through it. A foot slipped and she dropped to the ground, using her hands to grab chunks of grass and pull herself up.

Her heart raced in overtime. She could hear him just behind her. Something brushed her shoe— a hand? Fear and adrenaline moved her and she grabbed a hunk of grass over the top of the slope and launched herself over the side.

There was no time to waste for Alrik leaped over after her much smoother and faster than she did. Abby raced into the forest.

"Don't do this!" she called back to him. "You love me! I love you!"

No answer, only hard steps closing in on her. She jumped over fallen logs, raced through muddy grass, and ducked under low hanging branches that swiped across her face as she ran.

It was only a matter of time. She could never out run him. He was too big, too strong.

No sooner than she had that thought did he barrel into her. Surely, this is what it felt like to get hit by a truck, she thought.

Her breath wheezed out of her as her stomach collapsed into her spine as she went slamming to the ground, her head knocking against it so hard it struck twice. Her bones, everything, hurt from the fall. Her lungs seemed to take the brunt of the hit. It didn't help that he stayed on top of her, his weight keeping her from drawing in a deep breath.

"Alrik, don't do this," she begged. Her eyes watered. She didn't know whether from the pain of landing or the other pain trying to suffocate her.

Suddenly his body was off hers and she sucked in a long, much needed breath. Only he grabbed her by the shoulder and roughly flipped her over to her back.

"Ow!" she moaned as her head once against rocked back. She was going to be bruised black and blue if she made it out of this.

Footsteps sounded nearby. Abby peered behind Alrik to see the queen and her demons coming towards them. Of course she'd want to see him kill her.

Quickly, Abby sought his gaze only to find it bored and glossy as if no one was really there. "Baby, please don't do this. You have to help me. Please, I love you so much!" Her voice broke, but still she continued.

He sat over her waist, his hands holding her by the shoulders effectively pinning her down. The position was beyond uncomfortable but she managed to wriggle her hands up and touch his waist. For a second she thought she saw a flicker in his dark eyes, but she couldn't be sure.

"Alrik, listen to me. I can help you honey. Let me help you. Just get off me. I'll end the curse on you. I swear it."

"Kill her!" the queen ordered. She was now within twenty feet. The idummi swarmed around them, teeth bared in smiles. They bounced excitedly as they formed a circle around them. They were all ready for a show.

Big hands moved toward her and she acted on instinct. Abby lifted her hands and cast the very first spell he first taught her. Alrik went flying through the air as if jerked by a mighty force. His back slammed into a tree, cracking it down the middle. The tree groaned, shuddered, and then settled once more.

Alrik shook himself then started for her once more.

"Don't do this," she pleaded again.

He kept coming. She squared off against him.

"I don't want to hurt you!"

He stopped walking then charged for her. Abby couldn't move fast enough, not even to lift her hands use a spell.

Alrik reached her and deftly checked her body into a tree some fifteen feet or more behind her. He did this all with a hand at her throat, using his sheer strength to lift her feet from the ground and slam her spine against the tree. Her spine cracked at the pressure but she could still wriggle her legs so that gave her some relief—for a moment.

His grip on her throat tightened fast and hard. He meant business. He squeezed her throat, cutting off her air supply. Abby's hands flew to his wrist as she kicked him with every ounce of strength she had. When that didn't slow him down one bit, she dug her chin down and kept her neck taut— anything to keep her much needed air. Horrible, choking sounds came from her. She sounded...like someone having the life choked from them.

An unusual feeling came over her. Her vision tunneled, blood pounded loudly in her ears until it was all she could hear.

BOOM! BOOM! BOOM!

Alrik's face went in and out of focus like a camera zooming in and out. An intense pressure started filling her neck and eyes as if there was too much blood and it needed to escape.

He was going to kill her.

Abby used one last tactic. She swept her legs up until she could wrap them around his waist. Her gaze stayed as focused as she could on his face so she could watch for any signs of change in his eyes.

Something flickered in his gaze.

Hope sprung.

Her vision began darkening on the corners as a black fog crept in.

"I love you so much. Kiss me one...,"she gasped, "last...time..."

He blinked, his head tilting to the side. Then his grip loosened on her neck, not all the way but just enough for her to suck in a deep, ragged breath and for some of the fog to recede, and the pressure in her head to dissipate. His dark head leaned in and he pressed a chaste, soft kiss to her lips. Her breath caught.

Her eyes closed at the touch. Another part of her heart broke down. A sob escaped. She couldn't do this. She couldn't save him.

When he lifted his head, his face swam before hers. In a blink, her tears fell and his face cleared. In his eyes, she saw someone who was alert, fierce, and barely holding on.

His hold on her neck loosened to a feathery touch and then he thrust his hands in her hair. "Port home. Get out of here now!"

Then he pressed a hard kiss to her mouth and spun around. He stood protectively in front of her.

The queen bared her teeth. "Kill her I said!" she demanded.

Alrik's shoulders shook and he started to turn back around. She could see the battle in his body as he tried to fight the spell controlling.

Abby wanted to obey him, she really did. But, like hell she'd leave the love of her life to die down here alone.

Abby stepped around him, shot her hand out and then the fight really began.

Twenty-two

Pandemonium erupted.

Alrik fought the spell controlling him and lurched after the idummi. Horrible screams of death ripped through the air. The stale, bitter scent of blood filled Abby's nostrils like copper.

Abby had her target—the queen—and didn't let her out of her sight. Their gazes collided, ice versus fire.

Abby acted first.

Thrusting all of her power into it, she unleashed a fiery spell meant to burn and immobilize the queen simultaneously.

The queen swiped her hands in the air deflecting the spell. Abby tried again moving faster and pushing all of her power into it. The queen dodged it. She tried again and again only to have her spells deflected with ease.

The queen laughed as if this was all a game while sweat poured down Abby's face.

The idummi were dropping like dead flies around them from Alrik and his bare hands. But, there were still too many of them. Too much happened all at once. She just needed it to slow down for a minute so she could think.

The queen whispered in demonic calling forth dark powers so evil they made Alrik's icy magic look downright hot. Black smoke swirled out of the ground like tendrils of flame. Only this wasn't smoke.

Abby stepped back but the tendrils came for her, snapping at her like hands then they snaked around her ankles and wound up her legs. The tendrils squeezed tight like lengths of heavy rope. They solidified before her very eyes into something with mass, something heavy and strong like a hose. It latched on and yanked her sprawling forward.

Abby pitched to the ground. The tendrils were trying to squirm their way up to her hips. They'd encase her whole body if she didn't stop them.

Abby blasted the tendrils with a deteriorating spell and the tendrils withered away like dying flowers.

The queen glared at her, then looked around at her demons, most of which were dead, and raced back through the forest.

"Damn!" She really was a coward.

Abby ran after her with only one final glance at Alrik. He kept killing more and more idummi as they swarmed him. She trusted him to be well. She knew in her heart he'd overcome whatever they dished out. After all, she'd seen him fight against a band of rogue demons and those were trained fighters.

The queen raced back towards her swampy camp, her red gown a blur of bloody color in the green hued marsh.

Abby's heart drummed a thumping beat in her ears. Her breathing sawed from her throat and her neck hurt like a SOB. Each time she swallowed, heck, even just breathed with her mouth open it created aching sensations in her neck like the worst-case scenario of strep throat.

Abby reached the top of the slope that lead down into the marshy swamp and paused.

The queen was screaming in hysterics.

Idummi were leaving by the scores. What had been probably hundreds of demons had dwindled down to less than one hundred, if that.

Abby slowly made her way down the slope. This would end one way or another. Just between her and the queen.

The queen screamed in frustration. "AAGH! You won't leave me," she said darkly.

Her arms thrust out from her body, hands curling into fists she turned them as if she was ripping someone's heart out of their chest. The large crowd in front of her screeched in pain, their bodies jerking, and chests thrusting forward as if they were having their hearts torn from them. They collapsed to the ground shuddering. Dark green blood trickled from their mouths.

Abby could barely stand to watch.

The rest of the idummi stood watching the show with increased apprehension and fear. Several of them had curved knives at their waist and some even had swords at their hips or across their backs. Several started to step towards the queen's back. Abby stilled to watch. She cheered in her head.

Yes! Kill her! KILL HER!

The demons on the ground finally stopped screaming. Their bodies shuddered in the aftermath of death before freezing in the last position they'd ever be in.

The queen sucked in ragged breaths. Her hair no longer held the immaculate design it'd been in. The colored threads had come loose. The braid, if one could still call it that, was frazzled and fuzzy around her shoulders as if she'd been rolling around the ground. Her dress had torn at the sleeves probably from running through the forest with those low hanging branches snagging her. Green blood had splattered over the very bottom of her dress, ruining the fur trim.

Abby waited. The rest of the demons around her paced agitated, snarling. She could see their visible indecision. She prayed quickly to whoever might listen to her.

Let them kill her. Please let them kill her!

The queen turned around in a slow whirl with her shoulders held so rigidly that the muscles in her neck flexed to reveal a stark collarbone. She bared her teeth in a snarl as if ready to bite. With her arms held out straight from her body, she looked as if one little thing might set her off...only Abby didn't want to find out what she'd do once that happened.

"Kill him! Kill the girl! Kill them all!" ordered the queen.

Damn. Abby moved fast and ducked behind a boulder jutting out from the slope. Plastering her back against it, she waited straining to hear any footsteps. There was no time to waste. The idummi stormed back up the slope just a few paces behind the rock. Abby squeezed her eyes shut at the sound of the demon's howling war cry. They were revving themselves up for battle. The thought made her shake. Flattened her back up against the rock, she ignored the sharp points of it jabbing into her spine and back and hoped like hell they didn't spot her.

She had to act now. There were too many of them. Not even Alrik could take on that many demons.

She had no idea what she was doing. She shook down to her bones with a heavy cold as if she wore clothes that had been snowed on. Standing, she saw the demons had left and started for the queen.

The queen muttered to herself in soft Demonic whispers that Abby couldn't understand. She hovered near the black cauldron that hung over the fire then snatched a leather satchel off the ground and tossed chucks of herbs into it.

Abby didn't give her any sign that she crept up behind her. She just acted. Keeping her steps light she ran up on the queen.

Then with a hard jerk, Abby slammed her hands out in front of her using every fiery cell of magic inside her as if shoving someone. And she was in a way.

Abby's magic propelled the queen headfirst in a horrifying scene. With a bloodcurdling scream, the queen flew into the mighty fire. Abby's heart roared in her ears. The queen's terrible screams pierced something inside her, shocking her so all she could do was stand there and watch.

The red gown went up in flames. Her body rolled and jerked in the white-hot logs as if she fought to get away but couldn't. Flames licked at her hair and skin burning it away in sizzling, burning clumps.

Abby fell to her knees. She'd been shaking before but now she really shook. Her teeth chattered, arms trembled, and her stomach bobbed. It took everything in her not to keel over and vomit at that very moment.

Her stomach gave a vicious roll again, this one even harder as the smell of burning flesh filled her nose, and Abby couldn't hold it any longer. She doubled over and wretched as her entire body convulsed. Burning acid coated her tongue and stung her throat. After three heaves, she simply knelt there gasping like a fish out of water.

She'd done it. She'd done something so appallingly immoral. She'd really killed another person. Her stomach lurched again, but she tightened her throat to keep any more bile from rising. The action might have kept her stomach slightly in control but it did nothing to ease the pain around her neck from where she'd been choked.

Slowly she caught her breath and sat back.

Several things seemed to happen all at once.

What she saw sent an all new wave of fear through her while in the distance she heard mighty roars. Not a roar she'd heard before, but a different one. She heard not just Alrik's voice but also others.

Had Aidan and his men come? She could almost sigh with relief at the thought. They could help him fight back the horde of idummi. Yes, that had to be what she heard. Those were not the war cries of the idummi and certainly not of her Alrik. The rogues had come to help.

Then none of those sounds of war taking place atop and beyond the slope really registered in her mind. They were all thoughts rushed to the back of her mind.

She couldn't think of it any more.

Because in that moment, the queen was climbing out of the fire pit on her stomach. Her body moved at a twitchy, irregular pace. Her skin was charred black, her clothes burnt to ashen tatters across her enflamed body. Her hair...had been burnt off leaving a bloodied and darkened scalp where the flames had destroyed it. Yet she moved placing one elbow into the grass and tugging her body along as her legs dragged behind her as if she couldn't move them.

She alternated elbows until her entire body was out of the pit. Smoke clung to her body and drifted up from her like a smoking corpse. Yet she wasn't a corpse.

"Siradu shika gh'daburem!"

The demonic words registered in her mind. Abby didn't have time to try to understand the words because just then the demonic spell entered her body like a bomb and tore her insides to shreds.

"AAAH!" Her piercing screams tore through the night.

The spell...whatever it was...the queen had put something evil inside her. Agony engulfed her. She clenched her gut as she fell to the side curling into the fetal position. Right before she squeezed her eyes shut she saw the queen ever so slowly crawling towards her, one unsteady tug at a time.

The pain was the most intense feeling she'd ever felt. Like hot acid being poured inside of her. It kept filling her chest cavity and when that wasn't enough, she felt the molten-hot sensation pour into one leg then another. She just knew that if she sliced open her thigh right now some awful black tar substance would pour out.

Something was happening to her. She couldn't control herself anymore. Her body shook in violent seizures. No matter how many times she told herself to keep her eyes open and do something—she couldn't. Pain overtook her. She couldn't move, not even to save her life.

That rib-crushing, skin-squeezing pain covered her everywhere spreading like lava until it enveloped her in darkness.

She stopped being aware of much of anything then.

She could no longer hear the sounds of war taking place with Alrik. Was he dead? Were they all dead? Maybe that's why she couldn't hear anything.

No, that couldn't be right because she couldn't hear the crackling of the fire either or her own breathing. As she strained to hear, a soft high-pitched ringing started in her left ear. Her head twitched at the sound or at least she thought it did.

Were her eyes open? All she saw was black. Black nothingness.

Maybe this was death. Maybe she'd finally died. No!

Her body jolted, this time she knew she'd actually jerked because she felt her heart jump too.

She needed to find Alrik. He needed her help. She had to finish this.

She struggled to become aware, to come back to consciousness. She felt her body swimming as if floating listlessly beneath the surface. She swam towards that surface, each swipe of her arm through the murky area around her like trying to move through molasses. Finally something gave. Like a bubble bursting. She broke through.

Then, her eyes opened.

A gnarled creature glared in her face.

No, not a creature. The queen. Or, what was left of her.

Her face, colored in black ash and rosy burns grinned like a wild beast above her. Only the whites of her eyes and teeth could be seen among the fleshy red welts of the burns. In some places along her skull where there'd once been glorious hair, skin had melted to reveal the hot red layers of fresh skin beneath.

The queen held Abby by her shirt.

Abby screamed at the sight. Then she reacted and sent her fist fly up. She caught the queen's chin with a satisfying crunch of bone.

The queen fell off her and Abby moved. The spell the queen had casted on her hadn't lingered any longer. The intense pain had faded but she still felt weak as a kitten and feeble. Each motion felt sloppy. Even her punch felt like she couldn't have hurt a baby. Nevertheless, this was her last chance and Abby wouldn't fail. Not for her Alrik.

She and the queen rolled. Abby landed another punch square across her jaw. The queen's skin was still hot and the warm, gooey texture of her flesh made her skin crawl.

The queen's hand, now nothing more than skeletal bones and raw tendons, climbed over Abby's face. The warm sticky feeling nearly made her vomit but she held her gut in check.

Still the queen managed to grab a fistful of her hair and pull—hard. Abby grunted through the hair-tearing pain as she reached up to dislodge the hand.

She grabbed hold of the queen's burned, gnarled hand and yanked her fingers backward, hard. The queen exhaled a garbled shout of pain.

Abby heard a sound so lovely then she could have wept tears of joy.

"Abbigail!"

Never would she have thought that hearing him yell her name could make her smile.

She looked to the side and saw such a beautiful sight she lost sight of what she was doing.

Alrik came rapidly down the slope, Aidan and the rogue demons following behind him. He looked battle worn, but so strong and stunning.

I love you, she thought.

She made a mistake. One she didn't realize for all of the three seconds it'd taken her to turn her head and look up at him. That's okay it was worth it.

A blade slid into her chest so near to her heart. Her eyes, still locked on Alrik's face, flared in surprise. His dark eyes flashed then he roared and charged forward.

Abby looked down to see a knife sticking out from her chest. Blood oozed from the wound. Why was she so slow to act? She should be moving, acting now. Doing something. But what?

The queen's distorted face smiled up at her. "I win," she hissed.

Abby jerked at her words. Pain started numbing her like icy water filling her veins. "No you don't."

Abby pulled the blade from her own chest. It took her two tries for her strength was fading fast, and the skin of her chest caught the blade as if it didn't want to let it go. Finally, it came free. She palmed it in two blood-covered hands and stared into the evil eyes of the person who'd started this all.

"He wins," Abby said.

Then she slammed the blade into the queen's neck. The amount of blood that spurted from the wound almost seemed fake like something you'd seen in a horror movie. But this wasn't a movie and she'd really just shoved a dagger into another person's neck. Well, she'd also nearly burned the demon bitch too, so. Whatever.

Abby fell off the queen. She hadn't meant to but she had no control over her body. With each breath she took, more blood seemed to gurgle from her chest with a wet plopping sound.

Alrik's face swam before her. She smiled and reached for him. He grabbed her bloodied hand and ran a calming hand over her hair. A sigh escaped her it felt so nice. Whatever spell the queen had made him drink was gone. He had returned to his normal self.

"What have you done?" he asked in a hoarse voice.

She started to speak but was surprised to find she had to swallow a few times first. Her tongue felt heavy and dry. She needed some water. "I beat her. I killed her. Right?" God, she'd better be dead. Abby didn't know how many more times she could kill her.

Alrik leaned over her. It wasn't until that moment that she realized how cold she was. A shiver passed over her. His cheek pressed against hers, and then he kissed her. Even his cheek felt burning hot. She tried to purse her lips to kiss him back but couldn't.

"Yes, you killed her." Why did he sound so funny?

"What's...wrong?" She had to swallow again. Damn, her throat really hurt. After she felt better, she was going to really live in to him for choking her.

Her head rolled to the side but she didn't remember doing so.

Something was wrong.

It didn't dawn on her until then.

It really hadn't. She'd been so overjoyed to see him again—alive and strong.

So what the seer said was true. She would die. She actually was going to die now. Tears filled her eyes and spilled down her temples.

I don't want to die.

A sob climbed up her throat but she held it back.

Both of his hands covered her cheeks as he kissed her again. "I love you so much," he said, his eyes closed and his voice breaking.

He repositioned her so she lay in his lap. She sighed. This new position felt nice—much warmer and she got to be closer to him. His hand slid over her wound and she winced. Yeah, it hurt. He pressed hard to it.

"Why did you do it?" he croaked.

She hadn't been sure the first time she heard it, but yes, they were both crying. Abby tilted her face so she could see his eyes. She had to smile even though she could see his heart breaking in his eyes, could see the tears sliding down his face. She'd done that. She'd inadvertently hurt him when all she wanted to do was save him.

"Because," she gulped, her air supply growing shorter and the heavy feeling growing in her limbs getting worse, "I love you so much."

He pressed his forehead against hers. "You shouldn't have done it. You shouldn't have." He kept saying it over and over again.

It was the last thing she ever heard.

THE FALLEN KING

Twenty-three

He felt the life leave her body.

He could actually feel it as if her soul just walked out.

"Abbigail."

He shook her. Her eyes stared somewhere off the point of his shoulder.

"Sweetheart wake up." His voice broke. "Wake up, dammit!"

She didn't blink. Her chest refused to rise and fall again.

No, no, no. This couldn't be happening again. This couldn't happen again. NO!

"Somebody help me!" he shouted.

He set her body on the grass. His eyes caught sight of the dead carcass of his mother, and he shoved out his arm to push her away from his beloved.

He covered her wound with his hand and searched his memory for something. This couldn't be the end. There had to be a way.

Footsteps neared.

It was Aidan and his men. They looked solemn, their eyes heavy with sorrow. "Where's your healer?" demanded Alrik.

A man came forward to kneel beside her. He checked the wound and pressed his fingers to her neck but said as he'd expected.

"She's already passed on, my king."

The last of the words he ignored. He didn't give a shit if they respected him now. "You have to do something. Anything. Any spell any amount of power, name it and I'll do it."

He kept hold of her hand, kept squeezing it, but she wouldn't squeeze it back. His chest squeezed so hard it was a wonder his heart didn't start bleeding from the pressure. Tears kept coming. Why did she have to look so pale?

"My king, there is nothing you can do. She has gone from us. Let us bury her."

"NO!" he shouted. He wouldn't give up. He would figure out a way. His eyes swept over her face. "Give me a wet rag someone. Now!"

Within a few seconds, a demon pushed one at his face. He grabbed it started cleaning her face. She was so beautiful even in death, but blood marred her skin. He cleaned every spec of dirt and filth from her face and then started on her neck as his mind worked slowly, numbly. He couldn't contain his flinch at the horrible bruises covering her neck. From him!

Aidan stepped forward as he set to cleaning her hands. Dirt and blood had caked under her nails. That pain in his chest intensified. He'd done this to her. He'd taken her from her home and gotten her killed. And for what? His mother wasn't worth her life. She wasn't even worth a single hair off Abbigail's head.

"What have I done?" he whispered, squeezing her hand. He pressed it to his lips and kissed them as his eyes clamped shut. "Oh God, what have I done?"

Aidan stepped near him but didn't touch him. A good thing, he didn't know what he might do if someone laid a hand on him right now. Alrik kissed the palm of her hand and started cleaning the other.

"None of us have any spells to fix her. There are no herbs to push away death. Very few have such a white power to bring back the dead," Aidan said. He was speaking slowly. He'd cared for his Abbigail even in the short amount of time he'd spent with her. Alrik couldn't even blame him; she had that effect on people. He'd learned that first hand. "I've known very few who had that power... One is dead at my feet." He kicked the dead queen. "The other is alive before me."

Alrik nearly stopped breathing.

"But I can't heal anymore. The curse took that away from me before." Besides, he'd never actually done it. He knew it could be done in his bloodline.

He knew his brother could do it, had even seen him do it. His mother and even seen his father had the healing powers in their blood. But the curse had taken his white magic from him. "Look at me. I can't. Don't you think I'd save her if I could?"

A small smile lifted the corner of Aidan's mouth. "I think you need to look at yourself one last time. You might just be surprised."

A low tremble started in his gut then worked its way out. He knew what his words meant, but could it really be possible?

"Bring him a mirror," said Aidan.

The men talked amongst themselves and realized they didn't have one. So, someone brought forth his double-bladed axe. The steel was sharp and the fire reflected off it.

"Are you ready?" the demon asked.

No, he wasn't. He couldn't nod, couldn't even shake his head. He just sat there holding Abbigail's steadily cooling hand.

The demon shrugged then lifted his axe to face Alrik.

Alrik looked at his oblong reflection marked with specs of drying blood and at a face he hadn't seen in a thousand years.

Gold skin covered his face and neck. Bright violet eyes stared back at him as if he was looking into the face of a stranger. Brown hair with a good dose of red fell around his face in a wild array.

He kept hold of her hand but used his free on to touch his cheeks as if to make sure the reflection he saw matched up with him.

"It's real," he breathed.

"Yes, it is. You are cured," Aidan said.

He looked away. He was cured, but what for? What did it matter now? He'd lost the love of his life. He had no one to share this with. A hollow shell sat inside him as if he'd been carved out into a shell. He was nothing without her.

"Just because I look as I did before doesn't mean I'll have the powers as I did before."

Before...before he'd changed. When his powers hadn't been of rage and ice but of good things too.

"True," Aidan agreed. "But you could still try."

Yes, yes he would. Of course he would because if she died then he'd die with her.

Alrik tried to remember how to call forth healing magic.

He set his hands over her chest and closed his eyes.

He thought of closing her wound, of seeing her eyes blink, and hearing her heart beat. He let the thoughts course through him like blood until it was all he thought or felt. His hands started to warm and he focused harder and put all of his energy into it.

Hope sprung. He could do this.

Breathing ragged, sweat poured from his brow and still nothing happened. He sat back and wiped the sweat away. The demons and vampire watched him with a various mixture of grimaces on their faces.

"What?" Alrik asked at their strange looks.

Aidan looked uncomfortable. "It's been nearly half an hour and nothing's happened, Alrik. Why don't we just bury her and let us mourn?"

Thirty minutes? Impossible. It hadn't felt that long at all. Yet his muscles felt strained and tired in a way they hadn't before.

His gaze swept over Abbigail's cooling body and something fierce and raw came over him—a steely resolve.

"No, I'm going to do this. I can do this." Alrik leaned back over her as he placed his hands on her chest. He winced as he spotted the deep bruising on her neck. Disgust filled him. He didn't deserve her, but if she forgave him after he brought her back, then he'd grovel to her for the rest of his life.

Closing his eyes, he concentrated. He focused on the healing powers that existed in his blood. He called it forth as if beckoning a small hurt animal. His skin warmed. His mind rested in a place where time didn't exist. All that existed, all that mattered was Abbigail's bloody wound beneath his hands.

The heat grew. His muscles flexed and twitched as he physically forced the healing magic up and out of him. Ragged breaths tore from his burning throat. His arms shook as if he was holding up a building to keep it from collapsing. Even his head felt about to burst as if too much air filled it.

I'll bring her back. I'll bring her back, he chanted.

His blood started to boil. So much heat filled him he swore he breathed steam.

Then a blinding light covered him like rays of sunlight on bare skin. It was so hot it hurt him from its burn but he gritted his teeth and pushed through it.

I will bring her back. I will bring her back!

The light shifted its beacon to shine on Abbigail. In his magical eye, he could see the beautiful white light encase her body. At the center of her chest where his hands were he saw a glowing orange light emit from his hands as if they were on fire.

That light swirled around his hands slowly at first, then moving faster and faster. Alrik shook above her like a weak little flower in a mighty storm. His muscles convulsed with pain. Burning agony filled him in every inch of his body. He just wanted it to end or for it to kill him. Anything for it to be over. He'd never felt anything so intense before.

Just as he was considering letting go, of quitting, the spiraling orange glow shot inside of Abbigail's body.

His heart surged as if unchained from a heavy weight.

Her chest lurched up as if she'd been shocked by a great power. Then it snapped up again. And again.

A long ragged hiss of air sounded. He could almost see through her body to where her lungs expanded with air and then released it. His ears picked up on the most glorious sound of all.

Bum bum. Bum bum.

The beat grew faster and faster and then steadied out to a lovely cadence.

Her back arched deeply as her arms jerked and twitched.

"Huuuuuungh!" she gasped as her lungs filled with air.

"Yes, my love. Come back to me please," he begged raggedly.

Finally, she blinked. The blinding light started to fade as did the orange glow from his hands. Her chest rose and fell.

His arms still shook. He was terrified to lift his hands. What if it all stopped? What if when he took his hands away and she went back to that dead, spiritless woman she had been?

Her head moved and her gaze met his. Real shining eyes not glassy ones from death. His breath caught in his burning throat.

He let his hands move up to cup her face. Life didn't leave her. She was really alive, breathing, and gazing up at him softly.

Her eyes searched over his face. A small smile turned up the corners of her lips.

"You're beautiful," she said. Her voice sounded torn and ragged.

It was the loveliest thing he'd ever heard. Something he thought he'd never hear again.

"I love you, Abbigail Krenshaw. I won't let you go that easily." He kissed her, this time feeling her kiss him back. Another dark chain released from around his heart, freeing him.

Pulling back from the kiss, he pressed his forehead to hers. "You are mine now. There is no going back."

She tugged on a lock of his hair weakly and whispered, "As if I'd want to. Now why don't you take me home?"

Gently he lifted her into his arms. When he turned he stopped because all the demons stared at him with wonder in their eyes. Even Aidan's eyes held respect in them.

Slowly the vampire knelt on one knee and the others follow suit.

"Hail the fallen king!" Aidan said, his voice commanding.

His men followed suit. "All hail the fallen king!"

Alrik stood straighter. Another strange feeling came over him. One he hadn't felt in a long time— respect. Respect that he'd earned. As any true king would, he held his chin up high and nodded once in thanks.

The demons grinned up at him, even Aidan smiled though his was somewhat sadder.

Abbigail curled an arm around his shoulders and waved back to the group. "Bye everyone."

Alrik used the last of his strength and magic and ported them home.

Twenty-four

A few days later

Abby fidgeted like a kid who'd just stolen a cookie behind his mom's back. It was the nerves, they were driving her straight up the wall. But, what could she do about it? Nothing, she just had to deal. Ha, yeah. Deal. Today was only one of the biggest days of her life. She was being mated to Alrik by his brother Telal and she was meeting her half-sisters Chloe, Willow, and Lily for the first time.

They were all going to be there. Of course her mom would be there too. She'd already talked with her. Sure it'd taken a lot of explaining as to where she was, what all had happened, and why she was getting married. Yeah, that'd been a long story.

Abby started to breathe hard.

"Slow down. Just breathe in and out," she told herself.

It didn't help. She sat on her old bed, and put her face between her knees.

Maybe meeting her family so soon wasn't such a good idea after all. And where was Alrik? He was supposed to be back already. He had to go back to his old castle to make "arrangements" for the ceremony. Now that the curse had been broken, he and his brother seemed to be making amends.

Everything would be fine. She had healed up well, and Alrik had healed up gorgeously. The man had been sexy before but now she'd have to beat women away.

Suddenly the energy changed in the room as if all the atoms came together in one spot then exploded. Alrik stood in her living room looking wonderful and alive. She still had a difficult time adjusting to the golden skin, auburn hair, and violet eyes but she had no complaints. He looked so...angelic now. Okay, maybe that was exaggerating it a bit. He looked like a rugged good demon now and not one bent on world domination.

His eyes caught hers and she raced down the hallway and jumped into his arms. He caught her easily.

His mouth narrowed in and landed on hers. The kiss quickly swept her up. It was eager, wet, and a bit heady. She wrapped her arms around him and kissed him back with just as much energy. It felt like they hadn't been together in forever even though he'd left a few hours.

They'd both been recovering their energy for the better part of a week and neither had been able to be physically intimate, but now her blood spiked with arousal.

Apparently so did his because his tongue parted her lips with a sexy sweep and then dipped inside to lick her up. A ragged moan left her at the touch, and her hips rocked in response. He tasted delicious and felt so warm in her arms.

Yes, her body told her.

Strong hands walked down her spine to cup her ass. He held her like that with his hands kneading her through her jersey skirt as he walked with her. She didn't care where he took her. She trusted him.

"I want you," she whispered against his lips.

He tore his mouth away, his hot gaze colliding with hers. "We're supposed to meet them for the ceremony in less than an hour." He sounded pissed as if he wished he had hours with her instead. She had to agree.

Still…

She pressed her breasts against his chest. "An hour is more than enough time for us to both come…"

His hands clenched on her ass. She loved that little things she did could get some sort of a reaction out of him. His lungs expanded hard as he sucked in a sharp breath and then his mouth slammed down to hers.

Oh, yeeees!

Then they were walking backwards. Abby tightened her legs around his hips until her core lined up perfectly with the hard ridge tenting his pants. She rubbed herself against him and moaned. He rubbed her just right.

"Fuck," he cursed.

Her back hit the wall in the hallway as if he couldn't possibly make it all the way into the bedroom.

Hot lips and wet tongue kissed a path down her neck. An erotic shiver coursed through her body, pulling her nipples into hard points, making her sex dampen.

"I swear you wear these clothes just to torment me." He tugged the strap of her spaghetti strap tank to the side then kissed over her shoulder, across her collarbone and worked his way down to her breast.

"It's just a tank and skirt," she panted. Where they were going to celebrate, it was supposed to be warm.

His hands slid under her skirt. His touch burned the back of her thighs as his fingers curled around her. With a hard tug, he spread her legs even further then thrust his hips up into her, rocking his hard cock against her. The jersey cotton of the skirt and her scrap of satin panties did absolutely nothing to stop her from feeling every hard inch of him and she thanked God for small wonders.

"Hold on to me," he ordered.

She obeyed in an instant, ready to do anything so long as he continued to touch her. Her body was his to command, and he did so expertly.

Abby crossed her arms over his shoulders and held tight as he pushed her harder into the wall and braced her there so his hands could run free. He touched her everywhere. Long, strong fingers plumped and squeezed her ass, then ran a smoothing caress up her spine then back down. He ran circles over her hips, squeezed the curve of her waist where it met her hip. He touched her everywhere but where she wanted him.

Her mouth found his neck and sucked his warm skin into her mouth. "Alrik, hurry." She arched her hips against him purposely sliding along his cock. Blazing need burned inside of her. She needed to be filled by him to feel him filling her in only ways he could.

A growl left him from deep in his chest. The sound tickled her nipples.

"It's going to be hard," he growled.

Her head fell back against the wall. "Oh thank God."

He chuckled as his chin pushed down her top so her breast popped free and then his wet tongue circled her, and his teeth tugged. Each touch seemed to be directly tied to her clitoris and he knew it. Each little tug and pull felt like a seductive caress circling her wet bud.

His mouth opened wide and then he took her whole nipple into his mouth, sucking hard.

Hands moved between her thighs. Her breath caught in anticipation. Every muscle tightened in anticipation. She heard the hiss of his zipper and squirmed.

All the while, his cheeks hollowed as he sucked her nipple with that rough tongue, pulled on it with his soft lips. Her hands flew into his glorious hair to hold on.

"Yeees," she whispered raggedly.

Finally, what felt like forever later, his hands cupped her hips. She eagerly snaked her legs around his now naked hips. Her undulating hips found his hard cock poised and ready for her, but just as she pushed against him, his hands tightened on her to keep her still. The damn satin of her panties blocked her from what she wanted. If she had to get creative to get him inside her then she would.

Abruptly, he released her nipple then gave her a wet, hungry kiss. They both breathed hard after that. He pulled back and her eyes were slow to open. Her mind felt dazed like she'd spun around really fast in a circle and was about to fall down. When she opened her eyes his violet ones stared at her with so much passion and love her heart skipped a beat.

"I love you, Abbigail."

"I love you, too."

Her voice broke as he grabbed her undies in a fist and tore them from her body. Then he drove into her.

He did exactly as he said he would. He took her hard. He was unforgiving in his powerful thrusts. Abby could only hold on to him as he took her higher and higher. His hard cock filled her over and again bumping and rubbing over parts of her that made her wild.

Their lips met and fought, tongues lashing. She loved it. She loved everything about it. From how his hands cupped her ass so tight, from the raw hunger shining in his eyes, to the uncontrollable way he took her that just screamed: I can't get enough of you.

"One right now," he said, his voice ragged as sandpaper.

Then he ducked to pull her nipple back into his mouth.

That was it. Her entire body started to tighten. The warmth started inside of her where his cock worked her then pulsed outward on one heaving wave as she shattered.

He plunged into her as she fell apart in his arms, shaking and trembling. He tore his mouth from her nipple. "So fucking hot," he growled.

Then he slammed his mouth back to hers and pressed his fingers between her legs. She jerked.

"Alrik," she moaned as an all new warmth grew inside her. He rubbed his fingers across her bud in slow but sure circles working her up as his hips slammed into her, shoving her back into the wall.

"I want another one."

Her hands curled into his hair as her sex pulsed at his words. It was as if her pussy and his words were connected. He said something hot and then she responded in kind.

"Anything for you."

His sexy mouth curved up into a grin. "Yeah, anything for me baby."

Then he got serious between her legs and made her scream his name as she came. Only after she finished trembling in his arms did he thrust hard four more times, plant himself deep, and then jet inside of her.

"Don't set me down, I can't walk yet," she mumbled against his shoulder.

His belly deep laughter sent her into a fit of giggles and then he kissed her.

§

They couldn't stop smiling at each other like a bunch of love drunk fools.

"Are you ready then?" he asked.

"As I'll ever be."

He grabbed her hand, pulled her into his arms, and pressed his lips to hers. As he did, she felt the world shift and move as he ported them.

When she opened her eyes, they stood on a beach made of fine white sand. He'd asked her where she wanted to be mated at and all she could think of was the beach. Just like the beach where they'd spent their few days at, but with one stipulation. This beach had to be beautiful and hot.

She smiled up at him, unable to contain her excitement even as nerves ate at her stomach. Soon she'd meet her half-sisters and his brother and she'd be Mrs. Demuzi.

The water was such a light shade of blue it was nearly clear. The sky above mirrored the color with only a few puffy, cottony clouds in the sky.

"It's perfect."

His shoulders sagged. "Thank God."

She laughed. "You were nervous?"

"As hell. I had to hope you'd like this."

As if she wouldn't be happy being mated with him nearly anywhere. She just wanted to be attached to him permanently forever and ever.

Just then, people started porting in.

A pretty brunette accompanied by a tall, imposing man with long black hair pulled back from his face came first. Her belly looked rounded with child. A man with short wavy hair, definitely a demon, stepped back from them. Only demons could port like that, or a witch with enough power, or a good spell and a solid location. It looked as though her sister had her very own demon 'porter'.

A stunningly beautiful blonde woman carrying a toddler in her arms ported in next with two men. One, she could tell was a demon because he had long silvery hair, a straight aristocratic nose, and playful eyes.

"Thanks, Draven," she said to him. He nodded, grinning.

"Any time I get to touch you is a good time."

The woman rolled her eyes and the big man at her side growled. Abby's eyes popped wide. That was a real animal's growl. The man was a shapeshifter, she realized, and judging by the size of him, he had to be an alpha.

"I don't think your mate would like to hear about that," the woman retorted.

The demon named Draven winced. "Just a bit of teasing. Sorry, love, but no one actually stirs me like she does."

Another couple ported in this time with no backup demon because the demon was attached to the petite woman with an arm around her waist and his tongue deep in her mouth. Abby sucked in a breath. The resemblance between him and Alrik was unmistakable. Well, except for the fact that he had beautiful cerulean blue hair and she had yet to see his eyes. But, his skin was that glorious golden color. The woman in his arms moaned softly then popped her eyes opened and they darted right at Abby.

A blush colored her cheeks and then she pushed at who had to be Telal until he groaned and let her go. "Later," he whispered in promise.

According to Alrik, Lily was the youngest of the Bellum sisters and was mated to his brother Telal. Lily had a quick, happy smile on her face and a gorgeous pair of green eyes. Everyone came forward and behind the group, Abby watched her mom port in looking wobbly. She must have done it from a spell. Her mom spotted her and gave an excited wave. Abby couldn't fight her excited grin and waved back.

Introductions were made all around.

Lily and Telal came up first. Abby held out her hand but Lily pushed it away and pulled her into a hard hug. "Sister," she said.

Abby hugged her back, hesitantly. "It's nice to meet you."

Lily curled an arm around her shoulder and turned her to face the others. "It's our sister," she said like a judge who just banged the gavel making a judgment.

The two women, Chloe and Willow, eyed her suspiciously. "She does look like us," ceded the brown-haired one. "I'm Chloe by the way and this is my mate Tyrian. He's all vampire," she said like she won some great prize. The tall man started shaking his head. He looked strong like a warrior but held a command to his presence, and a wicked scar ran down the side of his cheek. Abby wouldn't be surprised if this vampire led an army.

The blonde woman narrowed her eyes. "I don't know..."

The strong, tanned, very good-looking shapeshifter at her side rested his hand at the back of her neck. A dominant touch. "Play nice, baby." He looked like he was trying not to smile.

The woman rolled her eyes. "Fine she looks just like us. I'm Willow. I'd shake your hand but as you can see, Mary's taking them up."

The little bundle in her arms was named Mary after their mother. Abby didn't need anyone to explain that to her. She'd already learned all about that from Alrik. Mary had been imprisoned in the demon's dungeon for some twenty years and had missed out on her daughters being raised. Of course, if that hadn't happened then Francis wouldn't have met her mother and Abby wouldn't be here. Naturally, Mary didn't exactly want to be here for this, she was still adjusting to normal life again after being rescued by her daughters.

Alrik was ate up over it. Over a lot of stuff really. But that was his past, and Abby firmly believed it wasn't his fault. It was the curse. They'd get through all the rough patches up the road together.

"Give her to me," the big man at her side said. Willow passed the baby to him and he held it as if he did that sort of thing all the time. He didn't look like the baby type, but he totally was. The man saw her gaze and smiled. He had a big smile, the kind that left you smiling back. "We're trying for another one. I'm Lyonis by the way."

"Abbigail Krenshaw."

"Soon to be Demuzi," Alrik corrected.

"Speaking of, shall we get this mating ritual started?" Telal said. He had a pleasant very deep voice.

"Yes!" Lily jumped in and started dragging her away. The other ladies followed as they broke away from the men and headed down the other side of the beach. "We'll be back!"

Abby tossed one last, panicked look over her shoulder at Alrik. He was smiling at her. A wicked smile that curled her down to her toes. She was really doing this. She was really going to be mated.

She was taken into the forest and undressed in a circle of red and white candles. They said it was for "purifying and love."

They were getting married in a demonic ceremony. That meant that her hands and feet were painted with a special tool called a lathu in special symbols and works. The paint was the color of chocolate. One sister held the bowl while Lily used the lathu to paint Abby's feat.

A breathtaking pattern of leaves and trees were painted from her toes up across her feet. It wasn't permanent though it was so beautiful she wouldn't mind it being so.

The intricate design worked up her foot then around her ankles. Small spirals came off the stems of the design. Intermixed with the leaves and open flowers in bloom were demonic words of love, bonding, and mating. After her hands were also done in the flowering design, she was dressed in a black gauzy dress that kept her arms and below her knees bare. She was told this ritual would be done barefoot.

Nerves fluttered around in her belly like butterflies.

Before she knew it, she was lead back to him. He stood all the way on the other side of the beach. She wished he was closer she didn't like having all these eyes on her. He looked amazing.

He'd changed.

Now he wore only a pair of fitted black trousers that stopped short of the knee and nothing else. All that beautiful golden skin was bared for the world to see. He didn't smile but wore a strong expression—that of a warrior being given his woman. His hands and feet were painted in the same design of leaves, vines, and words.

Finally, his hand was in hers. She wanted to say something, wanted him to say anything but they both stayed quiet as the ceremony started. Everyone took a seat in the sand behind them, except for Telal who stood before them to perform the ceremony.

Abby squeezed Alrik's hand and he squeezed it back, even harder. The nerves in her stomach abated at his touch and then she let out a deep breath. When she glanced back up at him, she saw a small smile playing at the corner of his mouth and she smiled back.

The ceremony took place in Demonish. Telal spoke of love and trust of faithfulness always. They were tender words. Words meant to be only spoken to one other person once in a lifetime.

Finally, Telal nodded to Alrik.

Then Alrik spoke. "I vow to always love you from now until the end of my days. Let these designs be a symbol of the ties that bind us together, of growth created out of trust, anger, friendship, and love. May these ties never break even after the paint washes away. May our love never sway against strife but grow stronger, and may they tie us closer for the rest of our days."

Tears fell from her eyes. When it came time for her to repeat the words, she fumbled over them until a fierce blush covered her cheeks. It was okay because he smiled down at her as if he couldn't be prouder.

Finally, she ended her part and her face was wet from tears and her cheeks bright red. "And may they tie us closer for the rest of our days."

Their little gathering stood and cheered. Alrik pulled her into his arms and gave her a kiss she would never forget. Not for the rest of her days.

"I love you, Alrik," she said against his lips.

His arms squeezed her. "And I love you, Abbigail Demuzi."

They clasped their painted hands together and started their life anew.

Read on for a preview of

Take Me
The Untouchables #1

Coming in January 2013
A paranormal erotic romance series

Dominic Blackmoore's lips devastated Felicity, sweeping her into a hazy, sensual storm where time ceased to exist. Where there was only him and her and the primitive energy of the world coaxing them to fulfill their duties as beings and lay with one another.

Then he pulled back pressing soft, but no less hungry kisses to her lips, across her cheeks, up her jaw to her neck where he kissed her rapidly thumping pulse. His ragged breathing sawed hotly against her skin sending a shiver through her body. His wet tongue darted out to taste just a tiny bit of flesh before retreating as if wanting to go slow and savor her.

"You'll make a perfect *bruid*."

Felicity blinked slowly as the fog lifted.

What?

She couldn't have heard what she thought she just heard. It had to be the lusty fog surrounding her combined with the potent brew he'd given her. Did